"You're married to Thorne but you slept with Forest."

Hope had some experience with fans who had trouble differentiating between actors and the characters they played, and apparently the girl with the blond braids was another one of them.

Instead, she simply acknowledged, "It wasn't one of Lainey's smartest decisions."

"You are a lying, cheating bi—"

"Missy!" one of the other girls interjected, clearly shocked by the outburst.

"She broke his heart." Missy's eyes were swimming with real tears as she drew back her arm, preparing to throw her iced coffee.

"No!" Tori protested, trying—and failing—to grab her friend's arm.

Hope braced herself for the frigid splash at the same moment someone stepped in front of her.

Michael.

She hadn't realized she'd spoken his name aloud until he turned to look at her.

His T-shirt was drenched with the cold brew and there was a furious expression on his mouthwateringly handsome face.

The achingly familiar face of the only man she'd ever truly loved.

Dear Reader,

The population of Haven, Nevada, has certainly grown since the first book in my Match Made in Haven series was published in 2018. Babies have been born, visitors have opted to stay and former residents have returned to their roots in the northern Nevada town.

Hope Bradford is one of those former residents—though she doesn't plan on staying in Haven for long. Just long enough for the smoke to clear after the implosion of her acting career, after which time she will return to Hollywood.

Michael Gilmore (MG to his friends) never wanted anything more than to live and work on his family's ranch. But whenever he envisioned his future, he pictured Hope by his side—until she decided to abandon Haven (and him!) for the bright lights of the big city.

Eighteen years later, an unexpected reunion of these high school sweethearts just might change all their plans...

And if the sparks that fly when they meet again isn't enough to remind them of the connection they once shared, the well-meaning interference of family members, old friends and one hundred pounds of Bernese mountain dog should do the trick.

I hope you enjoy this trip back to Haven, and Hope and Michael's story.

Happy reading!

xo

Brenda

The Rancher's Christmas Reunion

BRENDA HARLEN

HARLEQUIN
SPECIAL
EDITION

HARLEQUIN®
SPECIAL EDITION™

Recycling programs
for this product may
not exist in your area.

ISBN-13: 978-1-335-59427-3

The Rancher's Christmas Reunion

Copyright © 2023 by Brenda Harlen

For questions and comments about the quality of this book,
please contact us at CustomerService@Harlequin.com.

Harlequin Enterprises ULC
22 Adelaide St. West, 41st Floor
Toronto, Ontario M5H 4E3, Canada
www.Harlequin.com

Printed in U.S.A.

Brenda Harlen is a former attorney who once had the privilege of appearing before the Supreme Court of Canada. The practice of law taught her a lot about the world and reinforced her determination to become a writer—because in fiction, she could promise a happy ending! Now she is an award-winning, RITA® Award–nominated, nationally bestselling author of more than fifty titles for Harlequin. You can keep up-to-date with Brenda on Facebook and Twitter, or through her website, brendaharlen.com.

Books by Brenda Harlen

Harlequin Special Edition

Match Made in Haven
Captivated by the Cowgirl
Countdown to Christmas
The Rancher's Christmas Reunion

Montana Mavericks: Brothers & Broncos
The Maverick's Christmas Secret

Montana Mavericks:
The Real Cowboys of Bronco Heights
Dreaming of a Christmas Cowboy

Montana Mavericks: What Happened to Beatrix?
A Cowboy's Christmas Carol

Montana Mavericks: Six Brides for Six Brothers
Maverick Christmas Surprise

Montana Mavericks: The Lonelyhearts Ranch
Bring Me a Maverick for Christmas!

Visit the Author Profile page
at Harlequin.com for more titles.

To the WHVS Class of '88—thanks for the memories!

Chapter One

Hope Bradford glanced from the time displayed on her dashboard clock to the two-story clapboard house that was in complete darkness.

Of course, it was dark.

It was after two o'clock in the morning.

Tears burned the backs of her eyes as she gripped the steering wheel tighter.

Were they tears of relief? Regret?

Or maybe just exhaustion.

She'd been driving for more than nine hours, only stopping once en route to refuel her Corolla Cross—and herself.

Obviously she hadn't been thinking clearly when she'd decided to head out or she would have realized that she'd arrive at her grandmother's in the wee hours of the morning.

Or maybe she hadn't been thinking clearly for a while.

No doubt her agent would argue that Hope's thoughts had been muddled when she'd torpedoed her career, and while that was probably true, there was nothing to be done about it now.

Nothing but make the six-hundred-plus-mile journey from Sherman Oaks, California, to Haven, Nevada.

Was it Robert Frost who said that home was the place where, when you had to go there, they had to take you in?

Regardless of who'd spoken those famous words, there was the truth Hope had tried to deny for so long: even after almost two decades away, Haven was home.

And when she'd called her grandmother the previous afternoon, Edwina Bradford assured Hope that there would always be a room available for her, whenever she needed it.

She needed it now.

Desperately.

But she could hardly walk into her grandmother's house at two o'clock in the morning.

2:20

How long had it been since her last visit? Three years? Four?

She'd blamed her career for keeping her away for so long, and it was true that she'd been busy. But the bigger truth was that she hadn't wanted to come back. Hadn't wanted to remember the girl she used to be, the dreams she used to have, the boy she used to love.

And it wasn't going to do her any good to walk down memory lane now.

Instead, she decided to lean her seat back and close her eyes for the next five hours.

Edwina was always awake by seven a.m.—a habit ingrained after more than thirty years working at the local post office—and Hope knew that she wouldn't wake her if she knocked on the door then.

She'd just started to doze off when a knock on the driver's side door made her jolt. She instinctively scrambled for her cell, ready to call 9-1-1, when she recognized the face peering in her window.

Tears sprang to her eyes again, and this time she couldn't hold them back.

Edwina opened the car door as soon as the locks were disengaged, and Hope practically fell into her arms.

Even at this hour, her grandmother smelled of Chanel No 5, enveloping Hope in the scent of her past.

"I was starting to think you were going to stay in your car all night," Edwina remarked, hugging her tight.

"I didn't want to wake you," Hope said, immediately followed by, "What are *you* doing up at this hour?"

"I've got one of those cameras on the driveway. It sends me an alert if the motion sensor has been activated."

"I'm sorry I woke you. I was trying to avoid doing just that."

"I wasn't really sleeping," Edwina admitted. "I was waiting for you."

"But… I told you I would be arriving tomorrow. Actually today," she realized. "But much later."

"I know, but I could hear in your voice that you were itching to get away."

"You were right," Hope acknowledged, not so much

surprised as grateful to discover that her grandmother still knew her so well.

"Come on in," Edwina said now. "There are fresh sheets on your bed and clean towels in your bathroom."

Hope reached into the backseat for the duffel bag she'd filled with essentials. The other suitcases in her trunk could wait.

"I figured you'd have a thousand questions for me," she said, pressing her key fob to lock the vehicle.

"We'll talk in the morning." Her grandmother opened the door and gestured for her to enter. "Go get some sleep now."

She nodded, though she didn't hold out much hope that it would happen. Slumber hadn't come easily the past few weeks, and she'd inevitably awakened in the mornings feeling as tired and restless as when she'd gone to bed.

Not just restless but directionless—because if she wasn't Lainey Howard on *Rockwood Ridge*, who was she?

That was the question that had plagued her, every minute of every day, since the last meeting with the producers, the last phone call with her agent.

Or maybe Jenny Stanwyck was her former agent— because what was the point of having representation if she didn't have a career?

After another fierce hug from her grandmother, Hope made her way up the stairs to her childhood bedroom. And despite the concerns swirling in her mind, she was asleep almost before her head hit the pillow.

Michael Gilmore—MG to his friends—pretended not to hear any one of the chimes from his phone that announced at least five text messages while he mucked out stalls in the main barn at the Circle G Ranch Tuesday morning. It was a little bit harder to ignore the buzz of the device in his pocket when the calls started, but he managed to do so.

He didn't even pull out his phone to glance at the screen and check the identity of the caller. Because he didn't need to look at the screen to know.

Bernie—his hundred-pound canine companion— barked an admonition. Obviously the dog had heard the buzz of the phone in his master's pocket, too, and didn't approve of him ignoring it.

"I'm not in the mood to talk to anyone," he said, aware of the irony of the fact that he was, instead, talking to his dog. "Or not anyone who can talk back, anyway."

Bernie barked again.

"Always have to get the last word, don't you?" he grumbled, as he started to wheel the barrow filled with soiled straw out of the barn.

He gritted his teeth through the pain as he pushed forward, blaming the dampness of the air for the throbbing in his leg. He felt like an old man who could predict the weather by the ache in his bones, despite the fact that he'd only recently celebrated his thirty-fifth birthday.

He tipped the barrow to dump its contents, cursing the fact that the lingering effects of his injury had necessitated his demotion to the most basic—and unpleasant— chores at the family ranch.

Thirty minutes later, he was spreading fresh straw in the last stall when Bernie barked again.

A happy bark this time.

MG used to scoff when people said they could tell by a baby's cry whether it was hungry or wet or just wanting to be held. In the six months that had passed since Bernie had come into his life—two months after the accident that had threatened to change it forever—he'd been forced to reconsider.

The almost two-year-old Bernese Mountain Dog had been a gift from his cousin, Skylar, who'd decided that he needed a reason to get his sorry ass (her words) out of bed every morning. Bernie ensured he did that—in addition to offering company and companionship when MG wasn't in the mood to deal with the complications that accompanied same from a human source.

The dog's happy bark told MG that Paige Gallagher, his girlfriend of nearly three years and a physiotherapist at the clinic in town, had arrived at the ranch. Because the fact that he'd ignored her text messages and phone calls apparently wasn't enough of a hint that he wasn't in the mood to chat.

Through the window, he saw the silver 4Runner pull up outside the barn. Bernie, well trained by Skylar's husband—a former Marine—waited until the engine had shut off before racing outside to greet their visitor.

MG stayed where he was, wiping the sweat from his brow with the back of his hand and trying not to resent Paige's intrusion.

He knew that he should be grateful for everything she'd done for him.

Grateful that she cared.

And he was—both grateful and resentful.

She'd been the one to find him after he'd crashed his snowmobile during a late-night ride early in January. She'd called 9-1-1 and administered first aid while she waited for the ambulance to arrive.

He would have died if she hadn't shown up—and

that wasn't an exaggeration. It had been twenty degrees outside and his snapped left femur had broken through his skin.

He heard the soft lilt of her voice as she fussed over Bernie, could picture the huge dog rolling onto his back, inviting her to give him one of the belly rubs he loved almost as much as he loved Paige.

A few minutes later, she finally came into the barn. When she spoke to MG, there was no hint in her voice of the affection she'd shown to his canine companion.

"You missed physiotherapy this morning."

MG continued to spread fresh straw in the stall. "Was that today?"

"You know darn well it was today," Paige told him. "It's been every Tuesday and Thursday for the past seven weeks."

Which was an improvement over the three days a week that had been required for the first few months after the accident—and the reason he'd stayed with Paige at her apartment in town during that time. She would have been happy to let him stay even when his schedule was cut back to two days a week, but he'd been ready to move back to the ranch. More than ready to have his own space again.

And didn't that tell him everything he needed to know about their relationship?

"Kenzie said we could cut my therapy back to once a week," he hedged.

"*If* you continued to show improvement," Paige reminded him.

"As you can see, I'm doing just fine."

"Then why does your dad still have you mucking out stalls?"

"You'd have to ask him that."

"Maybe I will."

MG sighed. "Okay, maybe there's some sporadic discomfort, but I'm doing much better."

"If you want to make a complete recovery, you need to keep up with your therapy."

"You're right," he acknowledged. "Please tell Kenzie that I'm sorry I missed today."

"You can tell her yourself when you see her on Thursday."

He tightened his grip on the rake—for control of the pain as well as his frustration. "Fine. I'll tell her myself on Thursday."

She nodded. "Good. Now I need to get back to work."

"Did you really drive all the way out here just to nag me for missing an appointment?"

"If you'd responded to any of my text messages or answered any of my calls, I wouldn't have had to make the trip."

"When did you text? Or call?"

A smile tugged at her lips as she shook her head. "You're a horrible liar, MG." Then she rose onto her toes to brush her lips against his. "It's one of your more redeeming qualities."

"I have more than one?"

She shrugged. "Depends on the day."

"Ouch."

"Make sure you ice that leg when you go in," she told him. "And don't forget to do your exercises."

He caught her hand as she started to move past him, forcing her to halt in midstride.

She turned to give him a questioning glance.

"I'm sorry," he said.

Her brows lifted. "What, exactly, are you apologizing for?"

"I know I've been difficult—or more difficult than usual—since the accident."

"I can't disagree with that," she told him. "Lucky for you, I love you, anyway."

"I am lucky," he acknowledged, experiencing a twinge of guilt because he knew that Paige deserved a lot better man than him—but he couldn't seem to let her go.

She responded with a smile that was warm and sincere. "I figured you'd come to that realization eventually."

He tugged on her hand to draw her closer, then dipped his head to kiss her again. "I'll see you Friday."

"You mean Thursday?"

He managed a smile. "Yes, I will see you at the clinic when I'm there on Thursday, and then I will see you again on Friday—to celebrate your birthday."

"I wasn't sure you remembered."

"Have I ever forgotten your birthday?"

"No," she admitted. "But you've been dealing with a lot more than usual for the past eight months."

"You shouldn't cut me any slack for something that was my own fault."

"It was an *accident*," she said pointedly.

She was right. He certainly hadn't intended to run into a snowbank and flip his machine, but he never should have taken a ride in the dark of night when his mind wasn't on what he was doing.

Of course, Paige didn't know that he'd been distracted—or why. And it would serve no purpose to tell her that he'd been thinking of another woman.

The one who got away.

The one who, according to the internet, had just gotten engaged—for the fifth time—the day of his ill-fated ride.

Whether Hope Bradford would actually walk down the aisle with her most recent fiancé had yet to be determined at that point, but the fact that she'd accepted another man's proposal proved to MG—*again*—that she'd moved on with her life. Without him.

"I'll pick you up at seven," he said to Paige now.

Because—as the song said—if you couldn't be with the one you loved, you should love the one you were with.

Chapter Two

Hope awoke in the morning, not entirely sure where she was. It took her a minute to get her bearings, because the room in which she'd slept bore little resemblance to the one she remembered from high school and which had been unchanged on her last visit. She pushed back the covers and rose to her feet, turning in a slow circle to survey her surroundings from every angle.

Gone were the posters of NSYNC and 98 Degrees and Heath Ledger that had been tacked up on the formerly plum-colored walls, now painted a pale gray with just a hint of lavender. The purple-and-black-color-block comforter was gone, too, along with the twin mattress it had covered. In its place was a queen-size sleigh bed with a fluffy white eyelet spread and a trio of square throw pillows that she'd shoved to one side when she crawled beneath the covers. The black gauzy curtains had been replaced by white California shutters and the wall-to-wall carpet torn up to expose random width pine flooring, now with a whitewashed finish.

Obviously Edwina had made some significant changes since Hope's last visit to the old house on Queen Street, though the renovations had gone unnoticed the night before. Not even the remodel of the en suite bathroom had registered as she'd washed her face and brushed her teeth. But she took note of it now, admiring the soaker tub and separate walk-in shower, the marble-topped vanity and overhead chandelier.

The waterfall showerhead in the glass-walled enclosure tempted her, but not quite as much as the prospect of the coffee she knew Edwina would have brewing in the kitchen. After a quick brush of her teeth, she grabbed her favorite hooded terry robe and tugged it on over the T-shirt and boxer shorts that were her pajamas.

She made her way down the stairs, a little disappointed to note that they didn't creak like they used to. And curious to know what had inspired her grandmother to make so many changes.

Of course, Edwina had lived here for almost fifty years now, and this was hardly the first time she'd changed wall color or swapped out furnishings. But Hope couldn't help but wonder if that's all this was—or if her grandmother was, perhaps, attempting to make the house more marketable.

Edwina was only seventy-two years old, but it was a big house for one person, and only a few months earlier she'd commented to Hope about a friend—a recent widow—who'd sold her house to move into a new adult-lifestyle community that had opened up on the north side of town. Was it possible that Edwina was thinking of doing the same thing?

Frowning over the possibility, Hope paused at the bottom of the stairs when her caffeine-deprived brain belatedly recognized the sound of voices emanating from the kitchen. At first, she'd assumed her grandmother was watching TV or listening to the radio—then she heard Edwina giggle.

At least, Hope thought it was a giggle, but she couldn't be certain because she'd never before heard her grandmother giggle.

"Stop that, Dennis."

Dennis?

Who the heck was Dennis?

"Stop what?" A deep, obviously masculine, voice responded.

"You know very well what." Edwina's admonishment was followed by another giggle.

Hope stood frozen, torn between her desire for the coffee that she knew was only a few steps away and her desperation to not interrupt…whatever was going on between her grandmother and someone named Dennis only a few steps away.

The desperation to not interrupt won out, and she turned back toward the stairs.

The old floor groaned in protest of her abrupt pivot.

Because, of course, whoever Edwina had hired to fix the creaky stairs hadn't done anything about the floor on the main level.

"Is that you, Hope?" Edwina called out from the kitchen.

"I'll come back later," she said. *Much later.*

"Don't be silly." Her grandmother appeared in the

doorway, reaching out to take Hope's arm and draw her into the kitchen.

"I didn't realize you had company," she protested. "And I really don't want to interrupt."

"You're not interrupting anything," Edwina denied. "I was just making your favorite chocolate chip pancakes."

"Is that what you were doing?" Dennis asked, sounding amused.

Edwina sent him a look as she set a frying pan on the stove and ignited the burner beneath it.

Hope ventured a cautious glance in the man's direction. He was grinning, clearly unrepentant. He also looked vaguely familiar.

Almost like...her high school principal?

"Mr. Kirk?"

He nodded. "It's been a long time, Hope. I wasn't sure if you'd recognize me."

"Eighteen years," she noted.

"And now you've deprived me of the opportunity to make the introductions and mention that you're a three-time Emmy award–winning actor," her grandmother said, pouting just a little.

"She does like to tell people about those Emmys," Mr. Kirk confirmed.

"It's an honor just to be nominated," Hope said.

"Which has happened five times," Edwina pointed out, as she poured a mug of coffee from the carafe on the warmer for her granddaughter. "Cream and sugar are on the table."

"This is fine."

Her grandmother made a face.

"The camera adds ten pounds," Hope felt compelled

to explain. "And cream and sugar are extra calories I don't need."

"That sounds like your mother talking," Edwina remarked.

"She wouldn't be wrong," Hope pointed out.

"Well, there are no cameras here," her grandmother assured her.

And Hope was grateful for that, but she was also (perhaps foolishly) optimistic that she would be in front of the cameras again sometime in the not-so-distant future. Though, truth be told, there were also moments when she found herself wondering how she could even consider going back to Los Angeles now.

But the cast and crew of *Rockwood Ridge* had become more than friends over the past eight years. And being written out of the show was a bigger blow than simply losing a job she genuinely loved—though that definitely stung. The abrupt termination left her feeling as if she'd been excommunicated from her family.

Maybe she should have stuck around to tell her side of the story, she acknowledged now. Because running away gave the studio the opportunity to control the narrative when news of her departure from the popular show was made public—as she knew was likely to happen any day now—but she'd been feeling too raw to stay.

A couple of the writers had sent her text messages, lamenting that she'd been treated unfairly. But no one had stood up for her in front of the decision-makers. And so, feeling frustrated and unsupported, she'd packed her bags, called her grandmother and driven away.

"Next you're going to tell me that you don't want maple syrup and whipped cream on your pancakes."

Edwina's grumbling remark drew Hope back to the present.

"Actually, I don't want any pancakes," she said. "But thank you."

"You need to eat something," her grandmother told her, transferring the first pancakes from the pan to a platter beside the stove. "You're nothing but skin and bones."

She didn't think that was true, though it was undeniable that she'd lost weight. The stress of the past few weeks had taken its toll, as evidenced by the way her clothes hung loosely on her frame.

But she didn't want to talk about that. Not yet. And definitely not in front of Dennis.

Instead, she turned her attention to her grandmother's visitor and, in a deliberately casual tone, asked, "So what brings you by so early on a Tuesday morning, Mr. Kirk?"

"You're not in high school anymore, Hope. You can call me Dennis."

"Okay—what brings you by so early on a Tuesday morning, *Dennis*?"

Rather than answer her question, he shifted his gaze to the woman pouring more batter into the hot pan on the stove. "Do you want to take this one, Edwina?"

"I think I'd better," she said, setting a plate of pancakes in front of him.

"I didn't think it was a particularly difficult question," Hope commented.

"You're right," her grandmother agreed. "It's not. So I'll give you an equally straightforward and simple answer—Dennis didn't stop by this morning, he stayed here last night. And the night before that. And, in fact, several nights before that."

Hope's mind refused to connect the obvious dots that

Edwina's words laid out for her. There had to be another explanation.

"Are you saying… Have you started renting out rooms again?"

Edwina had occasionally taken in boarders over the years—partly because the income had helped pay the utility bills on the five-bedroom home, but mostly, Hope always suspected, because her grandmother enjoyed having other people around.

"Dennis hasn't been sleeping in one of the spare bedrooms—he's been sleeping with me."

The man in question pushed his chair away from the table. "I think I'm going to take my breakfast into the other room."

Edwina smiled indulgently at him. "You don't want your pancakes with a side of awkward family conversation?"

"Since I'm not actually part of the family, I'll pass."

"Can I pass on the awkward family conversation, too?" Hope asked, when Dennis had retreated from the room.

"Are you offended by the discovery that your grandmother has a lover?" Edwina asked.

"I'm not offended," she denied. "I'm just…surprised."

"Surprised that a seventy-two-year-old woman is sexually active?"

"Surprised that we're talking about this at the breakfast table."

"Since you're not having breakfast, it's just a table."

"Maybe I will have a pancake," she decided.

Edwina smirked as she transferred two pancakes from the platter to her granddaughter's plate.

Hope picked up the bottle of maple syrup and drizzled a stream of sticky liquid over her breakfast.

After Paige had gone and MG finally finished his chores, he sat down behind the desk in the office at the far end of the barn. His aching leg sighed with relief as he settled into the leather chair and signed into the computer. No way would he admit that it had been a mistake to skip his physical therapy, but he did down a couple of Tylenol before he navigated to The Home Station website to make a reservation for dinner Friday night. Next, he ordered flowers to be delivered to Paige on the same day. Then came the part he always struggled with—the gift.

He navigated to The Gold Mine website, hoping that something offered by the local jewelry store would catch his eye. Paige didn't wear a lot of jewelry to work—an occupational hazard, she'd told him—but she always put on a pair of fancy earrings and/or necklace and/or bracelets when they went out. And the few times he'd bought her something other than jewelry, she hadn't seemed too impressed by his efforts.

Such as when he'd decided to get her a copy of the latest Dierks Bentley CD a couple of years back, because he noticed that she often sang along to the radio when she was cooking. She thanked him, of course, then promised to give it a listen though she wasn't a fan of country music.

He'd tried again at Anthology Books, because Paige always had a book on her bedside table. He picked up a title that had topped the *New York Times* bestseller list for several months and was recommended by one of the clerks in the store. And screwed up again, because apparently she didn't like true crime stories.

His gift of a weekend in Napa Valley for a wine tasting had been much better received. But he'd known that it would be, because it had been Paige's idea.

But she'd dropped no hints this time, and so he was back to the tried-and-true gift of jewelry. Because *every day should sparkle*—according to the slogan on The Gold Mine's website, anyway.

He scanned the categories across the top of the page: "Bracelets & Bangles," "Earrings," "Necklaces & Pendants," "Rings," "Watches."

During the almost three years that he and Paige had been dating, he'd bought a few bracelets, several pairs of earrings, a chunky necklace and even a watch with an easy-to-read dial and three-hand quartz movement that she could wear to work. The one thing he'd never bought was a ring and it was the one thing—at least according to his sister, Olivia—that Paige really wanted.

He clicked on the "Rings" option, then—after only a brief moment of hesitation—"Engagement Rings" from the drop-down menu under that heading.

He'd resisted taking the next step for a long time, for a lot of reasons. But over the past eight months, MG had finally acknowledged the truth he'd been trying to deny for so long—he was going to end up married to Paige Gallagher.

There was no way out of it now.

Because how did a man break up with the woman who'd not only saved his life but indulged his whims and tolerated his moods?

If he could answer that question, he might have already extricated himself from the relationship. But as the answer continued to elude him, he'd been forced to acknowledge that there was no reason not to marry her.

No reason except that he didn't love her.

Couldn't love her.

Because his heart had been broken a long time ago and never fully mended. Because falling in love once and forever seemed to be the curse of being a Gilmore.

Eighteen years after saying goodbye to the woman he'd been certain he would love forever, he knew that it was long past time to move on with his life. He'd finally started to do so with Paige. And while he'd be the first to admit that she deserved better than him, for some reason, she seemed to want him.

So why shouldn't he—finally—give her what she wanted?

Why shouldn't he buy her a big fat diamond and ask her to marry him?

Because you don't love her.

MG ignored the warning that echoed in his mind.

Because even if it was true that he didn't love her with all of his heart and soul, the way he'd once loved Hope Bradford, he wasn't the same person now that he'd been then. He'd been more of a boy than a man when they were together. A boy easily influenced by feelings of attraction and affection for the most beautiful girl he'd ever known. A boy who'd let his heart remain broken for far too long.

But eventually the pieces had knitted back together—without needing surgical intervention or a rod and screws—and eventually he'd started dating again. That was when he'd discovered there were a lot of interesting and attractive women in town. Women he'd never noticed before because he'd been blinded by his feelings for Hope. But once he noticed them, he also found pleasure in their company. He never dated any one woman for very long, though, because he knew he wouldn't fall in love again and didn't want to mislead any of his partners.

Then he'd met Paige, who seemed to enjoy being with him as much as he enjoyed being with her, and who didn't put any demands on him. And somehow, without MG being fully aware of it, the weeks they spent together turned into months and those months became a year—and then two years. During that time, his brother Mitch had reunited with his childhood sweetheart—making him a stepdad to Elliott and Avenlea, Lindsay's children from her first marriage, and now a dad to their three-month-old daughter, Emeline. And within the same period, MG's sister, Olivia, had finally succeeded in snagging the heart of her best friend's brother (and long-time secret crush), becoming a stepmom to Adam's three sons—Easton, Hudson and Colton—in the process.

While bearing witness to these important family events, Paige had dropped a few tentative hints about her hopes for their future together. But she'd never made any demands or given him ultimatums, seeming content to let him discover—in his own time—that they were meant to be together forever, as she was certain they were.

Maybe she was right.

And maybe, finally, it was time for him to step up.

"Are you actually looking at engagement rings?"

MG glanced over his shoulder to find his sister standing there, and mentally cursed himself for being so wrapped up in his own thoughts, he'd failed to register her approach.

"What are you doing here?" he asked. "It's the middle of the day—aren't you supposed to be in school?"

"It's still August," she reminded him. "Classes don't resume until next week."

"Then shouldn't you be watching over your three stepsons who obviously aren't in school, either?"

"They're with their mom and stepdad—and baby sister—this week."

"Which apparently leaves you with too much time on your hands," he noted.

"Apparently," she agreed, glancing again at the images on the monitor again. "Are you finally going to give Paige a ring?"

"It's probably time," he acknowledged.

His sister frowned at that. "An engagement shouldn't be about time—like a participation medal for crossing the finish line of a marathon. It should be about loving someone so much that you can't imagine spending the rest of your life without them."

"If you ever decide to give up teaching, you could get a job writing greeting cards."

"I'm serious, MG."

"So am I." He clicked on a princess cut solitaire, enlarging the picture for her perusal. "What do you think of this one?"

"I think you're rushing things," she said cautiously.

"Says my sister who got engaged after one date and married only weeks later."

"To the man I've loved since I was fifteen," she reminded him.

"Well, not everyone is lucky enough to fall in love once and forever."

"You're right," she said. "But Gilmores do. Mom and Dad. Mitch and Lindsay. Me and Adam."

"Do you have a point?" he asked. "Or did you just come over here to be smug?"

"I came over because I heard something at The Daily Grind this morning that I thought you should know, too."

"I'm not interested in whatever the latest gossip is," he told her.

"You'll be interested in this," she insisted.

Though he remained doubtful, he said, "So tell me."

"Hope Bradford's back in Haven."

Chapter Three

MG refused to show any reaction to his sister's announcement, but he couldn't ignore the fact that his heart skipped a beat in response to her words.

After eighteen years, he'd thought the memories had begun to fade, but just hearing Hope's name had them rolling through his mind in bold, brilliant color.

Memories of a seven-year-old girl with bouncy blond pigtails and big blue eyes who walked into Mrs. Walton's first grade class the week of Thanksgiving. Memories of her silky-soft hair tickling his cheek when she leaned close to whisper in his ear. Of the softness of her hand when she gave his a reassuring squeeze before he walked to the front of the class to deliver an oral report. Of the sweetness of her smile every time she smiled at him.

Those were the early days, of course, when their friendship was new and innocent. But they remained close, even as their respective circles of friends expanded. And then, in the seventh grade, while he was hugging the wall of the elementary school gymnasium and wishing he was anywhere other than at the Seventh and Eighth Grade Valentine's Day Dance, Hope bravely breached the distance between them and asked him to dance.

To this day, he couldn't hear Jewel's "You Were Meant For Me" without remembering that dance—and Hope. He couldn't listen to the song without missing her and, at the same time, hating her.

Because the best times of his life were spent with her—when he believed that she loved him as much as he loved her. And the worst time was when she'd said goodbye—proving that her feelings for him weren't nearly as strong as her desire to see her name in lights.

He was happy that she'd gotten what she wanted, even if he'd been unsuccessful in his own pursuit of the same—because all he'd ever wanted was Hope.

"So?" He deliberately switched his attention back to the page of engagement rings, as if to prove to his sister that not only was he unaffected by her big revelation, he was, in fact, ready to move on with his life with a woman who was *not* Hope Bradford.

Olivia's gaze narrowed. "That's a pretty good imitation of not caring," she decided. "But I know that you do."

"Maybe I did," he acknowledged. "But my relationship with Hope was over a long time ago."

"And now you're going to propose to Paige to prove it," she guessed.

"Whether or not I propose to Paige has nothing to do with Hope."

"I sincerely hope that's true," Olivia said. "Because no woman should be seen as a consolation prize."

"I don't see Paige as a consolation prize," he assured her.

"Anyway," she said, "I didn't come here to meddle in your relationship with Paige but to warn you about Hope."

He felt his lips twitch. "If I run into her in a dark alley, I'm pretty sure I can handle myself."

"I guess we'll see, won't we?" she said. "Now I'm going to saddle up Dolly and take her out for a ride."

Then she kissed his cheek and walked out the door, and MG went back to perusing diamond rings on the website.

He'd been a little surprised—and a lot relieved—that Olivia hadn't asked him why he was looking to buy a ring when he had his maternal grandmother's hand-crafted platinum engagement ring to offer to his potential bride. But maybe his sister didn't know about Nonna's ring—a stunning old European cut diamond accented by three smaller gems on either side with diamond-studded openwork filigree.

It was a beautiful piece of jewelry, and he had no doubt that Paige would love it if he offered it to her. But it had come to him—as the eldest grandson—when he was dating Hope. And though he'd barely been seventeen at the time, he'd been certain the day would come when he would slide it onto her finger.

Obviously he'd been wrong about that, and even if he was completely over Hope Bradford—and he was, he insisted to himself—he knew there was no way he could ever give that ring to anyone else.

"How long are you planning to stay?" Edwina asked, when Hope ventured cautiously into the kitchen Friday morning. She was getting used to seeing Dennis with her grandmother—and she was happy to see Edwina happy—but Hope had already walked in on one sizzling kiss and wasn't eager to interrupt another.

"I haven't even been here a week," she noted. "Have I overstayed my welcome already?"

"You could never overstay your welcome," her grandmother said.

"Did I drive Dennis away?"

"Not at all," Edwina assured her. "He meets a group of old friends for breakfast every Friday morning."

"And you're not invited?"

"I'm invited. I opted to skip this morning because I wanted to talk to you."

"About what?" Hope wondered.

"About the fact that you're acting like a recluse," Edwina said. "You haven't gone out with your friends even once since you've been back."

"I'm here to spend time with you," she said, because it was true. But also because she didn't want to admit that she hadn't really kept in touch with any of her friends from high school.

"Even when I'm not home, you don't leave the house," her grandmother pointed out.

She shrugged. "There's nowhere else I want to be."

"You're hiding."

Hope retrieved a mug from the cupboard, intending to fill it with coffee from the carafe. "Maybe."

"There's no *maybe* about it," Edwina said, taking the mug from her hand. "And I'm not going to let you do it any longer."

"What's that supposed to mean? Are you kicking me out?"

"Just for a few hours."

"You're serious," Hope realized, panic beginning to claw at her belly.

"I am," her grandmother confirmed with a nod. "It's a beautiful day—walk over to The Daily Grind, get one of those lattes you like, breathe in the fresh air and bask in the sunshine."

A walk didn't sound like a bad idea, Hope admitted, as the panic started to subside.

If she wore a hat and sunglasses, it was unlikely that anyone would recognize her. In any event, as the producers had made clear, Hope Bradford wasn't nearly as big a star as she thought she was.

Not that she even considered herself a star, but the fact was, when she walked down the streets of LA, there was always somebody who recognized her as Lainey Howard from *Rockwood Ridge*. But this wasn't LA, and no one in Haven would expect to cross paths with a semifamous Hollywood actor.

And while Edwina brewed a decent pot of coffee, Hope missed her daily latte. She hadn't known what a latte was when she'd lived in Haven so many years before—and she doubted that anyone who worked at the local café back then did, either. But during the time that she'd been gone, Cal's Coffee Shop had become The Daily Grind and now offered an extensive menu of specialty hot drinks—including a skinny vanilla latte that she'd discovered on her last visit home.

"Okay," she decided. "I'll take a walk."

"Good idea," her grandmother said approvingly.

She changed out of her pajamas and into a pair of Alice + Olivia cropped trousers and an ivory crepe de Chine silk top by Gucci. Then she looked at her reflection in the mirror and realized that while she was perfectly attired for brunch with friends at The Ivy in Los Angeles, she was likely overdressed for a trip to the local coffee shop in Haven.

Rifling through the various tops and bottoms she'd brought with her from California, she was forced to admit that her wardrobe did not lend itself to blending in with the local residents. On impulse, she opened the bottom drawer of her dresser and discovered three pairs of very old jeans and several pairs of knit leggings in various colors.

She grabbed a pair of jeans and found a light blue scoop neck T-shirt in another drawer. When she needed to add a belt to ensure the jeans stayed in place, she was forced to acknowledge that she'd perhaps lost more than a few pounds in recent weeks. On the bright side, she decided that she wouldn't need to feel guilty the next time she indulged in Edwina's pancakes.

The T-shirt was a little baggy, too, but at least it wasn't falling off. She completed the look by tying her hair into a ponytail and pulling it through the opening at the back of her ancient Dodgers baseball cap. Another quick glance in the mirror told her that no one would look twice if they saw her walking down Main Street— and that she needed to add at least a touch of mascara to her lashes and a dab of gloss to her lips before she walked out of the house.

As she made her way down Queen Street toward the hub of town, she acknowledged that it was silly to be nervous. No one in Haven was likely to remember her, and even if they did, they had no way of knowing why she was in town. The news of her departure from the popular weekly drama had not yet been leaked to the press (though she knew it was only a matter of time) so there was no reason to worry about being asked questions she wasn't sure how to answer.

In any event, Edwina was right—it was a beautiful day. And though the sun was shining, the temperature wasn't unbearably hot, as it could be in the city.

Turning onto Main Street, she saw a trio of middle-school-aged boys riding bikes. A little farther along she passed a group of younger girls jumping rope in a driveway and, a little farther again, a giggling toddler wearing only a T-shirt and a diaper, running through a sprinkler on the patch of grass in front of a modest bungalow.

Hope felt a tug in the vicinity of her heart as she watched the young mother playfully chase her young child through the spray. She'd never given much thought to the idea of having a baby of her own until Bethany— one of her fellow cast members on *Rockwood Ridge*— gave birth to her first child the previous summer. The writers had worked her pregnancy into the show, allowing Bethany to share the joy of impending motherhood with the audience as well as the cast and crew.

After the baby was born, the new mom brought him with her to the studio, so that she could nurse him during breaks and cuddle him when she wasn't on set. Watching her friend, Hope had experienced an unexpected twinge of envy as she acknowledged, if only to herself, that she wanted what Bethany had—a husband and a family.

But three engagements had failed to lead to even one trip down the aisle, because Hope had realized that as much as she enjoyed being with Marcus (and later Justin and then Seth), she couldn't envision spending the rest of her life with him (or any of them)—and she didn't want to end up like her mother, who at fifty-three years of age already had six marriages under her tiny belt.

Pushing aside her melancholy, Hope pulled open the door of the coffee shop and stepped inside, inhaling the fragrant scent of fresh coffee and sugary donuts. She indulged herself by perusing the offerings in the glass-fronted pastry case, but when it was her turn to order, she only asked for a large skinny vanilla latte.

The woman behind the counter didn't even give her a second look as she took her order and her money, and the knots in Hope's stomach loosened as she moved down the line to wait for her drink. There were plenty of vacant tables inside the café, but Hope opted for the sidewalk patio area outside, settling at one of the small umbrella-topped bistro tables to enjoy her beverage.

Several other customers came and went as she sipped her latte, none of them paying her the least bit of attention, and she relaxed enough to remove her sunglasses and check out the gossip websites on her phone.

A group of four teenage girls—all slender and beautiful and wearing halter tops and very short shorts—walked past her table on their way into the coffee shop. They were talking and laughing, obviously making the most of their last few days of summer break.

She'd been one of those girls once. Young and carefree, comfortable in the company of her friends, optimistic about her future.

Oh, how times have changed, Hope mused, as she lifted her cup to her lips again.

A few minutes later, the same group of girls exited the coffee shop. The girl in the front—with brown skin and flat-ironed ebony hair that fell to the middle of her back—halted abruptly, causing her friends to mutter as they drew up short to avoid stumbling over her.

"What the hell, Tori?" a blonde with sunburned nose and shoulders demanded.

"It's Lainey Howard," the leader said.

"What?" asked a curly-haired brunette with sparkly cats-eye sunglasses.

"Who?" wondered a second blonde with her hair in two braids.

Hope shifted her attention back to her phone, pretending she didn't hear them.

"I don't think it's her."

"What would she be doing in Haven?"

"She grew up here."

"Well, yeah. But if you got out of this town, would you ever come back?"

That question was met with snickers.

"Excuse me."

Hope looked up.

"Are you Lainey Howard—from *Rockwood Ridge*?" The girl with the sparkly sunglasses asked.

She could deny it and maybe they'd move along. But she'd always enjoyed meeting fans of the show, and she thought those interactions were important for the fans to see that actors were real people, too.

"Actually, my name is Hope Bradford. But yes, I play—" *played* "—Lainey Howard on TV."

"I told you it was her," the girl identified as Tori said smugly.

Her friend with the braids looked more annoyed than impressed.

"*You're* Thorne Chesterfield's wife?" she said to Hope.

"Only on *Rockwood Ridge*," she said lightly.

Out of the corner of her eye, she saw a tall, broad-shouldered man with short dark hair on the sidewalk.

Though the presence of the girls around her table prevented her from getting a clear look at him, the way her heart jolted with recognition was proof enough of his identity.

Michael Gilmore.

"You're married to Thorne—but you *slept* with *Forrest.*"

The accusatory tone drew Hope's attention back to the girl with the braids.

"Who's Forrest?" Her sunburned friend was obviously not a fan of the show.

"Thorne's brother."

"Oh."

Hope had some experience with fans who had trouble differentiating between actors and the characters they played, and apparently the girl with the blonde braids was another one of them.

She could have pointed out that it was a story line developed by the writers with no input from the actors, or she could have said—quite honestly—that she'd never really slept with Forrest, but she suspected the teen wouldn't believe any of her explanations or denials.

Instead, she simply said, "It wasn't one of Lainey's smartest decisions."

"You are a lying, cheating bi—"

"Missy!" one of the other girls interjected, clearly shocked by the outburst.

"You don't understand! She broke his heart!" Missy's eyes brimmed with real tears.

"No!" Tori protested, trying—and failing—to stop her friend, who had drawn back her arm and was about to hurl her iced coffee.

Hope braced herself for the frigid splash at the same moment someone stepped in front of her.

Michael.

She hadn't realized she'd spoken his name aloud until he turned to look at her.

His T-shirt was drenched with the cold brew and there was a furious expression on his mouthwateringly handsome face.

The achingly familiar face of the only man she'd ever truly loved.

Chapter Four

"Ohmygod. I'm so, so sorry, Mr. Gilmore." Missy Sutherland fell all over herself apologizing to MG. "I didn't mean to spill my iced coffee on you."

Unfortunately the teen's earnest words did absolutely nothing to alleviate the discomfort of the cold, wet, sticky fabric now plastered against his torso.

"You didn't spill it," he remarked coolly. "You threw it."

"But… I wasn't aiming at you," she assured him.

"You were aiming at Ms. Bradford."

"She deserved it," Missy insisted, clearly not sorry for her actions   only regretting that he'd been caught in the crossfire.

If MG hadn't been so annoyed—and wet—he might have been amused by the contrast between her deference to him and her disdain for Hope. Because his long-ago girlfriend might be a Hollywood celebrity, but the Gilmores were akin to Haven royalty.

"What did she do to deserve it?" he asked the teen.

Her cheeks flushed and her gaze dropped to her feet. "She slept with Forrest."

"And Forrest is…your boyfriend?" he asked, as if he didn't know.

The girl's already crimson cheeks somehow got even redder. "No, he's—" she swallowed "—Thorne's brother."

"They're both characters on a TV show called *Rockwood Ridge*," Tori Spears spoke up to fill in the blanks for him.

Of course, he knew who both characters were—and also that Hope Bradford played Lainey Howard on the same show—but he wasn't going to admit to these teens (or the girl who'd trampled his heart when she left him for the bright lights of the big city) that he'd been known to watch *Rockwood Ridge* on occasion. (Or every Wednesday night at nine o'clock.)

"How old are you, Missy?"

Her brows drew together. "Why?"

"I was just wondering if the sheriff will charge you as a juvie or an adult."

"Charge me?" Her voice was shrill with indignation—and hopefully a little bit of fear. "For spilling my coffee?"

"For *throwing* your coffee," he said again. "That's assault and battery."

"I don't think it is," she said, though without much certainty.

"Brenna Flaherty is your aunt, isn't she? You could check with her when they give you your one phone call after you're arrested."

Missy's eyes filled with tears again. "You're not really going to call the sheriff, are you?"

He wanted the teen to understand that she was responsible for the consequences of her actions, but he didn't think she deserved to be hauled off to jail. Still, it wasn't really his decision to make, and so, finally, reluctantly, he turned to speak directly to Hope. "You were the intended target—what do you think?"

She held his gaze for a long minute, a whole range of emotions on display in her expression—none of which he could begin to decipher. Or maybe he didn't want to.

His personal history with his former classmate and long ago girlfriend turned Hollywood star was…complicated.

Or maybe it was only their breakup that was complicated.

Prior to that, their relationship had actually been quite simple. They were a couple of teenagers—young and in love and making plans for a future together.

Despite her involvement with the drama club throughout high school, Hope had never expressed an interest in a professional acting career. She had no interest in following in the footsteps of her mother, who'd been chasing fame and fortune for longer than Hope had been alive. But when she was presented with the opportunity to audition for a role in Hollywood, everything changed.

"I think Missy needs to at least pay for your dry cleaning," Hope responded to his question.

"Maybe—if I dry-cleaned my jeans and T-shirts," he remarked wryly.

"And probably watch a little less TV," Hope added. "Since she seems to blur the lines between fact and fiction."

Missy glared at her friends, who snickered in response to the comment.

"Missy's in the drama club at school," Tori supplied helpfully. "She's going to be a big Hollywood star someday."

"Bigger even than you," Missy said to Hope, clearly still miffed over her rejection of her fictional husband.

Before Hope could respond to that, the barista rushed out of the coffee shop. "I just heard what happened. Are you okay, Mr. Gilmore?"

"I'm fine," he said.

"And Ms. Bradford." Donna practically genuflected in front of Hope. "I didn't recognize you behind the sunglasses when you came in."

"That was kind of the point," she admitted.

"Well, please let me apologize for the drama—I'm sure you're visiting Haven to get away from all of that for a while."

"There's no reason for you to apologize," Hope assured her.

Donna turned to the group of teenagers as another employee came out with a mop and began cleaning the sidewalk.

"Missy Sutherland, you are banned from The Daily Grind for the next thirty days."

"What?" The teen was shocked. "Why?"

"Because actions have consequences," MG told her.

"But—"

"I could make it sixty," Donna warned.

"I'm a paying customer," Missy protested, at the same time Whitney said, "Shut *up*, Missy."

She stomped her foot. "This isn't fair."

"Do you want it to be sixty?" Donna asked.

The teen turned on her heel and stalked away.

Her friends exchanged glances.

"You can go, too," Donna told them.

The other three girls hurried after their friend.

"You must make phenomenal iced coffee," Hope remarked. "Missy seemed more upset about being banned from the café than she was by Michael's threat to call the sheriff."

Donna's lips twitched, as if she was fighting against a smile. "You really did that?" she asked MG.

He just shrugged.

Donna turned her attention to Hope again. "I'm truly sorry for the chaos and hope you won't shy away from coming back."

"Now that I've enjoyed one of your vanilla lattes, I might become a regular customer," Hope told her.

The barista grinned. "Then I will look forward to seeing you again."

"Me, too."

"Vanilla lattes, huh?" MG couldn't resist remarking when Donna had gone. "I guess even your coffee has gone Hollywood."

Hope picked up her sunglasses and slid them onto her face. "Is that supposed to be some kind of dig? Because lattes are available around the globe—and even here in Haven now, too, apparently."

"I don't need to ask if *that* was a dig," he noted.

She flushed. "I'm sorry."

"No, don't hold back. Tell me how you really feel about being home."

"I was actually really enjoying my visit—until about ten minutes ago."

"When I showed up or when Missy threw her coffee at you?"

"When Missy threw her coffee."

"She can be a bit of a drama queen, but that was over-the-top even for her."

"It sounds as if you know her pretty well."

"Not really. But I knew her mom. So did you," he reminded Hope. "She was Nina Conley back then. Married to Dallas Sutherland now."

Hope's brow furrowed, as if she was struggling to place the name. Which maybe shouldn't have surprised him, considering that she hadn't lived in Haven for almost two decades. Still, it was a bit of a slap in the face—as if Hope had simply put all of her friends out of her mind when she moved to Hollywood.

Although, to be fair, she and Nina had been classmates more than friends. And at least she'd immediately recognized MG—who had been one of her best friends for a lot of years, and more than just a friend for a while.

"You were in the drama club together," he reminded her.

That seemed to be the bit of information she needed to put the pieces together.

"She was the understudy for Juliet in our senior year."

He nodded. "And I don't think she ever got over you getting the part she wanted. When people around here started talking about *Rockwood Ridge*, she told everyone that the role of Lainey Howard would have been hers if only Mrs. Newman had cast her as Juliet in high school."

"Which completely disregards the fact that the Hollywood director who saw me onstage was only in town because he was with my mom—and she never would have shown up if I hadn't been playing the lead."

He nodded his agreement. "I'm just trying to give you a little context."

"I appreciate it," she said, then surprised him with a

follow-up question. "So how do you know so much about assault and battery laws?"

"I didn't always walk on the right side of the law in my younger days," he confided.

"I was at your side for most of those younger days."

"And then you were gone."

Her wince was almost imperceptible.

"Were you really arrested?"

"Yeah. I got into a fight at Diggers'. Ended up spending the night in jail."

"Who were you fighting with?" she asked curiously.

"Mitch."

"*Your brother* had you thrown in jail?" She sounded outraged.

"Duke had us both thrown in jail," he clarified.

The outrage subsided. "How did your mom and dad respond to that?"

"Let's just say that they didn't rush over to the jail to bail us out."

A smile curved her lips—and in it he saw a hint of the girl he used to know.

The girl he used to love.

"That actually doesn't surprise me," she mused.

Of course, it didn't—because she knew his parents.

Or she used to, anyway.

But that was a long time ago.

Ancient history.

"Well, I have to run," he told her.

"Wait," she said.

Against his better judgment, he did.

"Can't I at least buy you a cup of coffee before you go?"

"Huh?"

"Weren't you on your way into The Daily Grind when you intercepted Missy's throw?"

"Yeah, I was," he acknowledged. "Now I'm going to head to my brother's, because I can grab both a cup of coffee and a clean shirt there."

"Mitch doesn't still live at the Circle G?" she asked, sounding surprised.

"No. He moved to town when he and Lindsay got married."

"Lindsay... Delgado?"

"Yeah." Actually, Lindsay's surname had been Thomas when they married—because she'd married Mitch's best friend first—but MG didn't imagine that Hope was interested in those details. And he was mostly interested in getting out of his wet shirt.

"I'm happy to hear that they found their way to one another," she said. "I know Mitch had a huge crush on her in high school."

"Apparently he wasn't as good at hiding his feelings as he thought."

"It's nice to know that love can last." Hope's smile seemed a little wistful.

"As much as I'm enjoying this little chat, I really need to get a clean shirt so that I can run my errands." Not to mention that Bernie was waiting in the truck for him, and the longer the dog was left alone, the more drool MG would have to wipe off his seat.

"Right." She nodded. "Of course."

"It was good to see you, Hope," he said, and almost meant it.

"You, too, Michael."

"It's MG," he told her. "Only my mother calls me Michael."

"I always called you Michael," she said, as if he needed the reminder.

"That was a long time ago." His response was terse.

"I guess it was." That remark was accompanied by another wistful smile.

He turned away, refusing to let himself wonder about her regrets. He had enough of his own.

After Michael had gone, Hope wandered down the street, browsing in the windows of the shops. Haven's shopping district was a far cry from Melrose Avenue, but everything the town's residents needed for day-to-day living could be found along this central strip. As she moved from one storefront to the next, Hope found herself walking down memory lane as much as Main Street, as nearly every venue held memories of time she'd spent with him.

They'd lingered over mugs of hot chocolate at Cal's Coffee Shop (now The Daily Grind), shared platters of wings at Diggers' and held hands during movies at Mann's Theater. They'd perused the shelves at Anthology Books, admired the trendy window displays at Loose Threads and loaded up on snacks at The Trading Post when they were planning long afternoons on horseback at the ranch.

Throughout high school, they'd been practically inseparable. And the years they'd spent together had been some of the happiest of her life. And yet, when she'd been presented with the opportunity to leave Haven—to pursue an acting career she wasn't even certain she wanted—she'd jumped at it.

"What do you mean you're leaving?" Michael had asked, stunned, when she'd shared her news.

"My mom's boyfriend thinks he can get me a part in a movie he's making."

"But...you never said anything about wanting to be a professional actor."

"Maybe because I never thought it was a viable option."

"So you're going to chase the dream—just like your mom?"

"I have to," she said, desperate for him to understand. "If I don't, I'll spend the rest of my life wondering what if."

"That sounds like your mom talking."

"Well, maybe she knows what she's talking about."

"And what about the dreams we shared and the plans we made?" he'd challenged.

"I'm not giving up on those," she'd promised. "I just need to do this first."

"No."

"What do you mean no?"

"I mean that I'm not going to sit around waiting for you. If you want to go to LA, go. Just don't expect to come back and pick up where we left off."

"But... I love you, Michael."

"But do you love me enough to stay?"

She'd hated him for asking her that question.

For forcing her to make an impossible choice.

Because it wasn't a choice between the boy she loved and an unlikely Hollywood career. It was a choice between the boy she loved and the mother whose affection had always been denied her. And for the first time in her entire life, Debra Bradford was not only showing an interest but presenting Hope with the chance to build a real relationship.

In any event, she'd made her choice, and even if things

hadn't worked out the way she'd hoped, it would be foolish to regret that choice now.

So what if her life wasn't everything she'd once imagined?

In some ways, it was much, much better.

And if she occasionally felt a twinge in the vicinity of her heart when she attended a colleague's wedding or cuddled a friend's baby, she simply reminded herself again that she'd made her own choice.

And just because she was back in Haven now was no reason to get all melancholy over *what-ifs*.

She paused to admire the elegant lines of The Stagecoach Inn, a boutique hotel that also housed Serenity Spa and The Home Station restaurant. None of which had been here when Hope left town so many years ago.

Proof that, no matter how much the town seemed to be the same, all things changed.

Even her own wishes and dreams.

Chapter Five

MG had places to go and things to do, and he didn't have time to return to the Circle G for a clean shirt. Instead, he drove the short distance to Winterberry Drive, where his brother now lived with his wife and three kids.

"I won't be long," he promised Bernie, as he got out of the truck. "Try to drool *out* of the window rather than all over it, okay?"

The dog responded by thumping his tail against the seat.

"MG," Lindsay said, greeting him at the door with a tired smile. "What are you doing here?"

"Hoping to snag a cup of coffee—and a clean shirt from my brother's closet."

She finally noticed the brown splotch on the front of his shirt. "What happened to you?"

"Missy Sutherland."

His sister-in-law frowned. "I think I'm going to need

more of an explanation than that. Go help yourself to coffee while I see what I can find."

He left his boots at the door and proceeded to the kitchen. He was halfway through his cup of coffee when she returned with a clean shirt.

"Thanks, Linds."

"Now tell me how you ended up wearing Missy Sutherland's—" she eyed the brown splotch again "—iced coffee?"

He quickly summarized what had transpired outside The Daily Grind.

"So Hope Bradford is in town," she mused.

He frowned. "Out of the whole story, that's the part you focused on?"

"It's the most interesting part," she assured him.

"I'm not sure that's true."

"Because you don't want it to be true. Because you don't want to admit that you still have feelings for her."

"Feelings of nostalgia, maybe," he allowed. "She was a big part of my life growing up—but she's been gone for more years than I knew her."

"Uh huh," Lindsay said, in a tone that told him she was completely unconvinced by his argument. "How did it feel to see her again?"

After the first jolt of surprise, there had been too many emotions for him to sort through them.

Or perhaps emotions that he didn't want to sort through.

"It was…fine."

"Fine, huh?" A smile spread slowly across his sister-in-law's face. "I mean, you've never been a chatterbox, but sometimes what you don't say is more telling than what you do."

"And sometimes you talk in riddles that don't make sense to anyone."

"Correction—that you don't want to make sense of," she said.

He swallowed the last mouthful of coffee and set the mug in the sink. "The house is quiet today. Where are Elliott and Avenlea?"

"Their grandparents took them to Adventure Village."

"And Emeline?"

"Sleeping—finally."

"Oh." He didn't bother to hide his disappointment.

"If you want, you can tiptoe—*quietly*—into the nursery to take a peek at her before you go."

"A peek's not as good as a cuddle, but I'll take what I can get," he told her.

But first, he went into the powder room to change his shirt.

Then, tiptoeing—*quietly*—into the nursery, he peered at the sleeping infant. She was zipped into something that Lindsay called a sleep sack and stretched out on her back with her arms flung out at her sides. Her hair was dark, like her dad's, but her features—the delicate nose, Cupid's bow mouth, slightly pointed chin—were her mom's. (Thank goodness for that, Mitch had said sincerely when his daughter was born.)

His brother was hardly the first of MG's contemporaries to become a dad. Heck, Byron Chandler had knocked up Annabelle Lyons when they were still in high school. But it wasn't until Emeline was born and MG looked at his brother—with the woman he'd always loved and their beautiful family—and realized that his own life was sadly empty.

Sure, he had a girlfriend. And Paige was great. But

when he looked to the future, he didn't see himself perched on the edge of her hospital bed, holding their newborn baby in his arms.

Or he hadn't at the time.

But he was trying to picture it now—because he was pretty sure it was what she wanted at some point down the line. And after three years—including six months of rehab hell—she deserved a lot better than what he'd given her so far.

"You're going to have your hands full when she gets older," MG whispered to his sister-in-law, who was hovering in the doorway. "Because she's every bit as gorgeous as her big sister and her mama."

"And you're as much a flatterer as your brother."

He tiptoed out of the room again, pausing in the hallway to glance at his watch. "I'm also running behind schedule."

"Where are you off to now?" she asked, falling into step behind him as he headed down the stairs.

"To get a birthday gift for Paige."

"Isn't her birthday today?"

"Yeah."

Though he couldn't see her shaking her head because she was behind him, he definitely heard her sigh.

"Do you know what you're looking for?"

"I have an idea." He shoved his feet into his boots.

She handed him a dog biscuit from the jar she kept by the door.

"This is the reason Bernie always wants to come to town with me," he said, wagging the treat at her.

"And the reason I make sure I have dog treats is so that you bring him to visit, so Elliott and Avenlea don't bug me to get a dog of our own."

"Gorgeous *and* devious," MG mused.

She grinned. "We'll see you for dinner tomorrow at the Circle G."

He nodded, pretending his mom's planned "family dinner" to celebrate Paige's birthday hadn't temporarily slipped his mind.

Had he mentioned it to the guest of honor?

He was pretty sure that he had.

In any event, he knew Paige would be thrilled by the invitation.

It had taken Angela Gilmore some time to warm up to her eldest son's girlfriend when MG and Paige first started dating. She'd liked her well enough—or at least she claimed to when he asked her opinion—but she didn't think she was "the one" for him. Because she was confident that MG and Hope would eventually find their way back to one another, as Mitch and Lindsay had done.

But that was before the accident.

Before Paige saved his life.

After—everything changed.

Now his mother couldn't stop singing his girlfriend's praises. She was "an angel sent from heaven." He was lucky to have her. And when was he going to stop dragging his feet and put a ring on her finger already so that they could give Angela and Charles more grandchildren?

"I'm not supposed to pick up a cake or anything for this dinner tomorrow, am I?"

Lindsay chuckled. "No. Your mom asked me to take care of that."

"Okay, then." He kissed his sister-in-law's cheek. "I'll see you tomorrow."

Then he headed out to buy the ring that would make Paige (and his mother) happy.

* * *

Call a friend, Edwina had urged, even as she was pushing Hope out of the house.

And while it sounded like a good idea, the problem was that Hope had lost touch with all her friends from high school. She hadn't deliberately cut them out of her life—she just hadn't made an effort to keep the lines of communication open. Not even with Laurel Walsh who, aside from Michael, had been her best friend growing up.

And right now, Hope was genuinely sorry, because it would be nice to have someone to talk to and not feel so completely and desperately alone.

She could call Jenny, if she wanted to chat. The woman who'd been her agent for fifteen years had also become a good friend. But over the past few weeks, she'd been leaning on Jenny a lot. Probably too much. And though Jenny liked to tease that Hope paid her for her time, she knew that her agent went above and beyond the requirements of her representation.

Aside from Jenny, Hope knew that she could confide in Colin McCarragher, who was so much more to her than a costar on *Rockwood Ridge*. But Colin was completely incommunicado in the Ngorongoro Crater with his longtime girlfriend right now. And even if he had cell service in remote Tanzania, she wasn't going to interrupt his vacation just to confess that crossing paths with her first ever boyfriend had everything inside her tangled up in knots.

Colin knew about Michael, of course, because he knew all of her deepest, darkest secrets. Not that Michael was a deep, dark secret. In fact, once upon a time, he'd been one of the best parts of her life—and she'd walked away from him.

Not only because he'd forced her to make a choice, but also because she'd been afraid to trust that her feelings were real.

Because she'd been seventeen years old—and what did a seventeen-year-old know about love?

What did she know about love now?

Eighteen years and three broken engagements later, she was hardly an expert on the subject.

The only thing she knew for certain was that she wanted the kind of relationship her grandparents had shared. Edwina and Alistair had loved one another for forty-six years, forty-four of which they'd spent married. When her husband of more than four decades passed, Edwina had been certain she would never love again, because her heart had been buried with him.

Fast forward a dozen years, and her grandmother was having a passionate love affair with Hope's former high school principal. And while Hope was sincerely happy for her, she was also a little bit envious that Edwina had managed to do what Hope couldn't—risk her heart again.

By the time she'd walked the length of Main Street on both sides—to kill time, because she knew Edwina would be disappointed if she returned to the house too soon—Hope's stomach was rumbling. Or maybe it was the fact that she'd paused in front of Jo's Pizza that caused her empty stomach to take notice.

She pulled her phone out of her pocket to send her grandmother a quick text message.

Do you have any plans for lunch?

She didn't have to wait long for Edwina's reply.

Dennis just called. He's picking me up and taking me to Elko for a vintage car show.

Hope replied,

Sounds like fun.

Did you want to join us?

Did she want to be a third wheel on a date with her grandmother and former high school principal?
Not even a little bit.

No, thank you.

We shouldn't be too late.

Do you have a curfew that I'm not aware of?

Edwina replied to that with a string of laughing/crying emojis.

Stay as late as you want. I'm perfectly capable of fending for myself.

Then she tucked her phone away and walked into the restaurant.

"Hope Bradford!" Laurel Walsh's eyes were as bright as her tone when she greeted her childhood friend.
Except that she wasn't Laurel Walsh anymore, Hope reminded herself. She was Laurel Gibson now, mar-

ried to her high school sweetheart early in the fall after graduation.

But looking at her old friend, her curly dark hair secured in a high ponytail on her head and a bright red apron advertising Jo's Pizza over her clothes, Hope felt as if she'd been transported back in time eighteen years.

"I didn't know you were in town," Laurel said, breaching the distance between them to hug Hope.

"I'm visiting my grandmother," she explained.

"Edwina must be over the moon. And so am I." She drew back again. "Why didn't you reach out to let me know you were going to be around?"

"I wasn't sure if you'd want to hear from me," Hope admitted.

"Why wouldn't I?" Laurel asked, sounding sincerely baffled.

She shrugged. "Because I haven't been in touch in…a very long time."

The other woman waved away her explanation. "You were busy becoming famous. And I was busy trying to plan a shotgun wedding, because I got pregnant right after graduation."

"I'm sorry I couldn't make it back for the wedding."

"I was sorry, too," Laurel said. "But it was admittedly short notice and I knew you had a lot going on."

It was a generous interpretation of the truth—which was that she had a tiny part in a big movie. If she'd wanted to come back to Haven for a weekend, her absence probably wouldn't have been noticed. And even more than Hope wanted to attend her friend's wedding, she wanted to see Michael again. But Debra had encouraged her daughter to look forward not back, and Hope knew that saying goodbye a second time would be even harder than the first, so she made the easy choice and sent her regrets along with a gift.

"And anyway, me and Christopher split before Madison's third birthday—before we knew I was pregnant with Nikolas."

"I'm sorry," Hope said again.

"It's all good," Laurel assured her. "We're much better as friends than we ever were as husband and wife."

"You managed to stay friends even after the divorce?"

"We had to—for our children," Laurel explained. "But I'm sure you came in for lunch, not to listen to me blather on."

"Actually, I wanted to place a take-out order," Hope told her. "But it's been fun to catch up with you, at least a little."

"Then let's get you a table so we can catch up some more. The midday rush hasn't started yet, and I want to know what's going on with you."

Hope could have protested, but it was so nice to see her old friend—and such a relief that her old friend seemed happy to see her—that she let Laurel lead her to a table.

"I'll be right back with a menu," the server promised.

Her friend returned less than a minute later, with a menu and an extra-large pie loaded with toppings.

"That was fast," Hope said.

"Ha," Laurel said, setting the menu in front of her. "This pizza is for table seven."

Hope took a minute to peruse the restaurant's offerings while she waited for her friend to return. Jo's had been a popular spot when they were in high school, though the options back then had been cheese pizza, cheese and pepperoni pizza, three-meat pizza or vegetarian pizza. Now the menu was four full pages, including several crust options, more than a dozen toppings, plus salads, pastas and even a wine list.

After delivering the pie to table seven and checking on the diners at another table, Laurel returned with two glasses of water. She set one in front of Hope then slid onto the bench seat across from her with the other.

"There are days when I'm on my feet for the entirety of a six-hour shift, so I've learned to sit down when I can," she explained.

"I don't blame you," Hope said.

"So tell me what's been going on with you."

"Do you follow the *Hollywood's Hottest Gossip* blog?"

"I do," her friend happily confessed.

"Then there's nothing I can tell you that you don't already know."

"I'm sure that's not true," Laurel said. "Because *HHG* failed to uncover the reason behind your most recent broken engagement."

"Because it was nothing more than a mistake, quickly rectified."

"And they were very frustratingly skimpy on the details of your affair with Colin McCarragher."

"Because there was no affair."

"Seriously?"

"Seriously," Hope confirmed.

"Tell me that he's a good kisser, at least," her friend urged.

"There really isn't anything sexy or seductive about kissing someone in front of a camera crew."

Laurel pouted, obviously disappointed by her response.

"But away from the cameras, he is, indeed, a fabulous kisser."

Now her friend grinned. "I knew there was a reason that you guys positively smolder on-screen together."

"It was one seriously intense lip lock—after the wrap of my first season on the show," Hope confided. "But we both agreed that we didn't want to risk our professional relationship by getting personally involved. Since then, we've simply been good friends who work well together."

*Work*ed *well together*, she mentally amended.

"And we're good friends, right?" the server asked. "I mean, I know we lost touch for a long time, but we were always good friends."

"We're good friends," Hope confirmed.

Laurel grinned again. "So now I can say that I'm good friends with a good friend of Colin McCarragher."

Hope laughed. "Yes, you can."

"Now, good friend, have you decided what you want for lunch?"

Chapter Six

"Isn't this a surprise?" Olivia Gilmore said, lowering herself into the seat that Laurel had recently vacated.

Hope, who'd been checking her phone for any email or text message updates from her agent, tucked the device away to give her full attention to Michael's sister. "How are you, Olivia?"

"I'm doing well." Her tone was polite but reserved. "And you?"

"Can't complain," Hope said.

"No?" The other woman seemed surprised by her response. "Not even about the ruckus at The Daily Grind earlier today?"

"How did you hear about that?"

"I crossed paths with MG as he was leaving Mitch and Lindsay's," the other woman confided. "He stopped by there to borrow a shirt."

"He needed one," Hope acknowledged.

"And yet you appear to have escaped unscathed."

"Thanks to your brother."

"MG has always been a sucker for a damsel in distress."

"I don't think Michael would appreciate being called a sucker."

"Then he shouldn't act like one," his sister muttered.

"You seem to be annoyed with him…or are you annoyed with me?"

Olivia appeared to be waging an internal struggle, as if there was something she wanted to say but wasn't sure that she should.

Hope eyed her ex's sister carefully. "Have I done something to offend you, Olivia?"

"No," she admitted. "I just wish that you hadn't come back."

"Well, that's blunt enough."

"I'm sorry, but you being here now could screw everything up."

"I'm not sure what *everything* you're talking about, but my only reason for being in Haven is to spend time with my grandmother."

The other woman's brow furrowed. "Is Edwina unwell?"

"No, she's fine," Hope said, grateful that Michael's sister cared enough to ask. "I just hadn't been home in a while and I wanted to see her."

She smiled her thanks to Laurel when she delivered her pizza.

"Can I get you anything?" Laurel asked Olivia.

She shook her head. "I'm just waiting for my take-out order."

Laurel nodded and headed off again.

Hope transferred a slice from the serving tray to her plate. "Do you want a slice while you're waiting?"

"No, thanks." Olivia inched toward the edge of the bench. "I have to go, but there's one more thing you need to know."

Hope finished chewing and swallowed. "What's that?"

"MG's with someone now. Her name's Paige. She's terrific—and really good for him. And he's happy."

"Okay."

"They've been together almost three years, and any day now—probably tonight, in fact—he's going to propose to her."

"Then I guess congratulations are in order," Hope said, because what else was she supposed to say?

"I'm only telling you so that you don't think you can pick up where you left off with my brother."

"I can assure you that Michael wasn't a factor in my decision to come back to Haven and I have no intention of—how did you put it?—picking up where we left off while I'm in town."

"Okay, then." Olivia stood up. "Enjoy your pizza."

"I'm sure I will," Hope said.

But it was a lie.

The truth was that Olivia's pointed remark had killed her appetite.

It wasn't as if the news that Michael had a girlfriend was a big surprise. No doubt he'd had plenty of girlfriends over the past eighteen years. But to hear that he was planning to marry, which would inevitably lead to having a family, was like a kick in the gut. (And yes, she was aware of the hypocrisy, considering her three engagements, but that didn't make her feelings any less real.) Because there had been a time when she and Michael had planned for a future together. A time when the family he'd talked about wanting was their family.

Silly, teenage dreams, perhaps—though they hadn't seemed silly at the time.

Hope had been so head-over-heels in love with him that she couldn't imagine anything more wonderful than spending her life with him, and she'd been almost certain that he was planning to propose to her after graduation. Yes, they were young, but they knew what they wanted. He would continue to work at the Circle G with his dad and uncle and brother and cousins, and she would go to teachers' college. Or maybe she'd study business management or become an administrative assistant.

Okay, so maybe she didn't have all the answers at seventeen, but the one thing she knew without a shadow of a doubt was that she was going to be Mrs. Michael Gilmore and spend the rest of her life with the man she loved.

Now there was another woman who was undoubtedly dreaming of the same thing. Another woman who loved him and who he loved in return. Another woman who was going to wear his grandmother's ring.

Hope knew that she should be happy for him, because he deserved nothing but the best.

So why did the news make her feel empty inside?

"Is something wrong with your pizza?" Laurel asked, when she came by Hope's table again a few minutes later.

"No, it's great." Hope forced a smile. "Even better than I remembered."

"Then why aren't you eating it?"

"I guess I'm just not as hungry as I thought."

Her friend frowned at that. "Did Olivia say something to upset you?"

"No," she immediately denied, because she didn't

think Olivia had intended to upset her. Michael's sister had only told her the truth—a truth she needed to know, even if it made her unhappy to hear it.

"Did she tell you about MG and Paige?" Laurel's tone was sympathetic. "Not that I think you'd care that your high school boyfriend has a new girlfriend when you've dated several Hollywood hunks, but I remember you guys were really tight way back when."

Hope forced another smile. "A very long time ago."

Still, finding out that Michael had not only moved on but was planning to marry another woman hurt more deeply than she would have anticipated.

"So…do you want a box to take the rest of your pizza home?" her friend asked, after another moment had passed.

Though she'd lost all interest in the pizza, Hope forced herself to respond. "That would be great, thanks."

Hope's unexpected return to Haven had put a wrench in his plans, and MG wasn't happy about it. Not that he should be surprised. It was hardly the first time Hope had upended his agenda. But this time, he wasn't the only one impacted.

Thanks to his sister, he'd known that she was back, but *knowing* and *seeing* were two very different things. Hearing that she was in town had given him a little jolt, because it meant there was the possibility of crossing paths with her when he went into town, though he didn't do so very often—and even less so since the accident. Actually seeing her had jolted him all the way down to his toes, an unexpected—and unexpectedly intense—reaction.

Would it always be like this?

Would seeing her forever remind him of what they'd once shared? What they'd lost?

Except they hadn't really lost it, had they?

She'd chosen to throw it away.

She'd chosen the possibility of a career in Hollywood over the certainty of a life with MG. She'd shot for the stars—and become one. And he was happy that she'd gotten what she wanted, even if it meant that he never would.

He'd loved her for so long, even after she'd gone. But eventually he'd picked up the broken pieces of his heart and managed to put them back together, despite the fact that the biggest piece—the one he'd given to Hope when he was thirteen years old—had been missing

But he'd moved on. He'd had other girlfriends, other lovers. And with Paige, he'd started to believe that he could have a future. But that was before he saw Hope.

Seeing her had started an avalanche of memories that threatened to bury him. He'd loved her with an intensity of emotion that blocked out everything else. And when she'd left him, he'd been heartbroken.

Whatever her reasons for being in Haven now, he had no doubt that it was a temporary arrangement. That in a few days—or maybe a week or two—she'd move on again.

So he pushed the memories to the back of his mind and pushed open the door of The Gold Mine.

"Let me guess." Kelli Marshall, the store owner's daughter (and one of MG's long-ago, short-term girlfriends), pretended to muse as she tapped a neatly manicured nail against the dent in her chin. "It's not Valentine's Day or Christmas, so it must be... Paige's birthday."

"It is," MG confirmed.

"And are you looking for anything in particular?" She deliberately dropped her gaze to the display of engagement rings in the case directly in front of her.

"You seem to have something in mind," he noted.

She eagerly unlocked the glass door and pulled out a tray.

"A diamond solitaire is classic," Kelli told him. "And though it pains me to say this, because I know you can afford flashy, Paige wouldn't want anything too big or flashy that she couldn't wear at work." As she was talking, she spread a velvet cloth on the glass counter and set out three rings for closer perusal.

An annoying voice at the back of his mind asked him why he was looking at buying an engagement ring when he had one at home—the one that had come to him almost twenty years earlier.

That same annoying voice taunted him with the answer—because he'd already been in love with Hope when his grandmother died, and he'd shown the ring to her, promising that he would put it on her finger one day.

And even though that dream had turned to dust long ago, he still couldn't imagine giving the ring to anyone else. And so here he was at the local jewelry store, looking to buy a ring that held no memories of another woman.

He lifted one of Kelli's selections from the velvet and watched the light reflect in the facets of the diamond.

"That's a princess cut," she told him. "Classic and stunning."

He tried to imagine the look on Paige's face when she opened the lid of the box to reveal the princess cut diamond, but it was Hope's smile that he saw in his mind.

Hope's smile that took his breath away and made his heart beat just a little bit faster.

Dammit.

"What's wrong?" Kelli asked.

"Nothing."

Everything.

He set the ring back down on the velvet. "I'm just thinking that it might be too soon for a ring."

"You've been together almost three years," Kelli reminded him dryly.

"I know. But everything got turned upside down after my accident and I think we need some more time to get things back on track."

Because how could he buy a ring for Paige when he was thinking about Hope?

How could he promise to love Paige forever when he wasn't sure he loved her now?

Yes, he cared about her—there was no doubt about that.

And he was grateful to her for sticking with him, especially over the past eight months.

But thinking of spending the rest of his life with Paige filled him with more resignation than joy.

It wasn't her fault. She truly was an amazing woman: smart and beautiful and funny and kind. As far as he could tell, she only had one significant flaw: she wasn't Hope.

"Is this about Hope?" Kelli asked.

He scowled, annoyed by the question.

Annoyed that everyone in town seemed to think he was still hung up on his high school girlfriend.

And even more annoyed to acknowledge—if only to himself—that it might be true.

"Why would you ask me something like that?"

She shrugged. "I heard she was in town."

"Which has nothing to do with me and no bearing on my relationship with Paige."

It was a lie, of course.

But instead of calling him on it, Kelli returned the rings to the tray and the tray to the cabinet. "What's your Plan B?"

He picked out a pendant that she described as teardrop silhouette enhanced with a diamond-studded loop and a floating center diamond.

"I know it's none of my business," she said, as she wrapped the pendant, "but if you're never going to propose to her, you shouldn't keep stringing her along."

"I'm not stringing her along," he denied.

"I hope that's true." Kelli affixed a shiny bow to the top of the box. "Because for as long as I've known Paige, she's talked about wanting to get married and have a family someday."

"*Someday* is a rather vague timeline," he noted.

"Only to a man," she retorted. "To a woman over thirty, it's a rapidly approaching deadline."

Paige seemed happy with the flowers MG had sent to her at the clinic and equally pleased with his choice of The Home Station for dinner, at the conclusion of which they ordered dessert (mango pie with a shortbread crust and raspberry coulis) to take back to her house. After he'd opened a bottle of wine and she'd blown out the candle he stuck in the pie, he gave her the package from The Gold Mine.

A necklace box would never be mistaken for a ring box, and Paige's disappointment was evident in the wavering of her smile even as she carefully peeled away the tape that secured the paper. But when she finally unwrapped the gift, she said, "It's beautiful, MG. Thank you."

"I'm glad you like it," he said, picking up his fork to dig into his pie.

"The whole day was wonderful," she said.

"And in case I forgot to mention it, we're celebrating again tomorrow at the Circle G. My mom's making cannelloni and Lindsay's getting a cake—"

"I want a baby."

His fork slipped out of his fingers, clattered against his plate.

"A baby?" he echoed.

She huffed out a breath. "I'm thirty-three years old, MG."

"I know," he acknowledged cautiously. "That's why we're celebrating your birthday today."

"Did you also know that the quantity and quality of a woman's egg reserve begins to decline at thirty?"

This was not at all how he'd imagined the night proceeding—but the picture in his mind now was an out-of-control car about to plunge over a cliff, and he didn't have a clue how to rescue it.

"But your sister just had her first baby last year, and she's five years older than you," he pointed out.

"And before she got pregnant, she and her husband tried for over a decade to have a baby."

MG pushed his dessert away, his appetite gone. "Can we table this conversation for another day and focus on celebrating your birthday right now?"

Paige shook her head. "I think we've put off this conversation long enough."

He wiped his fingers on a napkin and folded it on top of his plate, mentally cursing himself for not having anticipated this. Maybe not tonight—how could he have guessed that she'd pick her birthday of all days to drop the *I want a baby* bomb—but he should have guessed that it was coming.

Maybe he would have been less surprised if she'd said *I want a ring*, but she'd skipped right past the prospect of an engagement and then a wedding to starting a family—while he was still trying to make his way over the buying a ring hurdle.

Paige pushed her plate aside, too. "I heard that you were at The Daily Grind with Hope today."

"I wasn't *with* Hope," he immediately denied. "We just happened to be there at the same time."

"So why didn't you tell me that you saw her?"

"Because I can't imagine how it's relevant to anything, including this conversation."

"Is that the only reason?" she asked skeptically.

"What other reason do you think there might me?"

She lifted her glass of wine, sipped. "I think—I thought—that you were finally ready to make plans for a future with me, until your ex-girlfriend's return sent you into a tailspin."

"I'm not in a tailspin."

"So tell me how you see things," she said. "Because I've never made any secret of the fact that I want to get married and have a family someday and, after almost three years together, it shouldn't have been a shock to you to hear that I want to have a baby."

"I just figured *someday* was a lot further down the road," he told her.

"I'm thirty-three years old," she said again. "I don't know how much *further down the road* I can go before it's too late."

"I'm sorry," he said, and he was. "I'm just not ready to be a husband or a father."

"I thought you were the one," she said, the quiet words filled with sadness. "And I really believe you could have been—but I'm obviously not the one for you."

"I don't know why you'd say that," he protested. "Don't we have a good thing going?"

"What's so good about it?" she challenged. "That I don't pressure you for more than you're willing to give? That I don't protest when you backtrack our relationship?"

"When have I ever backtracked our relationship?"

"You moved in here after the accident because it was convenient for you to get to the clinic for your physical therapy. But when I suggested we make it a more permanent arrangement, you dipped and twirled around the idea like you were on *Dancing with the Stars*. And then, as soon as Kenzie cut your treatments to twice a week, you packed your bags to go back to the Circle G."

"Because that's where I work, and if I lived in town, I'd have to leave before the sun was up in the morning to drive out to the ranch."

"Which is what your brother does," she pointed out.

She was right. Mitch did exactly what she was suggesting MG could do and had, in fact, been doing it— without a word of complaint—for almost two years now.

"Because it's not about what's sensible but about the effort you're willing to make to be with the one you love," Paige continued when he didn't respond. "And if you really loved me, the drive wouldn't be an obstacle— it wouldn't even be a consideration. Which is what got me thinking…and the more I thought about it, the more I realized that maybe you don't love me. Maybe you can't love me—because you never stopped loving Hope."

"How many times do I have to tell you that I'm not carrying a torch for my high school girlfriend?" he demanded, unable to keep the frustration out of his voice.

"She was more than that," Paige reminded him. "She was the first girl you ever loved, and when Gilmores fall in love, it's once and forever."

"Apparently you've heard the story of my parents' romance too many times."

"It's not just your parents," she said. "But also Mitchell and Lindsay and Olivia and Adam and…you and Hope."

"There's no me and Hope," he insisted. "If you need proof of that, consider the fact that she's been engaged to so many other men that I've lost count."

"But obviously you took notice."

"It's hard not to in this town, where she's an even bigger celebrity than Spencer Channing."

Paige gave no reaction to his mention of the former rodeo champion. She didn't even seem to be listening to him anymore—her mind apparently having gone down another path.

"Ohmygod." She looked at him now with wide eyes. "I really *am* a fool. I didn't even make the connection before."

"What connection?" he asked warily.

"Between Hope's engagement and your accident. I wondered why you would have gone out on your own in the dark. You aren't usually reckless, but you were acting recklessly that night—after pictures of Hope Bradford and Seth Hansen celebrating their engagement were plastered all over the internet."

"I acted recklessly because I'm an idiot," he said. "Just ask my mother."

Paige didn't crack a smile. "All I ever wanted was a life with you—but you're never going to love me the way I love you. And I don't deserve to be second best."

MG sat back, not sure what was happening. "Wait. Paige… Are you…breaking up with me?" he asked.

"I guess I am," she said.

He was stunned.

And secretly relieved.

Because she was right—he didn't love her the way she loved him, and he knew that he never could.

But after almost three years together, it didn't seem right to just walk out the door. Although the way she was standing there, dry-eyed with her arms folded over her chest, seemed to indicate that she was waiting for him to do just that.

Or maybe she wanted him to protest. To fight for their relationship. To fight for *her*.

"Maybe we should talk about this tomorrow," he finally said.

But she shook her head. "I'm done talking, MG." Her tone was sad but resolute. "You can't give me what I want and I'm not willing to settle for less."

She was right.

So he rose from the table and made his way to the door, pausing to touch his lips to her cheek. "I hope you find what you're looking for. And…"

She held his gaze, waiting.

"And *what*, MG?" she finally prompted.

"I… I am sorry, Paige. That I couldn't give you what you wanted." He walked out into the night and closed the door gently behind him.

Chapter Seven

The next week was fairly uneventful. Though Hope was still waiting on an update from her agent, she managed not to worry obsessively about what might or might not happen. Mostly, she enjoyed spending time with her grandmother and getting to know Dennis, and she even managed to chat with Laurel a few times on the phone, though they hadn't yet managed to mesh their schedules to get together.

Though her recycled-from-high-school wardrobe was doing the job of helping her blend in, she decided that she needed a pair of jeans that fit a little better—and weren't almost twenty years old.

"What do you say to a shopping trip tomorrow?" Hope suggested to Edwina as they tidied up the kitchen after dinner Thursday night. "We could make a day of it. Drive into Battle Mountain—or Elko, if you'd rather—browse the shops, have some lunch."

"Oh." Her grandmother sent a glance toward her boyfriend, who was putting away the dishes as she dried them. "That sounds like a lovely idea. Really lovely. But we…um…that is…"

"We're heading out tomorrow morning for a weekend getaway in Tahoe," he said, coming to her rescue.

"Which sounds even lovelier," Hope said. "But I sincerely hope you don't feel you have to leave town to get away from me."

"Of course, we don't," Edwina said.

"I actually made the reservations a few months back," Dennis said. "To celebrate our anniversary."

"Our first date was September ninth last year. And maybe a year isn't a big deal to you young people, but when you get to be our age, it's quite the milestone."

"And should be celebrated," Hope agreed. "We'll go shopping another time."

"I should have told you about our plans before now," Edwina said.

"Instead, she tried to get me to change our plans," Dennis confided.

"Well, I'm glad you didn't," Hope said. "Because I'm sure you'll both have a wonderful time."

"You'll be okay here by yourself?" her grandmother asked worriedly.

She smiled. "You do know that I live alone in California, don't you?"

"I know. That doesn't mean I approve."

Hope's tone was indulgent. "I'll be fine, Grams."

"I've made sure the fridge is stocked, but if you need anything—"

"I'll figure it out," she promised.

And that's how Hope found herself standing outside of Diggers' Bar & Grill Friday night.

Not because she wanted something different than what she could find in Edwina's refrigerator, but because she decided that spending a Friday night alone at home while her grandmother was on a romantic weekend away with her boyfriend was the very definition of pathetic.

Despite having made numerous visits to town over the past eighteen years, Hope honestly couldn't remember the last time she'd been to the local hot spot. Because when she came home to see her grandmother, she wanted to maximize her time with Edwina, which meant cooking and sharing meals together in the house on Queen Street.

She walked through the double doors that opened into an enclosed foyer that housed two entrances—one leading to the Bar and the other to the Grill. Hope opted for the bar, figuring a solitary figure occupying a single stool was less likely to be noticed than one taking up a whole table.

The interior of the restaurant was deliberately rustic, the wood floors scuffed and scarred from the steady traffic of bootheels, the walls covered with framed newspaper headlines announcing the discovery of gold and silver in the nearby hills, alongside miners' helmets, metal pans, coils of rope, pickaxes and other mining paraphernalia.

The bartender—none other than Duke himself, the owner of Diggers'—slapped a laminated menu on the counter in front of her.

She started to push the menu back to him, to tell him that she wasn't hungry, but at that exact moment, a server came out of the kitchen with a platter of wings and the scent of the tangy sauce teased her nostrils, reminding her that she hadn't eaten since breakfast—ten hours earlier—and that had only been a cup of yogurt and handful of berries.

She pulled the menu closer to peer at the offerings. Garlic bread, wings, nachos, fries, popcorn shrimp. Her mouth watered as she scanned the options—a veritable list of all the foods she'd mostly deprived herself of for the past eighteen years.

Her weight hadn't been a concern—at least not to Hope—when she first moved to Los Angeles. She'd been seventeen years old and naturally slender with an active metabolism. But like a lot of other people her age, she had some unhealthy eating habits: French fries from the high school cafeteria for lunch, pizza with her friends after drama club, plates of nachos dripping with cheese on date nights with Michael.

Moving to Los Angeles with her mom had been an eye-opener. Debra Bradford didn't have any junk food in her apartment—and if Hope brought any in, she'd toss it out. On the rare occasion that they went out for a burger and fries, it was one order that they'd split in half—followed by an extra workout after dinner to ensure that they burned off every single one of the calories they'd consumed.

Still, Hope hadn't worried about what she ate when she was away from her mother's critical eye. Not until a casting director took one look at her at an audition and decided to swap out the part she'd intended to read for in favor of another character, remarking that she appeared more suited to play the chubby friend rather than the main protagonist.

She hadn't had a French fry since.

Or a chicken wing.

Or garlic bread.

Or any one of the numerous menu items that called to her now.

"What can I get for you?" Duke asked, after preparing drinks for a trio of customers at the other end of the bar.

"I'll have the side of carrots and celery and blue cheese dip and a glass of the Stonechurch Vineyards pinot noir," she decided.

"The carrots and celery are available as a side with the wings," the bartender told her.

"But I don't want the wings," she said. (A blatant lie.) "I only want the veggies."

"Sorry," he said, not sounding sorry at all. "You can have the veggies with an order of wings or not at all."

"I'm happy to pay for the wings, but I don't want them."

"If other customers see me making an exception for Hope Bradford, they'll expect me to make an exception for them, too."

She blinked. "Who?"

A wry smile curved the bartender's lips. "I might not be much of a celebrity watcher, but I know everyone in town—and I know you're here visiting your grandmother. And since you obviously aren't one of my regular customers, it wasn't too difficult to figure it out, Hope."

"But... Hope Bradford is blond."

"Did you really think a wig would make a difference?" Duke asked. "Bartenders are an observant breed. And while it was a long time ago, so you might not remember, you used to come into the restaurant fairly regularly with your grandparents. And later, in the company of one of the Gilmore boys. MG, wasn't it?"

She sighed. "Maybe I should go."

"No one here's going to bother you," Duke promised.

"How can you be sure?" she asked warily.

"Because I won't let them."

She glanced at the menu again, because she really didn't want to go back to her grandmother's empty house. And despite her usual disguise having proven worthless, she believed the bartender when he said he wouldn't let anyone bother her.

"Okay," she decided. "I'll have a dozen wings with the carrots and celery and a glass of the pinot noir."

"How do you want your wings?"

It didn't matter, because she had no intention of eating them, but she decided to order them "hot" as she'd always done in the past.

"Can I give you a piece of advice?"

"Is it free? Or do I have to order more wings to get it?"

He chuckled. "This one's free."

"In that case, lay it on me."

"Do you like beer?"

"It depends on the beer," she said.

"Switch out the wine for a glass of beer—it will go down much better with the wings. And you'll look more like a local."

"I am a local," she reminded him.

"Hometown girl gone Hollywood."

"Fine—I'll have a beer instead of the wine."

He nodded approvingly as he tipped a glass beneath a tap.

She sipped the beer Duke set in front of her and found it surprisingly smooth and refreshingly cool.

A few minutes later, he delivered a plate of wings.

Her stomach growled as she picked up a carrot stick and dunked it in the blue cheese dressing.

She was nibbling on the crisp vegetable when, out of the corner of her eye, she saw someone settle onto the vacant stool beside her. There were several other empty seats at the bar, but of course the newcomer had chosen the one right next to her. Because some guys just couldn't resist making a move on a woman sitting alone.

But there was a sudden crackling in the air around her that told Hope it wasn't just "some guy" sitting beside her. Still, she didn't let herself glance over, not even when Duke wandered over to take his order.

But when he ordered a beer, her suspicions were confirmed, because she would recognize Michael Gilmore's voice anywhere—apparently even after eighteen years.

He accepted the beer Duke set in front of him with a nod of thanks and lifted it to his mouth. She reached for a piece of celery.

"You going to eat those wings?" Michael asked Hope when he'd set his glass down again.

"Why else would I have ordered them?"

He grinned. "That's your Donnalisa voice."

"I'm sorry?"

"Donnalisa in *Where R U*?"

"I didn't think anyone saw that movie," she muttered under her breath.

"Maybe no one outside of Haven," he allowed. "But your grandmother put up flyers around town to ensure everyone knew when it was airing."

"Didn't mean you had to watch it."

"Have you met Edwina Bradford?"

She didn't bother to respond to what was obviously a rhetorical question.

"And it wasn't a horrible movie," he continued. "I mean, yeah, there were some plot holes, and some unrealistic contrivances, but it was entertaining."

"That's a much better review than it got from any of the critics," she noted.

"Anyway, you don't have to worry that I'm going to blow your cover," he assured her, reaching across to steal a wing from her plate.

She slapped his hand away. "Do you often help yourself to food from other people's plates?"

"It's called sharing," he told her. "We used to do it all the time."

He was right.

And why was she hoarding wings she wasn't going to eat, anyway?

Maybe because being near him made her...uncomfortable.

Or perhaps *aware* was a more accurate description of what she was feeling.

Aware that he was sitting close—so close that their shoulders were almost touching. Aware of the breadth of his shoulders beneath the Henley-style T-shirt he was wearing. Aware of the calluses on the hand wrapped around his beer glass. Aware that those hands had once explored every inch of her body. Aware that she'd been naked with him, their bodies joined together in the most intimate way possible.

She slammed the door shut on the memories and slid the plate of wings closer to him, so that it was between them. A physical barrier of sorts.

"So what are you doing here?" she asked, because talking had to be safer than letting her mind wander down memory lane.

"Probably the same as you."

"I doubt that," she said. "Unless you're also contemplating the wisdom of all your life decisions."

"Sounds to me like someone's having a pity party."

"Maybe I am feeling sorry for myself." She stared at the glass of beer. "I should have had the wine. Beer always makes me melancholy."

"What have you got to be melancholy about?" he wanted to know. "From where I sit, it looks like you got everything you ever wanted."

"Well, the view is a little different from my seat," she said, then shook her head. "Anyway, that's enough about me." She lifted her glass. "Should we toast to your engagement?"

His brows drew together. "What?"

"Your sister told me that you were going to propose to your girlfriend. And… I saw you looking at rings at The Gold Mine last week."

He stared at her. "Were you were spying on me—just like everyone else in this town?"

"I wasn't spying," she replied indignantly—and perhaps a little defensively. "I was window shopping and, when I passed the jewelry store, I saw you there."

He swallowed another mouthful of beer. "I didn't buy a ring."

"Oh." She felt a giddy—and inexplicable—sense of relief.

"I bought a necklace. And she dumped me."

"Because you gave her a necklace instead of a ring?"

"Because she wants to have a baby."

"That couldn't have been a surprise to you," she remarked.

"Why not?" he challenged.

"Because most couples talk about what they want their future to look like—if and when they plan to get married, where they want to live, how many kids—if any—they want to have."

"Did you talk about all those things with Colin Mc-Carragher before you got engaged?"

"Colin and I talked about those things and a lot more," she said. "Because when you spend ten hours a day, six days a week for months at a time with someone, you have no secrets.

"But, in the interest of transparency," she continued, "I will confess that Colin and I were never engaged."

The look on his face clearly conveyed skepticism as he reached for another wing. "You're saying that all the gossip sites got it wrong?"

"The truth isn't nearly as important as the number of clicks," she told him.

He considered that for a minute as he lifted his glass again.

"Are you really not going to eat any of these wings?" he asked.

"I'm really not."

"Why?"

"Because there are ninety calories in a single chicken wing—more if it's breaded."

When he didn't immediately respond, she glanced sideways at him—and caught his gaze skimming over her in a slow and very thorough appraisal. Then his eyes lifted to hers and held for a long moment. Her breath caught in her throat and she felt a quiver low in her belly that she recognized as physical attraction.

But she shouldn't be attracted to him.

It was one thing to fall under his spell when she was

a teenager—when all the boys she knew wore Wranglers and cowboy boots. But she'd lived in California for the past eighteen years. In that time, she'd dated a lot of sophisticated urban men. But none of those men had ever made her feel the way she felt when she was with Michael.

"I know it's inappropriate to comment on a woman's figure, but it seems to me that you could afford to take in a few—or a few hundred—more calories."

"I have lost a few pounds in recent weeks," she acknowledged. "Without even trying."

"Maybe you should try to find them again."

She managed a small smile. "The only reason I ordered the wings is that Duke wouldn't let me have the side of veggies without them."

He inched the plate closer to her.

After a brief moment of hesitation, she picked up one of the wings.

"You always did prefer the drumettes," he noted.

And she realized that he'd automatically gravitated toward the wingettes.

MG gestured to Duke to bring them another round.

"And a dozen more wings," he said, when the bartender set their drinks in front of them.

"Can we get an order of garlic bread, too?" Hope asked. "With cheese."

Chapter Eight

"Look who's suddenly a wild woman," MG said, unable to resist teasing her.

Hope frowned at the beer in her glass. "Maybe I'm drunk."

He felt his smile slip. "How many of those have you had?"

She lifted her hand to her mouth to erase a smear of hot sauce. Watching the tip of her tongue lick the pad of her thumb made him feel as if he was seventeen again and wishing he had a textbook to carry in front of him as he traversed the halls of Westmount High.

"No need to worry," she said. "This is only my second."

Her remark yanked his attention back to the present, though it took him another moment to remember what they'd been talking about.

"Your second beer on an empty stomach," he pointed out.

"I'm eating now, aren't I?" she said, reaching for another wing.

"So it seems," he agreed, torturing himself further by watching her nibble the chicken off the bone.

He crunched down on a celery stick, in the hope that the noise of his chewing would prevent his imagination from running off again.

"Wings," Duke said, setting the plate on the bar. "And garlic bread with cheese."

Hope looked longingly at the bread, then glanced at the chicken wing bones on her plate.

Calculating the calories she'd already consumed, MG guessed.

He helped himself to a slice of bread, perfectly toasted with a generous layer of cheese melted on top.

She watched as he lifted the bread to his mouth and bit into it.

"It's good," he told her. "Crispy on the outside and soft in the middle with just the right amount of garlic."

She muttered under her breath as she reached for a piece.

"Don't accuse me of being the devil when you're the one who ordered the bread."

"A moment of weakness," she admitted.

"Or an acknowledgment of a long-denied desire?" he countered.

Their eyes met and held again, and suddenly MG was the one feeling weak—and wishing he'd turned around and walked out the door as soon as he saw her sitting at the bar. Because even with her wearing that ridiculous wig, he'd immediately known it was Hope.

And he'd never been able to resist her.

And looking at her in that cute little sundress and jean

jacket with cowboy boots on her feet, he felt as if he'd been transported back in time eighteen years.

He realized something else then, too.

That he'd missed her.

Every day since she'd been gone, he'd missed her.

When she'd first moved to California, he'd been painfully aware of her absence. But eventually, over time, he'd gotten used to her being gone. And he'd gotten over her.

He'd been certain of it.

Until each and every time she came back to visit.

It wasn't even necessary for their paths to cross—it was enough for him to hear through the always-reliable gossip mill that she was in town, and he'd realize there was still a piece of his heart that would forever belong to her.

Hope looked away first—turning her attention to the forgotten bread in her hand.

She took a generous bite, as if surrendering wholeheartedly to the temptation. Now her eyes closed and a low hum of appreciation sounded from deep in her throat.

Yeah, he definitely should have walked out the door when he saw her.

But he hadn't, so now he lifted his glass and swallowed a mouthful of beer.

"You're right," she said, her eyes still closed. "The garlic bread's good. *Really* good."

"Should I leave you alone with your French loaf?"

Her eyes popped open then and her lips curved a little. "Was I enjoying it a little too much?"

"I'd say that's probably a matter of perspective."

"I'm not accustomed to indulging my desires," she confided. "For food, I mean."

"But you are accustomed to indulging your...other desires?"

"No. I mean, I don't have other desires. Well, of course, I have other desires, but—" she closed her eyes again "—I'm going to stop talking now."

"Please don't," he said. "Things were just getting interesting."

She pushed her still half-full glass of beer away. "I've definitely had enough of that."

Duke obviously overheard her remark, because he set a take-out container on the bar so she could box up the leftover food. "Can I get you anything else?"

"Just my check, please," Hope said.

"Put it all together and give the check to me," MG said.

"You don't have to buy my dinner."

"A few wings and a slice of garlic bread hardly constitutes dinner," he chided.

"Well, it was *my* dinner. And I enjoyed it very much."

"I'm glad you did," he said, nodding his thanks to Duke when the bartender handed him the check.

He reached into his back pocket for his wallet, and paused when he heard a familiar laugh.

Turning toward the sound, he saw Paige at the take-out counter. She was with Gavin Trent, one of her co-workers.

Had she seen him?

No, if she had, MG was sure she would have come over to say hi. Just because they'd broken up didn't mean they couldn't be friendly toward one another.

But if she'd seen him with Hope, she might not be

feeling so friendly. Despite his repeated assurances that he no longer had feelings for his girlfriend from long ago, sitting at a bar and having drinks with her on a Friday night might suggest otherwise.

"Michael?"

He jerked his attention back to Hope. "Sorry?"

"Who is that?" she asked gently.

"That's Paige."

"Ah." She nodded sympathetically. "The girlfriend of three years."

"*Ex*-girlfriend."

"Who has apparently already moved on," she mused.

"Paige and Gavin work together." But even as he said it, Gavin whispered something close to Paige's ear, causing her to smile up at him. "And they're friends."

He watched as they walked out the door together.

"Well, it's good she has a friend to lean on." Hope pushed her stool back and lowered her feet to the floor. "Because breakups can be tough."

She staggered a little as she stepped back; he caught her elbow to steady her.

"Maybe you are drunk."

"I'm not drunk. My heel just caught on the edge of a tile."

"Are you driving?"

She huffed out a breath. "No, I'm not driving. My grandmother lives less than a ten-minute walk from here."

Which he knew, of course, because he'd spent almost as much time at the house on Queen Street—where Hope had lived with her grandparents while she was growing up—as his own when they were dating.

"I'll give you a ride home," he decided.

"I don't need a ride," she told him. "I can walk."

"It's late and dark," he pointed out. "And you haven't lived here in a long time."

"I'm not going to get lost between here and Queen Street," she assured him.

"I'm sure you're not," he agreed. "But I'll feel better if you let me see you home."

"Are you sure *you're* not drunk?" she challenged. "You've had just as much to drink as I have."

"And I weigh twice as much as you."

"Fine," she relented. "You can see me home."

He appreciated her acquiescence, though he had no intention of letting her wander the streets on her own. Though Haven thankfully didn't experience a lot of violent crime, he wasn't willing to take a chance with Hope's safety.

"Here we are," he said, using his key fob to unlock the doors of his truck.

She gave the glossy black dual cab pickup a leisurely once-over. "Nice vehicle. Yours?"

"No, I pilfered my dad's keys when he wasn't looking."

"It wouldn't be the first time," she noted.

He chuckled. "You're right. But it would be the first time in a lot of years."

It was a short drive to Edwina's house, but long enough that Hope had time to think back to various other occasions that Michael had driven her home—usually in his dad's truck. Sometimes he even drove all the way into town from the Circle G to pick her up after drama club and take her home. Then he'd walk her to the door, and they'd spend a long time lingering on the porch, kissing and cuddling, reluctant to say goodbye.

Or—if it was too cold to linger outside—they'd kiss and cuddle in the cab of his dad's truck, and he'd have to wait several minutes after she'd gone inside for the windows to defrost before he could drive away again.

Life had been so much simpler then—their future filled with possibilities and promise.

She'd loved him with every fiber of her being, and yet, when the opportunity presented itself, she'd taken off to Hollywood and left him behind.

Did he hate her for that?

They'd never really talked about it after the fact. Never really had a chance. Though their paths had occasionally crossed on her visits to town, their interactions had been limited to an exchange of pleasantries before they went their separate ways again.

The one exception had been her grandfather's funeral, a dozen years earlier. Michael had come to the visitation, to pay his respects, and he'd held her while she cried. Then he came back the next day for the service, and though he'd sat with his family, just knowing that he was there had steadied her. She'd looked for him afterward, to thank him, but he was already gone.

She knew where to find him, of course. And her grandmother wouldn't have objected to Hope borrowing her car to go to the Circle G. But the fact that he hadn't stuck around told her that he wanted his space, and she still cared enough about him to respect that.

It was only on this recent visit that she'd found herself wondering how her life would have been different if she'd stayed in Haven. If she'd stayed with Michael.

"You're awfully quiet all of a sudden," he remarked, as he turned off Main Street onto Queen.

"Just contemplating the road not taken."

"Apparently beer does make you melancholy."

"Being back in Haven might have something to do with it, too," she admitted.

He slowed the vehicle as he approached her grandmother's driveway. "The house is dark."

"I forgot to leave a light on."

"Where's your grandmother?"

"She's in Tahoe this weekend. With her boyfriend."

His brows lifted. "Edwina has a boyfriend?"

She nodded. "Do you remember Mr. Kirk?"

"The principal at Westmount?"

She nodded again.

"Are you saying that your grandmother is dating Mr. Kirk?"

"He told me to call him Dennis."

"Is that…weird?" he asked.

"Being on a first-name basis with our former principal or my grandmother dating our former principal?"

"Both."

"Yes," she told him. "And no."

"Well, that clarifies everything," he said dryly.

"I thought it would be weird," she admitted. "But they're really cute together. And it's nice to know that she could fall in love again, so many years after losing my grandfather."

"Are you sure they're in love? Maybe it's just sex."

"Please." She put her hands over her ears. "I do not need to hear things like that. I also don't need to hear the creak of her bedsprings in the night, which is why I've taken to sleeping with earplugs."

He chuckled. "Maybe you're just jealous that your grandmother is getting more action than you are."

"I'm definitely jealous. I haven't had sex in—" She

huffed out a breath. "I'm going to stop talking again now."

"Oh, no," he protested. "You can't leave a confession like that unfinished."

"I can and I am," she said firmly, reaching for the door handle. "Thanks again for dinner—and for the ride."

He unhooked his seatbelt. "I'll walk you to the door."

Hope didn't bother to protest, because she knew it would serve no purpose. And because she was curious to know if he would, after walking her to the door, be tempted to kiss her good-night, as he'd done so many years ago. But mostly because, after hanging out with him tonight, exchanging flirtatious banter and sharing heated glances, she wanted him to kiss her.

If she'd had any doubts that there was still a spark between them, those doubts had been put to rest when he'd taken her arm at the restaurant, the casual touch igniting a long dormant flame burning inside her.

"I'm feeling an odd sense of déjà vu," he noted, as he walked beside her to the front door.

She inserted her key and released the lock. "We've been here once or twice—or maybe a hundred times—before, haven't we?" she mused, turning back to face him.

"But not for a very long time."

His gaze dropped to her mouth; her breath stalled in her lungs.

"Michael."

She didn't know if his name was intended as a plea or a warning, but it had barely crossed her lips before they were covered by his.

And kissing Michael was pretty much the best thing ever.

There was comfort in the familiar—and they'd definitely been here before. But there was also excitement in discovering something new—because kissing Michael then wasn't the same as kissing Michael now. He was no longer a boy, but a man. More mature, more confident, more experienced.

His mouth moved over hers, hot and hungry, demanding a response that she was only too willing to give. She parted her lips so that he could deepen the kiss. His hands slid beneath her jacket, callused palms moving up her torso, branding her with his touch. His thumbs brushed the sides of her breasts, making her nipples tighten and her knees tremble.

She yanked the hem of his shirt out of his jeans, so that her hands could slide beneath the fabric, so that she could touch him, too. His skin was warm and taut over muscles that tensed and quivered in response to the light scrape of her fingernails. His hands curled over her bottom, pulling her closer as he continued to kiss her. She could feel the press of his arousal against her pelvis, and the answering ache deep inside herself as she kissed him back. Only when they were both desperate for air did he lift his mouth away from hers.

After a long minute, when she'd finally managed to catch her breath, Hope said, "Do you want to come in?"

Michael responded by reaching past her to turn the knob and push open the door.

Chapter Nine

Then they were inside the dark foyer and he was kissing her again. Deeply. Desperately. It was almost like being back in high school, except now she knew what might happen next. What she wanted to happen next. As everything inside her quivered and yearned, she had no doubt what she was yearning for—the joining of her naked body with his.

He pushed the denim jacket over her shoulders, let the garment drop to the floor. He trailed kisses down her throat, along her collarbone, the rasp of his stubble against her skin raising goosebumps on her flesh.

"I need to see you." He slapped a hand against the wall, hitting the switches for both the inside and outside lights. She blinked against the sudden brightness and reached to switch off the overhead fixture, so that they were illuminated only by the glow that emanated through the sidelights.

"That's better," he admitted.

His gaze moved over her—a slow and very thorough perusal.

"You take my breath away." The words were whispered against her lips as he lowered the zipper at the back of her dress. "You've always taken my breath away."

She didn't have a chance to respond before he was kissing her again, distracting her with his oh-so-talented mouth so that she didn't realize he'd tugged the bodice of her dress down until she felt his thumbs grazing her nipples through the thin lace of her bra, making her moan with wanton pleasure.

He unfastened the front clasp, freeing her breasts. Her head fell back against the wall as he traced circles around the taut peaks, causing them to draw into tighter points. She felt a similar tightening, low in her belly, a coiling of tension that ached for release.

"Michael," she said again.

Definitely a plea this time.

He responded by trailing kisses over her jaw and down her throat, before capturing one of those aching nipples in his mouth. He suckled gently, then not so gently. Another moan escaped her lips as liquid heat pooled between her thighs.

He shifted his attention to her other nipple, giving it the same attention, eliciting more moans of pleasure.

Then he abandoned her breasts and dropped to his knees in front of her. He pushed up her skirt and leaned forward to press his mouth to the already damp scrap of lace fabric between her thighs.

That was a new move—and one she heartily approved of.

When they'd finally been together, when they were

both seventeen, they'd been focused on the finish line. After years of foreplay, they'd both been eager to move on. And the act had been quick and enjoyable, if not exactly earth-shattering.

Apparently Michael had learned a lot about pleasuring a woman since then. And if they'd maybe rushed to this point, he certainly wasn't rushing now.

Her palms were flat against the wall, trying to hold her upright as the world tilted and spun. If not for his hands clamped on her hips, holding her in place, she was certain that she would have crumpled to the floor like her discarded jacket.

How long had it been since she'd had a man-made orgasm?

She honestly couldn't remember.

And really, it didn't matter.

What mattered was that she was on the edge right now.

Teetering on the precipice.

He continued to work her through the fabric—licking and nibbling and suckling.

It was too much—and somehow not quite enough.

Michael must have felt the same way, because he yanked down her wet panties, tearing them in his haste to put his mouth directly on her…and she flew apart.

Stars burst behind her eyes.

Rockets shot through her veins.

His hands remained on her hips, holding her steady as he licked every last drop of pleasure from her body.

When she finally stopped trembling with the aftereffects of the mind-numbing climax and managed to focus on him, she saw a very smug smile on his face.

"Michael," she said again, her voice hoarse.

He held her gaze as he started to rise to his feet, then his eyes slammed shut and a grimace took over his face.

"What's wrong?" she asked, immediately concerned.

"Nothing."

The word was tight, strained.

Obviously a lie.

Aware that she was standing in the foyer of her grandmother's house with the top of her sundress yanked down and the skirt bunched up, she adjusted her clothing as he straightened up, muttering a string of quiet curses under his breath and staggering a little as he did so.

"I'm fine," he said, forcing the words through gritted teeth, as if he was trying to convince himself as much as her.

"I don't understand," she admitted, feeling foolish and helpless and at a complete loss. "Are you hurt?"

"I said I'm fine," he snapped at her.

She recoiled at the harsh tone.

"Okay," she said, smoothing a hand over the front of her skirt. "In that case, why don't we go upstairs and—"

"No," he interjected.

"No?" she echoed.

"This was a mistake."

"A mistake?"

She felt like a fool, repeating his words. But her mind was spinning, struggling to make sense of what could have happened to make him withdraw so immediately and completely.

"I have to go."

And before she could respond to that, he was gone.

MG made his way back to his vehicle, gritting his teeth against the pain as he half dragged his left leg. He let

out another string of curses—not so quietly this time—
as he hauled himself into the driver's seat and tore open
the center console to rummage for the bottle of extra-
strength Tylenol he kept there. His refillable water bottle
was empty, so he swallowed a couple of pills dry and sat
back, waiting for them to work their magic.

He had prescription meds at home, but he hardly
ever took them anymore. It had been months since
he'd needed the stronger painkillers, because he'd been
(mostly) diligent about following the doctor's advice for
his recovery.

Until tonight.

Because being with Hope had always made him forget everything else.

He tipped his head back against the padded rest and
closed his eyes.

Christ, he ached.

And it wasn't only his bum leg.

He ached for her.

For Hope.

But maybe, instead of cursing the lingering effects of
his injury, he should be grateful that his knee had locked
up. Grateful for the physical pain that jolted him out of
fantasy and back to reality.

He was pretty sure Hope didn't know about his accident or injury.

Though her grandmother had come to visit when he
was in the hospital, wanting to see for herself that he
was going to make a full recovery before she reported
his condition to her granddaughter—he'd begged her
not to say anything to Hope.

*"Let her bask in the happiness of her engagement with-
out worrying about an old friend,"* he'd urged Edwina.

"She'll want to know. She'll want to see you," Hope's grandmother had insisted.

But MG had been adamant, and she'd finally acquiesced to his wishes.

And it hadn't been that he didn't want to see Hope, but that he didn't want her to see him in the condition he was in.

If he hadn't been enough for her when he was one hundred percent, he certainly wouldn't be enough for her now.

But even bigger than his fear of Hope seeing him in a hospital bed was his fear that Edwina would tell her about the accident—tell her that he'd almost died—and Hope wouldn't care enough to come back.

Thankfully, the doctors had assured him that, with proper treatment and follow-up care, he would regain full mobility. But they'd also warned there was the possibility of long-term issues, including stiffness of the knee or hip and soreness at the fracture site.

Which is exactly what had happened tonight and why he'd made a quick exit. He was sure Hope must be wondering about his reasons, and he felt a little bit guilty about his abrupt departure, but he'd been in no mood to stick around to explain.

He shook off the memories, started his truck and pulled out of the driveway, heading toward home where he knew Bernie would be waiting.

Dogs, he'd learned over the past six months, weren't only man's best friend but truly loyal companions. Bernie didn't pout if he was out late and didn't nag if he left dishes on the counter. He also didn't let MG wallow in his own misery for too long. Whenever he sensed that MG was in a mood—and the dog was eerily intuitive—

he'd sidle up close to him (or even crawl into his lap!) and cuddle.

Yes, his cousin Sky and her husband, Jake, had gifted him with a hundred-pound canine cuddler.

"I don't need a dog," he'd told her, when she first brought up the subject.

"Yes, you do," she'd insisted. "Because your disposition is so miserable, no human beings want to be around you."

"Then why are you here?"

"Because I love you, you idiot."

"Was name-calling a required course for your counseling certification or did you take it as an elective?"

"You're not my patient—you're my cousin. And you're an idiot," she'd told him again.

Six weeks later, she'd introduced him to Bernie.

Six months after that, he'd finally admitted—if only to himself—that he was glad to have him.

And when he pulled into the driveway leading to the renovated bunkhouse that was his home on the Circle G, Bernie was on the porch, waiting for him.

The dog stayed put until MG had turned off the engine, then trotted over to the driver's side of the truck to greet him. MG carefully lowered his left leg to the ground, wincing only a little as pain shot from his knee to his hip.

Bernie whined deep in his throat.

"I'm okay," MG told him, rubbing the thick, soft fur on top of the dog's head.

Bernie didn't seem completely convinced, as evidenced by the fact that he stuck close to MG's side as he made his way to the house.

He tossed his wallet and his keys on the counter, then opened the fridge to grab a beer—one of only two bottles left on the shelf. Next he reached into the cupboard above the sink for the Tylenol that he kept there. His gaze caught on the prescription bottle and he considered the stronger medication, for just a second. But the pills he'd taken in the truck had already taken the edge off the worst of the pain, so he popped a couple more and washed them down with a swallow of beer.

"Anything good on TV tonight?" he asked Bernie.

The dog responded by hopping up onto the sofa.

"I guess we'll find out, won't we?" MG said, settling beside his canine companion.

He leaned forward to set his bottle on the table and spotted a piece of paper tucked beneath the coaster. He immediately recognized his brother's scrawl on the page.

Mom and Lindsay were making gnocchi tonight—
and the kids were hanging out with Grampa—so
I stopped by to have a beer with my brother. You
weren't here, so I drank mine and yours.

MG was chuckling as he tossed the paper back onto the table.

Well, that explained where his beer had gone.

He and Mitch used to hang out frequently, before Lindsay moved back to town, a young widow with two small children. After that, the quiet nights with his brother became fewer and farther between. Since Emeline was born, they'd ceased to exist entirely.

Of course, MG understood that parenting three kids—one of them an infant—required all hands on deck. Truth be told, he envied the hell out of his brother, because Mitch had everything he'd ever wanted. The woman he'd always loved and a family with her.

It was what MG had always wanted, too.

And why he knew Paige had been right to call him on his "someday" BS. Because as much as he hadn't wanted to admit it, even to himself, he had been stringing her along.

Not that he didn't enjoy being with her, because he did. But because he knew that she was looking forward to a future with him and he just couldn't see it. After Olivia and Adam's wedding, followed closely by the announcement that Mitch and Lindsay were expecting a baby, he'd realized that he wanted what each of his siblings had found—and he knew he wouldn't find it with Paige. So he'd decided to make a trip to California in the New Year, to see Hope and determine if there was any chance—and any way—for a future for them together.

He'd booted up his computer to book a flight to LA when he saw the reports of her engagement, and all of his hopes had been trampled to dust. Though it wasn't the first time she'd been engaged, the news of this engagement, so closely on the heels of his admitted desire to give their relationship another chance, hit him hard. He'd had a couple of beers and brooded over the headlines. Then, desperate to escape his memories and regrets, he'd climbed onto his snowmobile and gone for a ride.

The months that followed had been a dedicated effort to reclaim his mobility and his life. And he'd mostly succeeded. Though he still made the trip into town once a week for therapy with Kenzie Channing, he was mostly "Back in the Game" (the name of the local sports medicine clinic).

So much so that he'd completely forgotten about the lingering effects of his injury when he'd dropped to his knees in front of Hope tonight. All he'd been able to think about was touching her, tasting her, pleasing her.

He'd been seventeen the first time they were together, and a complete novice when it came to lovemaking. Because he'd been in love with Hope since seventh grade, and while his friends were learning the ropes with various girls they dated, MG was waiting for Hope to be ready to take the next step with him. And despite their passion escalating along with their feelings for one another, she'd wanted to wait—mostly because she didn't want to be a teenage mom like her own mother.

She wanted to marry him and have a family with him someday, but not before she'd finished high school. MG had been in complete agreement in that respect, and so he'd gotten pretty good at taking care of his own needs while knowing almost nothing about satisfying hers.

When the day finally came that she whispered *yes* instead of *no* against his lips, he'd wanted nothing more than to be inside her. And the experience had been every bit as amazing as he'd anticipated—at least for him. Afterward, he'd realized that it hadn't been quite as spectacular for his partner. Not that Hope had complained. In fact, she'd assured him that it had been everything she'd expected—which, he later decided, told him that her expectations had been ridiculously low.

They'd made love three more times over the two weeks before Hope packed up and moved to LA. Before he knew that she wanted to leave Haven. To leave him.

He'd learned a lot in the eighteen years that had passed since they were first together, and when Hope invited him into the house, he'd been determined to give her more than he'd given her before—a better memory of her first lover to take back to LA. Because he no longer had any illusions that she would stay.

He'd wanted to pleasure her—and he had.

She'd completely come apart for him.

Sitting at home now, with his dog's head in his lap and the game on TV, he could still taste her on his lips.

And he was still hard as a rock.

He was also achingly aware that he'd likely blown any chance of a different ending—or another beginning—with Hope.

Hope tossed and turned all night.

And it was Michael's fault.

After the mind-blowing orgasm he'd given her, she'd expected to sleep like the dead. But while her body had been sated, her mind had been spinning. Trying to figure out what had happened to make him rush off.

When she'd invited him to come inside, she'd thought—hoped—that the night would end with them both in her bed. She couldn't have guessed that things would accelerate from zero to sixty faster than a Bugatti Divo, and while she had absolutely no complaints about their interlude in the foyer, she'd hoped it was only a prelude of more to come. (No pun intended!)

Instead, he'd taken very good care of her…and then he'd walked out.

And she wanted—*needed*—answers.

Which was why she was at the Circle G before ten o'clock the next morning.

She parked near the barn, where she suspected she was most likely to find him—or someone who might steer her in the right direction. She turned off the engine and dropped her keys into her Telfar Circle Bag, then got out of her car, straightened the hem of her ribbed V-neck cashmere sweater (Giorgio Armani), brushed an imaginary speck of dust off her stretch crepe skinny pants (Carolina Herrera)—having dressed carefully in some of her favorite designer labels to give her the confidence of her Hollywood image so that she didn't make the mistake of acting like a smitten seventeen-year-old (again!) when she confronted Michael.

She turned on her Romy flats (Jimmy Choo) and started toward the barn, stopping abruptly in her tracks and letting out a startled yelp when she saw the enormous animal blocking her path.

It was a dog, she realized, pressing a hand to her racing heart.

A bigger dog than she'd ever seen, but definitely a dog, with a fluffy tricolored coat, floppy ears and beautiful dark eyes.

"Um…hi, there," she said.

The dog's tail waved.

That was a good sign, wasn't it?

Still, she wasn't foolish enough to step forward.

"Guard dog?"

He tilted his head at that.

"No," she decided. "You're definitely a lover more than a fighter."

"That's what all the girls say."

Chapter Ten

Hope's heart jolted at the sound of his voice, but she turned slowly—casually—to face the speaker.

Not Michael, she immediately realized, but Mitchell.

The cool smile she'd affected immediately warmed and widened.

He was grinning, too, as he made his way toward her. "Welcome back, Miz Hollywood."

"It's good to see you, Mitchell."

"You're the sight for sore eyes," he told her.

"So why don't I get a hug?"

"Because I don't want to mess up your fancy duds."

She responded to that by hugging him.

He gave in and squeezed her tight.

"Damn, it's good to see you," he said, drawing back to look at her again. "But what the hell are you doing here?"

"I'm here to see Michael."

"And now I'm going to have to kick his ass for not telling me that you were coming."

"He couldn't tell you what he didn't know," she said.

Mitchell's brows lifted at that. "He's working on some charts in the office. Do you know where it is?"

"I'm sure I can find it."

"Bernie will show you the way," he said.

"Bernie?"

The big dog lumbered forward, tongue lolling, tail wagging.

"I guess you're Bernie," she said, tentatively offering a hand for the dog to sniff.

"That's Bernie," Mitch confirmed.

"Yours?"

He shook his head. "MG's. He got him after... I mean, he got him about six months ago."

Hope's gaze narrowed. "You started to say something else—that he got him after...what?"

"After Sky's husband finished training him," he said. "That's what Jake does—he trains dogs."

"Well, he seems to have done a good job with Bernie," she acknowledged.

He nodded. "Bernie—go find MG."

The dog started toward the barn.

"You can follow him," Mitch said to Hope. "He won't steer you wrong."

"I will." She gave Michael's brother another quick hug. "In case I don't see you again before I go."

"You always know where to find me."

She nodded and turned to follow the dog into the barn, walking between the rows of freshly cleaned stalls, past the tack room and feed storage to a partially open door at the far end of the building.

Bernie pushed the door with his nose, to open it wider, then trotted inside.

"Got tired of chasing rabbits, did you?" Michael asked, chuckling as he rubbed the dog's ears.

Then he must have caught a glimpse of her, standing in the doorway, because his laughter cut off and he straightened in his seat. "Hope."

She stepped into the room. "Hello, Michael."

"What are you doing here?"

"I thought we should talk about last night."

"There's nothing to talk about."

The dismissive tone hurt, and she hated that her own reflected it when she responded. "How can you say that?"

"Because it was fun, but it didn't mean anything."

"Maybe it didn't mean anything to you," she allowed. "But it meant a lot to me."

He exhaled a weary sigh. "I should have guessed that a Hollywood actor would turn a simple orgasm into some kind of complicated drama."

She sucked in a breath. "Why are you doing this?"

"What do you think I'm doing?"

"Being deliberately hurtful."

"I'm sorry if that's what you think. I'm only trying to be honest."

"If you really believe that, then you're lying to both of us," she said. "Because whether you want to admit it or not, there's something between us still. And what happened last night proves it."

"Or maybe it was just the dress," he said.

"The dress?"

"Looking at you, in a dress that you wore in high school, reminded me of the girl you used to be. And the boy I used to be. And I guess I was enticed to take a walk down memory lane."

"We obviously have different memories, because you'd never before done what you did to me last night."

He shrugged. "I've learned a few things since you've been gone."

"Apparently."

"Don't get me wrong—last night was fun," he said again, as if that might appease her. "But it would be a mistake to think it was anything more than that."

"Was it fun for you, though?" she wondered aloud. "I mean, it could have been, if you'd let me reciprocate…"

The heat that flared in his gaze appeased her far more than his words had done, because it proved that he wanted her, even if he didn't want to want her.

"…but you didn't stick around long enough for that—or anything else."

"It was late," he said. "And I knew Bernie was waiting for me at home."

"Really?" She glanced at the canine, snoring now beside the desk. "You're going to blame the dog?"

"Man's best friend."

But her gaze had caught on something else when it moved away from Bernie: a cane, hooked on the edge of the desk.

It could have belonged to Jack Gilmore, Michael's grandfather. Or Charles, his dad, or David, Charles's brother. All of them lived and worked on the Circle G and had access to this office and the desk at which Michael was currently seated.

But the presence of the cane combined with the flash of pain she'd seen on Michael's face when he'd risen to his feet the night before and his uneven gait as he walked out the door convinced her that the walking aid belonged to him.

"So your quick retreat had nothing to do with—" she picked up the cane "—this?"

His scowl was all the confirmation she needed.

"I asked if you were hurt," she reminded him. "And you said you were fine."

"Because I was. I am."

"But something happened," she guessed. "And I need you to tell me the truth, Michael. Please."

"Jesus, you are not going to let this go, are you?"

"You should know me well enough to know the answer to that question."

"But I don't," he said. "I don't know you at all."

"It's been a long time," she allowed, "but have I really changed so much?"

"Considering that you're standing there in an outfit that undoubtedly cost more than my monthly truck payment, I'd have to say *yes*."

She lifted her chin defiantly. "I'm not going to apologize for the fact that I make a lot of money."

"No one's asking you to."

"And I'm not going to let you sidetrack the conversation by making it about me when I asked about you."

"You might be a celebrity in California," he replied in a distant tone, "but here, you're just a trespasser."

"Apparently you haven't changed at all, because you still lash out when you're hurting, just like you did when we were kids."

"I have work to do here, Hope."

"I'm not leaving until you tell me what happened."

"Are you saying that you will leave if I tell you?"

It hurt to think that he was so eager to get rid of her.

But she was now so desperate to know, that she would have agreed to almost anything.

"I'll leave if you tell me," she promised.

He nodded. "Okay. I crashed my snowmobile and broke my leg. A compound fracture of the femur, to be more specific."

"Ohmygod." She felt weak all of a sudden, but there were no chairs in the room aside from the one he was occupying, so she leaned back against the filing cabinet. "You crashed your snowmobile? What were you thinking?"

"I didn't actually do it on purpose," he said dryly.

"When—" She had to swallow before she could finish her question. "When did it happen?"

"Early January. I had months of therapy afterward, to restore my mobility, and most days I manage to forget that I've got a rod and six screws in my leg. Other days—" he shrugged "—it can stiffen up and then I use the cane for a little extra support."

"The accident must have been big news around town."

"It was," he agreed. "Nothing the gossips love more than a Gilmore doing something stupid."

"Or a Blake," she noted.

"A Gilmore doing a Blake would be stupid," he said, in an apparent effort to lighten the mood.

He was referring, of course, to the age-old feud between the town's two founding families. Having grown up in Haven, she was familiar with the story, which started when ancestors of each family came to Nevada some hundred and fifty years earlier to settle the same parcel of land. Rather than admit they'd been duped, Everett Gilmore and Samuel Blake agreed to split the property along the natural divide of Crooked Creek. The

Gilmores, having arrived first and already started to build their homestead, took the prime grazing land, leaving the Blakes with less hospitable terrain. As a result, the Blakes struggled for a lot of years—until gold and silver were discovered in their hills.

Although both families ended up ridiculously wealthy—the Gilmores making their fortune in ranching and the Blakes through mining—the animosity between them had remained for a long time. It was only in recent years that they'd finally managed to bury the hatchet.

"I wonder why my grandmother never told me about the accident," Hope said now.

"Probably because I asked her not to."

"What? When? Why?"

He glanced away. "She came to visit me in the hospital—said she needed to see for herself that I was okay before she told you the same thing. And I asked her not to mention the accident."

"But why?" she asked again.

"Because I was okay and I didn't think you needed to be bothered by news about an old friend."

"You were a lot more to me than that."

"Maybe," he allowed. "Once upon a time."

"And now?" she asked softly.

He was quiet for a minute, as if considering the question.

"Now I need you to go so I can get back to work."

MG hadn't been entirely sure that Hope would honor her side of the bargain, but she did. After he told her about the accident, she left. And he was glad that she was gone—the last thing he needed was the distraction of a woman who wasn't going to stick around.

But he was glad she'd shown up today, because seeing her here at the ranch, in those fancy clothes, was a reminder to MG that they lived in different worlds. She'd gone Hollywood, but he was still—and would always be—a cattle rancher.

And now that she was gone, he could turn his attention back to the breeding charts he'd been working on. But the scent of her perfume—probably something as pricey as the ridiculous shoes on her feet—lingered in the air and stirred his blood.

It was the same perfume she'd been wearing last night. Slightly spicy and dangerously seductive and—

"What was that about?"

MG scowled as Mitch walked into the room. "What was what about?"

His brother rolled his eyes. "Why was Hope here to see you?"

"I ran into her at Diggers' last night and gave her a ride home. She forgot her leftover garlic bread in the truck and came to get it." The first part of his explanation, at least, was completely true.

"She drove all this way for some leftover garlic bread?"

"You've had the garlic bread at Diggers'—wouldn't you travel twice as far to get some?"

"So why didn't I see her carrying a take-out container when she left?" Mitch challenged.

"Because I ate the garlic bread when I got home last night. Which reminds me—you owe me a couple of beers."

"And you owe me a shirt."

"I can go dig it out of my laundry hamper right now, if you want," MG said.

"Thanks, but I'll wait until you've had a chance to wash it. Though now that I'm thinking about it…you ran into Hope in town the day you dropped by to borrow that shirt, didn't you?"

"Yeah. So?"

"So maybe the universe is sending you a message," Mitch mused.

"And what do you think the message is? That I should stop going into town?"

"Ha! And no."

"Come on," MG said. "You're obviously itching to tell me what you think the message is."

His brother shook his head. "I think I'm going to let you figure this one out on your own."

"How was your weekend?" Hope asked, when Edwina and Dennis returned home late Sunday afternoon.

"Absolutely fabulous."

His enthusiastic response caused her grandmother's cheeks to turn pink.

"Hopefully you're going to share more details than that— though not too many details," Hope hastily clarified.

Dennis chuckled. "I'll take our bags upstairs and let Edwina fill you in."

"I just made a pot of tea," Hope said. "Do you want a cup?"

"I think I'd rather have a nap," Dennis said with a wink. "I'm exhausted."

"Those are the details I don't need," Hope told him.

"It's not what you're thinking," Edwina chided. "We were up late last night, walking under the stars."

"Is that what the old folks are calling it these days?"

"Who are you calling old?"

Hope laughed as she poured the tea into two mugs.

"Definitely not you," she promised. "Now tell me more about this fabulous weekend."

While they sipped their tea and nibbled on cookies Hope had baked, Edwina described the flowers in the hotel room and the view from the balcony; she raved about the candlelight dinners and luxurious spa treatments—including a couple's massage.

"I felt totally spoiled and so very lucky," Edwina confided.

"He's the lucky one," Hope said. "And if he's smart, he won't ever let you go."

A little bit of her grandmother's glow faded then.

"What did I say wrong?" Hope immediately wanted to know.

"Nothing," Edwina assured her. "But there was one little…hiccup…over the weekend."

"What kind of hiccup?"

"While we were strolling along in the moonlight last night, Dennis proposed."

"And that was a hiccup?" Hope asked cautiously.

"Yes," Edwina confirmed. "Because I told him that I had no intention of ever getting married again and apparently he thought I was just being coy."

"Did he have a ring and everything?"

Her grandmother nodded. "He even got down on one arthritic knee."

An offhand remark that, of course, made Hope think of Michael on his knees and—

Nope.

She wasn't going to think about that right now.

And maybe not ever again.

Because he'd made it clear that while he'd had a good

time with her, there wasn't going to be a repeat performance.

"Are you all right, dear? You look a little flushed all of a sudden."

"I'm fine," Hope hastened to assure her grandmother. "Just wondering how you responded to his proposal."

"I told him to get up off the ground and stop acting like a fool because I knew I hadn't fallen in love with a fool."

"You didn't really say that."

"I most certainly did," Edwina said. "I then reminded him that I've never been the type to play games and if I wanted to get married, I would have said so."

"How did he respond to that?"

"He closed the ring box, tucked it back in his pocket and apologized for thinking he knew what I wanted better than I did."

"And that was that?"

"That was that."

Hope sipped her tea. "Was it a nice ring?"

Edwina laughed softly. "It was a beautiful ring."

"So tell me something…if you love Dennis and he loves you—why don't you want to marry him?"

"Because I lost the love of my life when your grandfather died, and while I was happily surprised to learn that I could fall in love again, I don't want another husband. There was a special bond between me and Alistair, and though the vows we exchanged promised only *till death do us part*, there is a piece of my heart that will only and forever belong to him."

Hope's heart gave a wistful sigh.

"Did you ever wonder why I was engaged three times but never got married?" she asked her grandmother.

"Was it only three? I thought it was five."

"It was only three," Hope confirmed.

"Well, of course, I wondered," Edwina said. "And I suspected that one—or maybe more—of your mother's six marriages might have soured you on the institution."

"They were likely a factor," she admitted. "But a bigger factor is that I wanted to know, before I exchanged vows with someone, that it was going to be forever—like you and Grampa. And until I meet someone who loves me the way he loved you—and who I love as much as you loved him—I'm not going to start planning a wedding."

"You don't think it's possible that you've already met that someone?" Edwina asked.

Hope didn't let herself hesitate before she shook her head. "No. But I've got my fingers crossed that it will happen."

"I'm glad to hear that. Now tell me about your weekend."

"It was mostly quiet and uneventful," she said, choosing to disregard one mind-blowing orgasm and one heart-breaking conversation, neither of which she intended to discuss with her grandmother.

Edwina's gaze narrowed. "Did you leave the house at all?"

"I went to Diggers' Friday night—ran into Michael there." She'd hesitated to add the last part, but she knew that Edwina would find out eventually, because there were no secrets in Haven.

"And how is he doing?" her grandmother asked, her tone deliberately casual.

"He seems to have recuperated quite well after his accident."

"He told you about that?"

"My question is—why didn't *you* tell me about it?"

"He asked me not to."

"You should have told me, anyway."

"I would have gotten around to it eventually," Edwina said. "Just like I'm sure you'll eventually get around to telling me why you're not in any hurry to go back to Los Angeles."

Hope dropped her gaze. "I will," she promised. "Just... not yet."

"Well, I'll be here, whenever you're ready to talk."

"Thanks, Grams." Her phone vibrated in her pocket, and she pulled it out to look at the screen.

Her heart dropped into her stomach when she saw that the incoming text was from her agent. Drawing a deep breath, she swiped to open the message.

Copy of press release from studio to follow. Distribution scheduled for noon tomorrow.

Which meant she was going to have a lot of questions to answer tomorrow, whether she was ready to talk or not.

Chapter Eleven

MG hadn't seen or heard from Hope since her Saturday afternoon visit to the Circle G. Unfortunately, that didn't stop him from thinking about her. Being a rancher didn't leave a lot of time for leisure, but most of the day-to-day responsibilities were routine, which meant that while his hands were busy, his mind was free to wander. And too often his mind wandered in Hope's direction.

By his estimation, she'd been in Haven for almost three weeks already—longer than any other visit in recent memory and further evidence, to his way of thinking, that she would be packing up and heading back to California any day now. And then he could stop wondering if he might catch a glimpse of her every time he went into town, as he seemed to be making too many excuses to do these days.

He didn't need an excuse Wednesday afternoon, because he had his now once-a-week physical therapy. But he found himself leaving half an hour earlier than usual, so he could stop at The Daily Grind to grab a coffee before his appointment. And if he took more than a casual glance around as he walked out with his coffee, who would notice?

He sat outside, enjoying his java in the sunshine before walking down the street to Back in the Game. He nodded to the receptionist, then took a seat in the waiting area. There was usually a neat pile of magazines in the center of the table, so that patients could thumb through the pages while they waited to be taken into a treatment room, though they usually remained untouched as most patients focused on their phones.

Today, MG noticed that the table was littered with tabloid newspapers—and all of the biggest headlines were about *Rockwood Ridge* and/or Hope Bradford.

Hope Bradford's Out! Donovan Kessel's In! Shake-up on the Set of Popular TV Drama

Where's Lainey Howard? TV Star Hope Bradford MIA

Hope Bradford—Television Darling or Hollywood Diva?

Real Life Drama in Rockwood Ridge

He reached for the closest paper and unfolded it to begin reading the article.

Fans of the popular network television series *Rockwood Ridge* have a lot of questions after the studio announced that three-time Emmy award winner Hope Bradford would not be returning for the show's ninth season.

Lainey Howard, a recurring character in the first two seasons, quickly became a fan favorite resulting in the actor's promotion to regular cast member. Lainey Howard has been the focal point of several major story lines in recent years, and fans have laughed and cried and loved and hated along with the girlfriend-turned-lover-and-finally-wife of mainstay character Thorne Chesterfield. (Expertly portrayed by Colin McCarragher, who has also been awarded with three Emmys for his work on *Rockwood Ridge*.)

Inside sources have suggested that the departure of Ms. Bradford is linked to the arrival of Oscar winner Donovan Kessel on set for the upcoming season, though reps for both actors declined to comment. The details of Mr. Kessel's character are being kept under wraps by the studio, though it has been teased that he will seriously shake things up in *Rockwood Ridge*.

Disgruntled fans of Lainey Howard would argue that he already has.

"You're reading old news."

MG glanced up to find Paige standing across from him. "Sorry?"

She gestured to the paper in his hand. "The internet blew up about Hope Bradford's unexpected departure from *Rockwood Ridge* on Monday."

"Did it?"

"I sometimes forget that you're not on Twitter or Instagram." She lowered herself to perch on the edge of a chair across from him. "Did you really not know?"

"I really didn't know." He folded the paper and tossed it back onto the table. "How are you doing?"

"I'm good," she said.

"You look good," he told her, and meant it. In fact, if he'd had any concerns that she might be nursing a broken heart as a result of their breakup, there was certainly no outward indication of it.

"Thanks," she said. Then, "How are you doing?"

"Good."

She stacked the papers, straightened the magazines. "So what do you think…is this incredibly awkward?"

He shrugged. "Not incredibly."

She picked up a discarded gum wrapper, crumpled it in her fist. "Do you think it will get easier over time?"

"I do," he said.

A smile twitched at the corners of her mouth. "Just when I'd given up thinking I'd ever hear you say those words to me."

He lifted his brows. "Glad to know you can joke about our breakup."

She shrugged. "I think we both know it was a long time coming."

"I know most of my friends thought you would kick me to the curb long before you did."

She didn't even try to hold back her smile this time. "Mine, too." She rose to her feet then. "Kenzie's just finishing up with another patient, but she'll be with you in a sec."

He nodded. "Thanks."

She started to turn away, then paused to say, "It was good to see you, MG."

"You, too, Paige."

Then she disappeared down the hall as Kenzie appeared to usher him into a treatment room.

Hope supposed she should be grateful that the studio had given her a heads-up, via her agent, about the press release. It was possible that Fallon Newbridge might have tried to reach out to her directly—after her last meeting with the studio heads, the associate producer had sounded sincerely regretful when she said goodbye—but Hope, anticipating the fallout of the eventual announcement, had gotten a new cell phone before she left town and her agent was the only one in LA who had the number.

And Jenny had been in contact—via email or text message or both—every day since the news broke that Hope Bradford was out at *Rockwood Ridge*.

Just checking in to see how you're doing.

I'm okay.

Do you want to chat?

Not necessary.

You could fight back, you know. Tell your story. The whole story.

It was something Hope had considered at various times over the years—and more frequently of late. But she imagined that what happened with Donovan Kessel when she was barely eighteen would be twisted into a classic case of he said/she said, and Hope had no desire to have every aspect of her life picked apart and her character denigrated by his legions of fans.

And then I'd be not only unemployed but unemployable.

You didn't do anything wrong.

And that was only one of the reasons that Hope loved her agent—because Jenny always had her back, no questions asked.

But if she went public with the truth about what Donovan Kessel had done—or tried to do—she knew that she couldn't expect the same support from anyone else. The reporters and bloggers and influencers wouldn't be at all deferential. They'd come at her with not only questions but accusations, calculated innuendos and outright lies.

To what purpose? Hope asked herself. To prove that she wasn't a diva?

There were so many more and much worse things they could—and would—say about her if she broke her silence.

I think I'd rather just lie low and wait for the story to run its course.

Anyway, she'd made her choice eighteen years ago—and there was no way to change the past.

But the future was yet to be written and she could do anything she wanted going forward.

Anything except continue to play the part of Lainey Howard on *Rockwood Ridge*.

When Hope made her way to the kitchen Saturday morning, she discovered that her grandmother wasn't alone. Over the past few weeks, she'd gotten used to seeing Dennis sitting across from Edwina, and it turned out that she actually enjoyed talking to her former high school principal—so long as she didn't think about the fact that he was sleeping with her grandmother.

This morning, however, Dennis was nowhere to be found. Instead, someone else was at his usual spot at the table.

"Good morning, Hope."

"Good morning, Mother."

She dutifully crossed the room to touch her lips to Debra Bradford's cheek, then gratefully accepted the mug of coffee Edwina held out to her.

"Thanks, Grams."

She kissed her cheek, too, before lifting the mug to her lips, desperate for the caffeine to wake up her brain so that she could handle the imminent confrontation with her mother.

Because there was always a confrontation with her mother.

Debra Bradford had been bitten by the acting bug at a young age and hopped on a bus for an open casting call in LA when she was only sixteen years old. Her parents freaked out when they discovered their daughter was missing, but Debra had left a note clearly outlining her plans and the sheriff had advised her parents to wait for her to come home.

Though Debra didn't get the part she'd coveted, she

was nonetheless offered a minor role in the film, and that was enough to convince her she was destined to be a star. Eight months later, when filming finally concluded, she returned to Haven for Christmas—four months pregnant.

She refused to tell her parents anything about the father of her baby. She also refused to let her unplanned pregnancy derail her career. Not even the revelation that her solitary scene had been left on the cutting room floor could dissuade her.

She stayed in Haven only until she gave birth. And then she packed up and returned to California, surprising everyone when she took her baby girl with her.

Hope's early memories of Tinseltown were fuzzy. She remembered an apartment in a high-rise building with a fountain in the courtyard out front and a bedroom with tall windows and a closet filled with toys. She also recalled a lady named Lashonda who would babysit whenever Debra had to go to an audition. (Though she never managed to snag what she would consider a breakthrough role, Debra worked fairly steadily back then.) And there was a man—Hope called him Uncle Steven—who was a frequent visitor to the apartment. She liked when he came over, because Debra smiled a lot when he was there. He also usually brought flowers for Debra and a toy or book for Hope. Sometimes he stayed all night, cuddling with Debra in her bed. (In retrospect, Hope knew they were doing more than cuddling, but as a child, she'd had no reason to question the explanations her mother gave.) There were other men who occasionally came for sleepovers, too, but Hope didn't remember any of their names.

She had a happy life in LA, right up until her seventh

birthday. That night, Uncle Steven brought a cake and lots of presents and she went to bed with sugar coursing through her system and a smile on her face. She woke up in the night, though, with a sore tummy and the sound of loud voices coming from behind the closed door of her mom's bedroom. She didn't understand most of what was being said, but the words *liar* and *whore* stuck in her brain.

The next day, Debra told her they were going to have to leave the apartment with the fountain in the courtyard. Hope tried not to cry—because Debra always got mad when she cried—but she had to know if Uncle Steven would still come to visit if they lived somewhere else. When Debra told her that she probably wouldn't ever see Uncle Steven again, Hope couldn't hold back her tears. That was when Debra packed up most of her clothes and toys, tossed them in the backseat of her car and took her on a road trip to visit Gramma and Grampa.

"How about pancakes this morning?"

Edwina's question jolted Hope back to the present.

"Pancakes?" Debra echoed, sounding horrified. She looked at her daughter, her eyes wide. "You haven't been eating pancakes, have you?"

"Gramma's pancakes are hard to resist," Hope remarked.

"Not that she hasn't tried," Edwina said.

"If you want to salvage what's left of your career, you'll lay off the carbs," Debra warned.

Hope swallowed another mouthful of coffee. "Is that why you're here, Mother? To offer unsolicited career advice?"

"I'm here because I found out about you being cut from *Rockwood Ridge*. And I have to say, it was quite upsetting to have to hear that news from my makeup artist."

"I'm sorry. I should have reached out to you," Hope said. "But I know how much you hate being disturbed when you're on location."

Debra sniffed—an acknowledgment more than an acceptance of the apology. "But mostly I'm here because I wanted to make sure that you were okay."

"You could have called," Hope pointed out gently. "You didn't need to fly all the way out here."

"I could have called," Debra agreed. "I wanted to see you."

Hope refilled her mug before she ventured to ask, "How did you know I was here?"

"Where else would you go?"

A very good question, she admitted.

But while Debra obviously hadn't had any trouble tracking her down, Hope felt confident that her presence in Haven remained a closely guarded secret, as only a very few of her closest friends knew of her connection to the northern Nevada town.

"If not pancakes—how about eggs and bacon?" Edwina suggested.

"You know I don't eat breakfast," Debra reminded her mother.

"Hope?"

She shook her head. "Thanks, Grams. But I'm not feeling very hungry this morning."

"Of course, you're not hungry," Debra said, her tone oozing with false sympathy. "Your career is on the precipice and you need to focus on pulling it back."

Hope was pretty sure her career had already tumbled over the precipice, but the bigger issue—at least from her perspective—was figuring out if there was anything left to salvage. Or even if she wanted to.

"Seems like a task that could be helped along by a good breakfast," Edwina muttered, not quite under her breath.

"Food is not the answer to all the problems in the universe," Debra said.

"Tell that to the more than eight hundred million people in the world suffering from chronic hunger."

"Fine—you can make your pancakes for them. Hope and I have other plans."

Hope nearly choked on a mouthful of coffee. "We do?"

"We do," her mother confirmed. "Now go put some decent clothes and some makeup on."

"Why?" she asked warily.

"Because we've got an appointment for mani-pedis at Serenity Spa."

"I'm not in the mood for a mani-pedi."

"Which is further proof that you need to get out—pamper yourself a little. The key to feeling better is looking better."

Hope could have dug in her heels and refused to go to the spa with her mother, but she'd learned long ago that giving Debra what she wanted was the quickest route to peace. So she put on some decent clothes (a twill and silk cardigan by Dolce & Gabbana with wool trousers by MaxMara and Tory Burch loafers) and makeup—just some lightweight foundation, a touch of sun-kissed bronzer on her cheeks, a swipe of mascara over her lashes and a subtle tint of color for her lips. Products she never used to leave home without in LA, but hadn't worried about as much now that she was back in Haven.

Well, except for her sunscreen, without which she never ventured outdoors.

"Now you look more like yourself," Debra said. "But aren't you going to do something with your hair?"

The messy bun wasn't Hope's favorite look, either, but it was quick and easy and not unstylish.

"You said our appointment is for one o'clock. If I take the time to fuss with my hair, we'll be late."

"Darling, we're Debra and Hope Bradford—not just local but real celebrities. We're not going to be turned away from the spa if we're a few minutes late."

Hope knew it was true, but she'd never been one to exploit her star status, as her mother was wont to do. Still, she retreated to the bathroom again to remove the fastener, brush out her hair and straighten it.

As she was fussing, she recalled a feature in *People* magazine about the millions of young women across the country who attempted to emulate the style of Hope Bradford. Apparently they wanted her hairstyle, her wardrobe, her handbags and shoes, her famous boyfriends and her beach house. There was no mention of any of them wanting her mother.

"Much better," Debra announced when her daughter reappeared.

Edwina rolled her eyes behind Debra's back, and Hope was filled with a rush of love for the grandmother who'd always loved her unconditionally.

Despite all the drama preceding their arrival to the spa, Hope was able to relax once they were there. They were greeted by Andria, the owner, and offered glasses of champagne, which they sipped while their feet soaked and soft music played in the background.

All in all, it wasn't a bad way to spend a few hours in her mother's company, Hope decided.

"Smile." Debra leaned close as she extended her arm to snap a photo.

Hope automatically curved her lips.

"And that's how you show the world that all those nasty rumors don't bother you," Debra said approvingly, her thumbs moving over her phone screen.

"Right now I'm hiding from the world," she reminded her mother.

"Nonsense."

Her dismissive tone set off Hope's radar.

"What are you doing?" she asked.

"Just dropping a quick social media post."

"Let me see that." She grabbed her mother's phone, her heart dropping into her stomach when she saw the Instagram app was open—and displaying the photo that Debra had snapped only moments earlier. Beneath the selfie of the two of them, her mom had added several tags: #motherdaughtertime #SerenitySpa #noplacelike-home #HavenNV.

"Ohmygod." Hope felt as if she was going to throw up the champagne she'd just drunk as she realized there were already twenty-nine likes and three comments on the post. "I can't believe you posted this. No, I can believe it... But for a few brief moments, I actually thought you were here to offer some maternal comfort and compassion."

"What are you going on about?" Debra might have frowned, if her regular Botox treatments didn't render the furrowing of her brow impossible.

"I came to Haven so that I could figure out my future in private... How could you announce my location to the whole world on Instagram?" Her voice shook with anger—and hurt.

"Privacy is overrated."

She felt the sting of tears. "That wasn't your decision to make."

Her phone pinged with a message from her agent.

What happened to lying low?!?

Hope didn't bother to respond to the question, because Jenny obviously knew that Debra Bradford was what had happened. And while she wished she could storm out, her experience with the paparazzi had taught her the dangers of giving in to emotional impulses.

Do you need a rescue?

She decided to respond to that one—to ensure her agent didn't worry.

I'll keep you posted...

Colorado is supposed to be nice this time of year.

When Hope decided to leave LA, she'd considered her properties in Vail and New York City as potential destinations. But *Architectural Digest* had done a feature on the chalet a few years back and *The New Yorker* magazine had included her Central Park West apartment as part of a holiday spread a few months later. As a result, Haven was the only place she'd felt confident she could enjoy a degree of anonymity. Sure, she was likely to be recognized by some of the residents—as the coffee-throwing incident at The Daily Grind had demonstrated—but her previous visits to town had assured her that her desire for privacy would be respected.

Apparently by everyone except her own mother.

"You don't understand how crucial it is to stay in the public eye," Debra went on, seemingly oblivious to her daughter's distress. "I know your last appearance on *Rockwood Ridge* was only a few months ago, but you don't want casting directors to forget about you."

"Maybe I do," Hope told her.

"Don't be silly, darling."

"Why is that silly?"

"Because if you're not an actor, what are you?"

It was the question she'd been asking herself since she'd thrown her suitcase in the trunk of her car and driven away from Los Angeles. And she was no closer to an answer now than she'd been four weeks earlier.

Chapter Twelve

Debra left Haven before noon the following day, but the damage had already been done. By the time she sashayed out the front door of the house on Queen Street—and she did, indeed, sashay—there were two news crews, a handful of network reporters and at least twice that number of celebrity bloggers stationed outside, clamoring for a sound bite—or at least a photo—of the former star of *Rockwood Ridge*.

The fact that they weren't there for Debra didn't faze her at all. Because she knew that in the absence of her daughter (who was peering through a crack in the blinds from her bedroom window upstairs), they would take any little tidbit they could get to feed the hungry fans—and hungrier critics. So she paused, posed, beside the limo that pulled up in front of the house to take her to the airport for her return flight to Toronto.

"Ladies and gentlemen." She held up a hand and flashed a practiced smile. "I can hardly answer any of your questions if you insist on talking over one another."

A woman in a red dress stepped forward, indicating that she would take the lead.

"Casey Willcott for *Hollywood's Hottest Gossip*," she said, speaking into a personal recording device. "Can you confirm, Ms. Bradford, that this is the house where you grew up and where your daughter, Hope Bradford, is currently hiding out?"

"This is where I grew up," Debra confirmed. "But my beautiful and immensely talented daughter—a chip off the not-so-old block, some would say—isn't hiding out. Hope is merely taking a little time to consider her various and numerous options."

"Tom Logan, *Channel Six News*. What do you have to say about the rumor that Hope Bradford was fired because she refused to work with Donovan Kessel?"

"If you want me to respond to all the rumors regarding my daughter, we'll be here all day and I have a plane to catch."

"Can you tell us where you're headed, Ms. Bradford?"

That question, from a young man with mop of curly dark hair, earned a wide smile because it was a question specifically about Debra.

"I'm going back to Toronto to continue filming *A Holiday Wish* with Jason Sterling, Pamela Lang and Reggie Osborne."

"You've worked with Jason Sterling previously," the woman from *HHG* remarked.

"This will be our fourth movie together," she confirmed.

"And you were romantically linked with Mr. Sterling during the filming of each of the last two, were you not?"

She responded to that question with a coy smile and two words: "Was I?"

Then, with a last wave to the gathered celebrity watchers, she climbed into the limo and made her escape.

Hope wasn't sorry to see her go.

She was, however, sorry to see that the crowd across the street from her grandmother's house remained.

MG couldn't help but feel a pang of sympathy for Hope as he skimmed through the article he'd stumbled across when he decided to look up the local movie listings and instead typed her name in the search bar. More than a week after the news first broke of her departure from *Rockwood Ridge*, Hollywood had yet to uncover a bigger scandal and so Hope's name and face continued to dominate the celebrity sites.

He had no doubt that Debra Bradford had taken and posted the photo of her and her daughter at Serenity Spa. (And she was probably really irked with the blogger who posted it to a celebrity sightings site and cut Debra out of the picture.)

He wondered if Hope knew what they were saying about her online—the good, the bad and the ugly. And there was a lot of ugly. Apparently for every fan of Hope Bradford there were two or three haters who seemed to take pleasure in throwing dirt at her while hiding behind obviously made-up screen names.

Was it all just part and parcel of being a celebrity?

Had she known what she was getting into when she agreed to go to LA eighteen years earlier?

Whether she did or didn't, she'd made her choice.

And while he could—and did—have some sympathy for the situation in which she now found himself, there was nothing for him to do about it.

But when he made a quick trip into town to pick up a few things from the hardware store on Tuesday, he impulsively detoured down Queen Street on his way back and discovered there was a news van parked directly across from Edwina's house.

He shook his head, baffled by the fact that her firing from a TV show was news.

He knew she wasn't the first actor to ever be "released from her contractual obligations," so what was the big deal?

He supposed the popularity of both the show and her character had some bearing on the popularity of the story. Add to that the name recognition of an Oscar-winning actor and the result was immediate clickbait.

And he was as guilty as anyone else for scrolling from one story to the next. Which was how he'd ended up watching an online interview with Donovan Kessel, *Rockwood Ridge*'s newest hire.

"I can't say that I'm familiar with Hope Bradford's work, but I've heard that she's a talented actor and I was disappointed to learn that I wouldn't have the opportunity to work with her on *Rockwood Ridge*."

"Unnamed sources at Moonshine Pictures claim that Hope Bradford chose to leave the high profile role of Lainey Howard rather than work with you," the off-screen interviewer said. "Can you comment on that?"

Kessel seemed surprised by this revelation and took a minute to consider his response. "I do have a reputation for being someone who demands one hundred percent from not only myself but all those around me on

every project, no matter how big or small. I can understand how another, less experienced, actor might find
that intimidating."

"You're suggesting that she was daunted by the prospect of working with a big-name actor? You don't think
her refusal to work with you might have been based on
something more personal?"

"I don't know how it could be when I'm sure I've never
worked with Hope Bradford before."

"But Hope Bradford did have a minor part in *Shadow
Games*."

"Did she?" He seemed to consider this revelation.
"Well, that movie was made…almost seventeen years
ago, I think…and the lead actors don't often interact
with the rest of the cast, so I'm sure you can understand
why I wouldn't have any recollection of her on the set."

MG clicked to end the playback of the interview and
then he picked up his TV remote to cancel his scheduled
DVR recording of *Rockwood Ridge*. Because he had
no interest in the show if there wasn't any chance that
Lainey Howard would appear on his screen.

Hope sat cross-legged on the sofa in her grandmother's
living room, her hands fisted in her lap, seething as she
listened to Donovan Kessel essentially label her an inexperienced rookie who couldn't handle playing in the big
leagues. Maybe she hadn't been in the business quite as
long as he had and she didn't have an Oscar, but she had
eighteen years and three Emmys under her belt.

He thought she was intimidated by his stardom? She'd
had the privilege of working with countless blockbuster
stars and award winners—several of them much big-

ger than Donovan Kessel—and none of them had ever complained.

"I'm sure you can understand why I wouldn't have any recollection of her on the set."

His easy dismissal made her want to throw something at him, and she realized that the remote control was in fact clenched in her fist. But if she gave in to the impulse, the only damage she'd do would be to Edwina's television, not the smirking face of Hollywood heartthrob Donovan Kessel.

Was it possible that the incident that had such a profound impact on her life had been completely forgotten by him?

Or was he simply spinning the story for his fans—as he was so good at doing?

The problem was that his interview didn't only spin the story, it also fed the frenzy.

"Wasn't he on TV yesterday?" Edwina asked, settling into her favorite recliner.

"He's been on TV every day for the past week and a half, milking the story for every drop of publicity he can get out of it."

"What are we watching?" Dennis asked, settling onto the opposite end of the sofa, closest to Edwina's chair. "Oh, it's Donovan Kessel," he said, answering his own questions. "I really like him in those *Shadow* movies."

"Shh," Edwina said to him. "Hope's trying to watch this."

"Further to our interview with Donovan Kessel last week, *HHG* tracked down other members of the cast and crew who worked on *Shadow Games* with Donovan Kessel and Hope Bradford. Donovan Kessel, as I'm sure you all know, played Quincy Shadow in that movie and each of the *Shadow* sequels, and Hope Bradford is credited as 'girl in laundromat.'"

"Really?" Dennis looked at Hope, grinning. "You were 'girl in laundromat'?"

She couldn't resist smiling back, because he was seriously adorable and she loved that he loved her grandmother. "I had three lines—'How late are you open?' 'I need quarters for the machine' and 'That's gonna leave a stain.'"

Dennis chortled with glee. "I remember that scene now. Especially that last line—when the blood splatters all over the clothes you're folding."

"Shh," Edwina said again.

They fell silent as clips from interviews with various cast members and crew were shown. Some confirmed Donovan's story, that he and Hope never would have had an opportunity to cross paths. Others went further to recall that Hope was practically brand-new to Hollywood, young and inexperienced but eager to learn.

"And completely in awe of Donovan Kessel," a former production assistant claimed.

"Seriously crushing on him," the costume designer asserted. "Of course, all the girls on set were seriously crushing on him, because he was Donovan Kessel."

The half-hour celebrity "news" program wrapped up by reminding viewers they'd be able to catch Donovan Kessel in his new role as Dalton Jones on *Rockwood Ridge* when the series returned in January.

Hope handed the remote to Dennis as she rose from the sofa.

"Where you going? I thought we could all watch *Shadow Games* together," he said.

"I want to do some reading before bed—but you guys go ahead."

"Before bed? It's eight o'clock," Edwina pointed out.

"It's been a long day."

Her grandmother opened her mouth as if to say something else, then closed it again.

Hope kissed her cheek. "Good night, Grams."

"Sweet dreams."

Then she surprised Dennis by dropping a kiss on his cheek, too.

"Ahh, you're a sweet girl, Hope Bradford."

"I was raised right," she said, winking at her grandmother as she exited the room.

Making her way up the stairs, she heard the echo of the costume designer's words in her head. *Of course, all the girls on set were seriously crushing on him, because he was Donovan Kessel.*

It was undoubtedly true, and the actor's star had only risen higher since the making of *Shadow Games* seventeen years earlier. Which was why *he* was doing interviews to promote *his* new role in *her* TV show and *she* was hiding out in Haven, Nevada.

It felt good to be back in the saddle and doing some real work around the ranch, MG decided. Even if he was currently hot and sweaty and desperately in need of a shower before he headed into town for his physical therapy appointment.

He wasn't surprised to find Bernie lazing on the front porch when he got back to the bunkhouse, but he was surprised to find his mother puttering around inside.

"Mom? What are you doing here?"

"Oh. Michael." Angela Gilmore smiled brightly. "I didn't expect you to be back so soon."

"It's Wednesday," he reminded her. "I have my now once-a-week physical therapy."

"You've made so much progress, I sometimes forget..." Her words trailed off and she shook her head. "No, I'll never forget. But I'm grateful you're doing so well."

"Can you tell Dad that I'm doing well? Because he's still got me mucking out stalls every morning."

"I think that assignment has less to do with accommodating your injury than punishing you for being an idiot."

"Because needing three surgeries, a rod and half a dozen screws to repair my broken leg wasn't punishment enough?"

"You go ahead and have your shower," Angela said, ignoring his obviously rhetorical question. "I won't be too long finishing up here."

"Finishing up what?" he asked, still baffled by her presence in the bunkhouse.

"I'm just giving your brother's bathroom a quick cleaning and putting some fresh sheets on his bed."

"Mitch hasn't lived here in more than two years," he reminded her.

"Which is why I knew it would be perfect."

"Perfect for what?" he asked warily.

"Not what—who," she told him.

"Okay, perfect for who?" he prompted, when she didn't immediately volunteer the information.

She smiled brightly. "Hope."

"Hope," he echoed.

"Hope Bradford," she clarified, in case he knew someone else named Hope. "Edwina was telling me that she can't step out the front door without someone snapping a photo and uploading it to one of those gossip sites. As a result, she hasn't left the house in days. So I suggested that she could stay here, where she'll have plenty of space to move around freely and do as she pleases."

"I'm sorry," he said, certain he couldn't have heard her correctly. "You did *what*?"

"I invited Hope to stay here."

Apparently he *had* heard her correctly.

And his mother had apparently lost her mind.

"You invited Hope to stay in my cabin?"

"Yes. And why shouldn't I?"

"*Because. It's. My. Cabin.*"

"With both a spare bedroom and a spare bathroom," she reminded him. "You probably won't even know she's here most of the time."

As if.

"No," he said firmly.

Angela's brow furrowed. "What do you mean *no*?" she demanded.

"I mean that I don't want Hope staying here."

"Why not?"

"Because."

"Because isn't a reason," she chided.

"What do you think Paige would say if I told her that Hope was staying here?"

"Why are you concerned about what Paige would say? Didn't she break up with you?"

"And one of the reasons she did is that I didn't want to live with her, because I like having my own space."

"There's plenty of space, Michael. And I'm sure Hope won't need to stay more than a few weeks."

"A few weeks," he echoed.

She was talking as if it was a done deal.

Which made him realize that it likely was—at least as far as his mother was concerned.

"Have you already told Hope that she could stay here?"

"Of course."

"And she agreed?" he asked dubiously.

His mother shrugged. "I think she's pretty desperate."

"Why didn't you offer her Olivia's old room?"

"Because we're in the process of redoing Olivia's room," she told him. "Wait until you see the L-shaped quad bunk beds that we've ordered."

"Why do you need four beds?"

"For all the grandsons to hang out together."

"So Hope could have her choice of four beds if she stayed at the main house."

"The beds aren't going to be delivered until sometime next month and we only just picked out the new paint. Not to mention that there are constantly people in and out of our house—the poor girl wouldn't have any peace."

"I don't know that anyone else would refer to Hope Bradford as a poor girl," he said dryly.

"You can't know what it's like, to live in the spotlight the way she does."

"It's what she chose."

"She chose to make a living as an actor," his mom acknowledged. "I don't think that decision automatically forfeits all expectation of privacy."

"Fine. Hope can have the cabin. I'll move back to the main house and sleep in my old room."

"We've got a crib set up in your old room," she reminded him.

"So I'll sleep on the sofa bed in Dad's office."

Angela sighed. "If you think it will be too hard to stay here with Hope, if the memories of your youthful heartbreak are still too raw, then of course you can sleep on the sofa bed in your dad's office," she said. "And if that's the case, then I'm sorry I issued the invitation. But you've been adamant that whatever feelings you had for her were gone a long time ago, so I didn't think it would be a problem to let an old friend stay."

He gritted his teeth, because she'd neatly boxed him into a corner and she knew it.

"I'm going to shower," he said, walking past her to his bathroom and slamming the door.

As Hope took a tentative step out of the bedroom and into the main living area of the bunkhouse, she realized that she'd made a mistake of monumental proportions.

"You can stay at the Circle G," Angela Gilmore said, when she stopped by to have coffee with Hope's grandmother and Edwina confided that Hope didn't want to leave the house because of the news van still parked outside.

"Oh, that's not necessary," Hope had protested. "Any day now, one of the Kardashians will announce she's having a baby or one of the Real Housewives *will confess to an affair and this will all blow over."*

"That's what you said a week ago," Edwina reminded her.

"Access to the Circle G is on a private road," Michael's mother pointed out. "No news van would dare venture past the gates. And we've got plenty of space."

Hope was undeniably tempted. She loved her grandmother dearly and had so many wonderful memories of this home, but not being able to walk out the door for even a breath of fresh air made her feel trapped.

"Don't you think you should check with Mr. Gilmore before you go throwing open the doors of your home?" Hope suggested.

"Charles won't have any objection," Angela assured her.

It occurred to her that Michael might, but she knew that he'd moved out of the main house several years back, so she didn't think he'd object too strenuously when it was unlikely their paths would have much opportunity to cross.

Well, the joke was on her—because when Angela invited her to stay at the Circle G, apparently she hadn't been referring to a spare bedroom in the main house but the empty room in the bunkhouse. Which Hope hadn't clued into until Angela drove right past the brick-and-stone two-story structure that she'd frequently visited in the past and pulled into the short gravel driveway leading to a single-story building with a wide front porch that Hope knew had once been a bunkhouse—and was now where Michael lived.

"Am I not staying in the main house?" she'd asked, when Angela turned off the engine of her SUV.

"Goodness, no," Michael's mother had responded. "You wouldn't have any peace and quiet there. In addition to five grandchildren traipsing in and out at all hours, the upper level is something of a construction zone right now as we're renovating and redecorating some of the bedrooms."

She'd wanted to protest, but what could she say?

She did, however, venture to ask if Michael knew that

he was going to have a new roommate, and his mother assured her that he did.

Then Angela had opened the door to the bunkhouse, shown Hope to her room and given her a quick hug before hurrying back to her home to get started on making dinner.

Hope had taken a few minutes to unpack her bags—pleased to discover that she had her own en suite bath so Michael wouldn't grumble about her stuff being all over his bathroom counter and she wouldn't have to worry about him walking in when she was in the shower. Okay, maybe the latter wasn't a cause for worry so much as wishful thinking, because her long-ago boyfriend and now roommate had made it perfectly clear that he wasn't interested in exploring the chemistry that continued to simmer between them.

After her clothes were put away and her toiletries organized, she'd sat on the edge of the bed, wondering what she was supposed to do now. Angela had told her to make herself at home, but she didn't feel entirely comfortable walking around Michael's house when he wasn't there. On the other hand, she'd probably feel more inhibited about browsing his bookshelves and peeking in his refrigerator when he was home, so perhaps she should do some exploring now.

The layout of the bunkhouse was fairly simple—the two bedrooms, each with its own bath, were at the back of the building. Michael's bedroom shared a wall with the powder room, on the other side of which was a sizable living area with leather sectional and chair, an enormous television and river rock fireplace. Hope's room—formerly Mitchell's—shared a wall with the mud/laundry room, on the other side of which was a decent-sized kitchen, obviously recently updated with granite countertops, stainless steel appliances and a separate prep counter/island. There was also a separate dining room, with two large windows, one of which looked out onto the side yard and the other the front porch.

She glanced at her watch—and sighed to discover that her leisurely perusal of the space had taken all of three minutes.

Now what was she supposed to do?

She didn't want to watch TV and she was too restless to read. And though she wasn't hungry, she suspected that Michael would be when he came in, so she opened the refrigerator to take stock of its contents and figure out a dinner plan.

Chapter Thirteen

MG wasn't in a hurry to go back to the Circle G when he left Back in the Game, and the fact that he was avoiding his own home because he knew that Hope would be there only added to his annoyance.

Maybe he'd call a buddy and make plans to meet for a beer and a bite at Diggers'. That would kill a few hours. Except the last time he'd been to Diggers' had been with Hope, and he definitely didn't want to be thinking about that night and how it ended versus how he'd hoped it would end, especially when he had to go home and climb into a bed that was less than twenty feet away from the one in which she'd be sleeping.

So the Diggers' option was definitely out, but there was no reason he couldn't stop by to say hi to his brother's family. No reason except that it was getting close to dinnertime and he didn't want Lindsay to think he was trying to mooch a meal. Not to mention that if Mitch knew about their mom offering his old room in the bunkhouse to Hope, his brother would immediately guess that MG was avoiding her—and he wouldn't be wrong.

Which left MG grumbling behind the wheel of his truck but headed toward home.

He started to lift his hand to knock on the side door, then dropped it to grasp the knob. It was his house, dammit. And he wasn't going to let the presence of some Hollywood celebrity reduce him to knocking on his own damn door.

He took off his boots in the mudroom and set his hat on a hook. "Let's go figure out dinner," he said to Bernie.

Except that Bernie wasn't there.

His canine companion always met him at the door when MG walked through it at the end of the day— unless he was walking through the door with him.

"Bernie?" He made his way through the laundry room and into the kitchen where the dog was sitting by Hope's sexy bare feet with crimson-painted toenails. "There you are."

His uninvited houseguest swiveled her head, looking surprised but happy to see him. "Were you looking for me?"

"Oh. Um. No." He pointed to the dog. "I was looking for Bernie."

Her easy smile faded. "Oh."

"He's usually at the back door when I come in."

"My fault," she admitted. "He's been hanging around the kitchen while I've been cooking, hoping for a handout. But don't worry—I haven't given him any treats. Though I did drop a piece of carrot on the floor and he gobbled it up before I could get to it." She gave the dog a look, and

Bernie had the decency to feign shame for half a second before his eyes shifted to the counter again, obviously hoping for something else to fall.

"What are you making?"

"Penne with sausage and peppers, garden salad and garlic bread."

He looked at the dining room table, already set with plates and cutlery. There was a bowl of salad with serving tongs and an open bottle of pinot noir and two wine glasses waiting to be filled.

"Are you expecting company?"

"No."

"Then why are there two place settings?"

"I thought you might want to eat, too," she said lightly.

That was unexpected. "You're cooking dinner—*for me*?"

"I'm cooking dinner and *sharing it* with you," she clarified.

"Why?" he asked.

"To show my appreciation for you not saying *no* when your mom asked if I could stay here."

He ignored the wine on the table and opened the fridge to pull out a bottle of beer. He twisted off the cap and tossed it into the garbage. "Is that what she told you?"

Her brow furrowed. "It's not true?"

He tipped the bottle to his lips, swallowed.

"I guess, at the time she spoke with you, it probably was true," he allowed. "Because she hadn't yet shared her harebrained scheme with me."

"Harebrained scheme?" Hope echoed.

He swallowed another mouthful of beer. "You can't honestly think this is a good idea."

"Maybe not a good idea, but definitely the best of my limited options. Otherwise, I wouldn't be here."

"You're here because you're desperate," he pointed out. "At least, that's what my mom said."

"I could have gone back to Los Angeles," she said, though with a decided lack of enthusiasm for the idea.

"Except that there must have been a reason you left Los Angeles."

"I got fired," she said, as if he hadn't heard the news.

"I'm sorry," he said.

She moved to the table to pour a glass of wine.

Her hand wasn't quite steady as she lifted the bottle, and she immediately set it down again, as if she didn't want him to see that she was rattled.

He moved to the table and poured the wine, then picked up the glass and put it in her hand.

"Thank you."

"I'm not a good roommate," he warned her. "I like my space and I get grumpy when people are in it."

"I'll try to remember that."

"It's nothing personal."

Her lips twisted in a wry smile. "I'm not sure I believe that."

"It's not," he insisted.

"Well, you don't have to stick around for dinner, if you have other plans."

"No other plans."

She lifted the pot off the stove and dumped the pasta into the colander in the sink. "Then you can grab the plates off the table."

He set his bottle of beer on the table and grabbed the plates. "What else can I do?"

"Get the garlic bread out of the oven," she said, as she filled his plate with pasta.

He slipped his hand in the oven mitt on the counter and opened the oven door.

"No cheese on the garlic bread?"

"I wasn't feeling completely wild tonight."

Of course, that remark reminded them both of the night they'd crossed paths at Diggers'. When they'd shared wings and garlic bread—with cheese—and he'd taken her home afterward.

She ducked her head, so that her hair curtained her face, but not before he noticed that her cheeks had gone red.

Interesting, he mused, as he transferred the bread to the serving plate, that the woman whose face had graced countless magazine covers and who'd bared most of her body on the movie screen for anyone who could buy a ticket to see was still capable of blushing like the schoolgirl he remembered her being.

After setting the bread on the table, he returned to help her with the pasta, then gestured for her to sit before he did the same. While Hope served herself some salad, he dug into the main course, clearing almost half his plate before lifting his head to say, "This is really good."

"You sound surprised," she noted.

He dipped his fork into the pasta again. "I guess I just assumed you didn't cook."

"Why would you assume that?"

He shrugged. "Maybe because you don't look like you eat."

"I'm eating right now," she pointed out to him.

"I've seen you put exactly two bites of salad in your mouth—the rest of the time, you've been pushing the lettuce around in your bowl. You haven't even sampled your pasta."

"I guess I lost my appetite along with my career."

"I'm sure it's not that bad," he said. "How can it be when Hope Bradford is synonymous with Lainey Howard—and anyone who's a fan of *Rockwood Ridge* loves Lainey Howard."

"Or they did, until she slept with her husband's brother."

"To give her husband the baby he desperately wanted."

Hope seemed taken aback by his quick response. "How do you know that?"

Dammit.

"I, uh, must have heard my mom and grandma talking about it. My grandmother is a huge fan of the show. And Grandpa might grumble about having to watch it, but I don't think he's missed an episode, either."

"I should stop by and see your grandparents while I'm here."

"They would be thrilled," he told her. "And it's not like you can make plans to do much else without a vehicle."

"Your mom suggested I leave my car at my grandmother's, to preserve the illusion that I'm still there."

"A good plan," he acknowledged. "Except that you're now stranded here."

"At least I'm stranded somewhere I can go outside and feel the sun on my face."

"Just so long as you don't expect me to chauffeur you to get your nails done or meet friends for lunch."

"Considering that I had my nails done last week and, aside from Laurel, I don't really have any friends in town, neither of those tasks is on my immediate agenda. But even if they were, you can rest assured that I don't expect you to chauffeur me anywhere. In fact, the only time I've been in your truck since I came home was the night you insisted on driving me back to my grandmother's house from Diggers'."

And there it was—another reminder of the night he was desperately trying to forget.

She dropped her gaze to her plate. "I'm sorry. You've made it clear that you don't want to talk about that night."

He lifted the last forkful of pasta to his mouth, then dragged his bread through the sauce on his plate.

"Did you want more pasta?" she asked. "I made plenty. Probably too much, actually."

"No, thanks." He shook his head. "I don't think I could eat another bite."

She jumped up to clear their plates, despite the fact that hers was mostly untouched.

"Do you want me to put the leftovers in the fridge or freezer?"

"I'll deal with the leftovers—and the dishes," he told her, pushing away from the table.

"You don't have to do that," she protested.

"You didn't have to make dinner, but you did—and she who cooks does not clean up afterward."

"Your mother's rule?" she guessed.

"You know it."

"Well, I won't tell her if you don't," she said, scraping her plate.

MG carried the salad to the kitchen.

The space was plenty big enough when he was moving around on his own. Trying to maneuver around Hope, though, it suddenly felt like very tight quarters. As he reached past her to drop the napkins in the garbage, he couldn't help but notice the hint of cleavage visible in the low vee of her top. When he stepped around her to put the plates in the dishwasher, he caught a whiff

"One Minute" Survey

You get up to **FOUR** books <u>and</u> a Mystery Gift...

ABSOLUTELY FREE!

YOU pick your books – WE pay for everything!

See inside for details.

Dear Reader,

Your opinions are important to us. So if you'll participate in our fast and free "One Minute" Survey, YOU can pick up to four wonderful books that WE pay for when you try the Harlequin Reader Service!

As a leading publisher of women's fiction, we'd love to hear from you. That's why we promise to reward you for completing our survey.

IMPORTANT: Please complete the survey and return it. We'll send your Free Books and a Free Mystery Gift right away. And we pay for shipping and handling too! ← *We pay for EVERYTHING!*

Try **Harlequin® Special Edition** and get 2 books featuring comfort and strength in the support of loved ones and enjoying the journey no matter what life throws your way.

Try **Harlequin® Heartwarming™ Larger-Print** and get 2 books featuring uplifting stories where the bonds of friendship, family and community unite.

Or TRY BOTH!

Thank you again for participating in our "One Minute" Survey. It really takes just a minute (or less) to complete the survey… and your free books and gift will be well worth it!

If you continue with your subscription, you can look forward to curated monthly shipments of brand-new books from your selected series, always at a discount off the cover price! Plus you can cancel any time. So don't miss out, return your One Minute Survey today to get your Free books.

Pam Powers

of that damn perfume. And when she bent over to retrieve a fork that had fallen to the floor, the delectable
curve of her bottom brushed against his groin, causing
all the blood in his brain to immediately migrate south
and the wineglass he was holding to slip out of his hand.

She jolted upright when she heard the crystal shatter.

Thankfully the pieces seemed to be confined to the
sink into which the glass had fallen.

"Hope," he said through gritted teeth. "Please. Get.
Out. Of. My. Kitchen."

"What did I do?" she asked, sounding both confused
and contrite.

"You didn't do anything. You're just…in my space."

She took a step back.

"Also, your feet are bare," he pointed out in a gentler
tone. "And I don't want you to cut yourself on any shards
of glass that might have fallen to the floor."

"I'm sorry."

"I don't want you to be sorry. I just want you to…go
watch TV or something."

She backtracked out of the kitchen, retreating to her
bedroom, he guessed.

He exhaled a weary sigh and began picking shards of
glass out of the sink. As he turned to drop them in the
garbage, he saw Bernie looking at him reproachfully.

When he finally finished tidying up the kitchen, he
discovered that Hope was curled up in the living room
with a book in her hand. And Bernie, *his* supposed best
friend, was curled up with her, his big head on her thigh.

MG settled in at the opposite end of the sofa and
reached for the TV remote.

Hope lowered her book and shifted to face him.

"I'm sorry," she said again.

"Why are you apologizing to me?"

"Because I didn't think to question your mom when she told me that you didn't have an issue with me staying here."

"Forget about it."

She shook her head. "I can't. But I can find somewhere else to stay."

"That's not necessary," he said.

"You shouldn't be made to feel uncomfortable in your own home, and obviously having me here makes you uncomfortable."

"Don't worry about it, Hope."

She lifted a hand and absently stroked the dog's flank. Bernie tipped his head back to look at her adoringly. *Traitor.*

Hope glanced at him. "Did you say something?"

Apparently he had, though he hadn't intended to say the word out loud. "I was just, uh, talking to the dog."

"Is it okay that he's on the sofa?"

He had to laugh at that. "You want to tell him to get off?"

Her lips curved a little at the corners. "No."

"He pretty much has the run of the house," MG told her. "The only place he isn't allowed is on my bed."

"Why not?" she wondered. "Does he steal the covers?"

"I wouldn't know, because I refuse to let him up there to find out."

"Well, you can share my bed," Hope said.

Unfortunately, that time *she* was talking to the dog.

Michael was already gone when Hope ventured out of her bedroom the following morning. She decided that it was probably a good thing. Even better, there was a

Keurig on the counter and a carousel of coffee pods beside it. She selected a French roast and popped it into the machine.

She was savoring her first sip of the freshly brewed coffee when a knock sounded on the front door. She froze, wondering if she was supposed to answer the summons and if it would be completely inappropriate to open the door she was wearing a short robe over striped satin boxer shorts and a rib knit tank top. Before she could answer either of those questions, the door opened and Angela Gilmore walked in carrying a tray of something that smelled like sugar-coated heaven.

"I hope I'm not stopping by too early," Michael's mother said. "But I've got homemade cinnamon rolls fresh out of the oven."

"In that case, I'd say you're right on time."

"Sit, sit," Angela urged. "I'll get plates and forks."

Hope sat.

Angela, obviously comfortable in her son's kitchen, selected a pod and set her own coffee brewing while she gathered plates and cutlery.

"Did you sleep well last night?" she asked, joining Hope at the table.

"Like a baby."

"I'm so pleased to hear it. Some people, accustomed to the noises of city living, can have trouble adjusting to the unnatural quiet of the ranch."

"No trouble at all," Hope assured her. "Though I haven't slept well for more than a week, so that might have factored into it, too."

The older woman smiled as she lifted an enormous cinnamon bun out of the tray and transferred it to a plate.

"I'm sorry that you've been going through such an ordeal."

Hope shrugged. "I really have no cause for complaint."

"Just because the studio paid you a lot of money doesn't give them the right to treat you so horribly," Angela said indignantly, as she slid the plate across the table to Hope.

"I appreciate the support—and the sugar rush—but there's no way I'm going to be able to eat all of that."

"Not with that attitude," Angela agreed.

Hope couldn't help but laugh. "Seriously—can't we split this?"

Angela grumbled some more, but she finally relented and cut the pastry in half.

Hope lifted a bite of flaky pastry, dripping with icing, to her mouth. "Ohmygod," she said, speaking around the mouthful of food. "This is...amazing."

"They're a big hit with all the grandkids," Angela admitted.

"I can see why."

The other woman cut into her half of the roll. "Charles would be happy to have them every day, but I usually only make them when we have company."

"I can't imagine eating something like this every day," Hope said. "But it certainly is a delicious treat."

"I'll wrap half of them up for the freezer—otherwise Michael will finish them off before the weekend. And speaking of the weekend, we're having a family dinner Saturday night for Elliott's birthday—and that includes you," she said firmly.

"But I'm not family," Hope protested.

"Maybe not. Technically," Angela allowed. "Though there was a time when I thought...hoped..." She smiled, then shrugged. "In any event, you're always welcome in our home."

"I appreciate that," Hope said. "But I'm not sure Michael will want me there. No doubt he would appreciate a break from bumping into me every time he turns around."

"There was a time when you and Michael couldn't stand to be away from each other," his mother noted.

"First love is intense," she acknowledged, careful to keep her tone light. "Then I went away and broke his heart—and mine, too."

"You did what was right for you at the time," Angela said. "But what was right for you at seventeen might not be right for you at thirty-five."

A realization Hope had recently come to herself.

"Anyway, dinner will be on the table for six, but you're welcome to come any time before that."

"I'm not coming at all unless you let me bring something," Hope said.

"How about a green salad?"

She grinned. "My specialty."

"So what's it like—sharing a cabin with Hope?" Mitch asked, as he and MG worked with their cousin Caleb to vaccinate the new calves.

"Not much different than sharing a cabin with anyone else—except she smells a lot better than you ever did," MG said.

Caleb chuckled at that as he opened the chute to release the inoculated calf.

"You sleeping in separate beds?" Mitch pressed.

MG slanted him a look. "What do you think?"

"I think he'd be less grumpy if he was living out his high school fantasies," Caleb chimed in.

"I think you should shut up and focus on inputting the data," MG told him.

"I can multitask," his cousin assured him.

"Seriously, bro—what's holding you back?"

"For starters, she came out to the ranch for privacy, not to be hit on. Not to mention that her career recently imploded, and what kind of man would try to take advantage of a woman feeling vulnerable and uncertain about her future?"

"Good reasons," Caleb said with a nod.

"But did you notice that, in enumerating his reasons, MG never said he wasn't interested in her?" Mitch asked their cousin.

Caleb nodded again. "I did."

"She's Hope Bradford," MG noted. "Who wouldn't be interested?"

"Except that you're not interested in the celebrity—you're interested in the girl you've been in love with since high school," his brother said.

"And you broke up with Paige more than three weeks ago," Caleb chimed in again.

"So I should jump into bed with the first woman to catch my eye?" he scoffed.

"She *was* the first woman to catch your eye," Mitch reminded him. "More than twenty years ago. And anyway, Paige has obviously moved on, so why shouldn't you?"

"What do you mean—Paige has obviously moved on?"

Mitch and Caleb exchanged a glance.

"You haven't heard?"

"Heard what?"

"She's been spending a lot of time with Gavin Trent," Caleb said.

"Well, I hope he treats her better than I did," MG said.

"You really don't mind that she's moved on?" his brother asked.

"Why would I mind? She deserves to be happy."

"So do you," Caleb told him.

"And so does Hope," Mitch added.

Chapter Fourteen

Hope was admittedly apprehensive about the "family dinner" Angela had insisted she attend. And the closer it got to zero hour on Saturday, the more she paced.

"Do you have one of those Fitbit things and you're trying to increase your step count for the day?" Michael asked her.

"No." She stopped pacing. "I guess I'm a little nervous."

"Why?"

"Because your whole family's going to be there—including your grandparents, as your mom informed me today."

"You've met them all before," he reminded her.

"I haven't met Olivia's husband. Or his kids. Or Mitch and Lindsay's kids."

"Adam's a good guy," Michael assured her. "The kids, though…you should probably be worried about them."

"What? Why?"

He chuckled. "I'm kidding."

"Well, it wasn't very funny."

"And Adam's kids might or might not be there—they spend every other weekend at their mom's place."

"I still don't think I should go."

He shrugged. "Okay."

"It's really okay if I skip out?"

"Your call," he said. "As in—you're going to have to call my mom and tell her you're a great big chicken."

"I'm not a great big chicken," she said indignantly.

"Then why are you acting like one?"

"FYI, that's an uninformed cliché. The truth is, chickens will fight bravely and ferociously to protect their families."

"Does that mean you're coming to dinner or not? Because I'm out the door in ten minutes."

She huffed out a breath. "I'm coming. Because I'm not a chicken but I am afraid of your mom."

"We're all afraid of my mom," he told her. "She's small but mighty."

She managed to smile at that. Then she glanced down at the ruffled blouse and cropped pants she'd donned for the occasion. "Just give me five minutes to change."

"What's wrong with what you're wearing?"

"Just give me five minutes," she said again.

"No." He caught her hands as she started to walk by, halting her in her tracks.

Over the past few days, he'd been careful not to touch her—seeming to go out of his way to avoid the possibility of even accidental physical contact with her. So the fact that he'd reached out would have stopped her in her tracks even if he wasn't holding her in place.

"There's nothing wrong with what you're wearing," he said. "So tell me why you're twisted up in knots about sitting around the table with my family? Or is it the menu that has you worried? Are you concerned your system will go into carbohydrate overload?"

She lifted her chin defiantly. "I'm not afraid of lasagna. I even tackled one of your mom's cinnamon buns the other day."

"She said you tackled half."

"It was a big half."

"And you're ducking the question," he pointed out.

He was still holding her hands—not so tightly that she couldn't have pulled them out of his grasp, but with a deliberate pressure that offered silent encouragement and support. And it felt nice. Really nice.

She dropped her gaze to their linked hands. "I guess I'm just a little concerned that I won't live up to their expectations," she finally confided.

"You did prepare a thirty-minute dramatic monologue for our after-dinner entertainment, didn't you?"

"I know you're joking," she said. "But sometimes when people meet someone they've seen on TV, they think they know that person or they expect her to be like the character, and they're disappointed when it turns out that she's not."

"Nobody's going to be disappointed in you, Hope."

"You can't know that."

"Sure I can," he said. "Because I know all of them—and I know you."

"Okay," she said, not entirely convinced but willing to be persuaded.

"Let's go then."

"As soon as I grab the salad out of the fridge."

"You're bringing your own dinner?"

"Ha. Your mom asked me to make it."

"Which should prove that she doesn't see you as a celebrity, because there's no way she'd ever ask Julia Roberts to bring a salad to dinner."

And somehow, that made Hope feel better about the evening ahead.

"Since when do you get out the fancy dishes for a family dinner?" Michael wondered aloud, as he surveyed the table covered with an Irish lace cloth and set with gold-edged plates, gleaming silverware and sparkling crystal.

"Since your mother overheard mine grumbling that she wouldn't have given away her mother's dishes if she'd known they wouldn't be used," Charles said, coming into the room.

"Good timing," Angela told her husband. "I need three more chairs."

"Who else is coming?"

"Easton, Hudson and Colton."

"I thought this was their weekend with their mom."

"It was supposed to be, but Brooklyn's sick."

"Brooklyn's their half sister," Michael explained to Hope. Then to his dad he said, "I'll get the chairs."

"Thanks."

"What can I do to help?" Hope asked.

"Can you count out three more sets of cutlery?" Angela asked. "Top drawer of the sideboard."

Hope found the cutlery while Angela shifted the place settings around, adding three more to the table.

"I'm actually glad they're going to be here," Michael's mom confided to Hope. "Without them, we were twelve—or thirteen, counting Emeline—and my mother always said it's bad luck to set a table for thirteen."

"Now you've got sixteen—and still room for more," Hope noted.

"Room to grow," Angela said, with a wink. "Because I haven't given up hope of more grandbabies in the future."

"You might want to wait for Lindsay to wean the baby before you make comments like that within her earshot," Michael warned, returning with the requested chairs.

"I'm not putting any pressure on your sister-in-law," Angela promised. "It's still possible your sister might change her mind about adding to her family. Or—if pigs learn to fly—you might actually decide to get married and start a family."

"Can I get you something to drink?" Charles asked Hope, in an obvious attempt to shift the direction of the conversation. "We've got beer, wine, juice boxes—"

"Those are for the kids," Angela admonished.

He shrugged.

"I'd love a glass of wine," Hope decided.

"Red or white?"

"Red, please."

Charles had just stepped out of the room when a child's voice called out from the front of the house, "We're here!"

"And so it begins," Angela said, a happy smile on her face.

Hope soon realized that the "it" to which she'd been referring was the influx of company. Mitch and Lindsay and their kids were barely through the door when Jack and Evelyn—Michael's grandparents—showed up, followed closely by Olivia, Adam and their kids.

"You're definitely going to want this now," Charles

said, pressing a glass of wine into Hope's hand as Michael finished introducing her to the newer family members.

She smiled her thanks as Angela shooed everyone toward the dining room with instructions to find a chair and sit in it. Though there was no apparent assigned seating, obviously each of her guests had a usual spot at the table, and they crisscrossed paths to get to it—which left Hope to take the empty seat beside Michael.

Evelyn and Olivia helped bring out the food—platters of antipasto, trays of lasagna and baskets of warm bread. The din of talking quieted a little as everyone focused on filling their plates—then their stomachs. But through bits and pieces of conversation, Hope discovered that Elliott and Hudson, in addition to being cousins by marriage, were best friends and in the same class at school. She also learned that Colton didn't like his first grade teacher as much as he'd liked Ms. Gilmore, his kindergarten teacher, and that Avenlea had just started school in Ms. Gilmore's class.

"There used to be two Miz Gilmores at our school," Easton explained to Hope. "Then Olivia married our dad and became Mrs. Morgan, so now there's only one."

"That one being Brielle Gilmore, Caleb's wife," Michael clarified for her.

"Formerly Brielle Channing," Mitch chimed in.

"Whose mother was a Blake," Olivia added.

"Well, she's a Gilmore now," Evelyn said, in a tone that declared the end of that subject.

"Are you disappointed that you didn't get to see your sister this weekend?" Angela asked Easton, following her mother-in-law's cue.

"Nuh uh." The boy answered without hesitation, adding an emphatic headshake to his response.

His brothers echoed the gesture.

"She cries *all* night," Hudson complained.

"I know what *that's* like," Elliott assured his friend.

"You cried a lot when you were a baby, too," his mother pointed out.

"Maybe," he allowed. "But I didn't have an older brother or sister that was kept awake by my crying."

"No, just a mom and a dad," Lindsay responded dryly.

"Yeah, but as a parent, that's your job," he said.

"One that doesn't pay nearly enough."

"I don't know," her husband said, winking at the little girl in the booster seat beside him. "The hugs and kisses are pretty great."

Avenlea beamed at him, so much joy in her smile that Hope found herself smiling, too, despite the ache in her heart.

"What's your class like this year?" Jack asked his granddaughter.

"Busy," Olivia said. "Of course, the first few weeks back after summer are always an adjustment, but in addition to that, I got stuck with after-school duty twice a week this year. Which is why I wanted to talk to Dad about possibly moving Dolly over to Morgan's Glen."

"Why don't you want her to stay here?" Charles asked.

"Because I won't be able to get over here to exercise her as often as I'd like."

"She's not being neglected," Angela promised. "I've been taking her out."

"That makes me feel a little better," Olivia said.

"How about you, Hope? Have you been riding at all since you arrived?" Evelyn asked.

She shook her head regretfully. "I have not."

"Why not?" Michael's grandmother wanted to know.

"To be honest, it's been so long since I've been on the back of a horse, I'm not sure I remember."

"It's not something you forget," Evelyn assured her. "Like riding a bike—except it's a horse."

"Which is a heck of a lot bigger than a bike and with a mind of its own."

The family matriarch chuckled. "It is indeed."

"So what are your plans now that you're back in Haven?" Jack asked.

"She's not *back*. She's visiting," Michael interjected to clarify before Hope even had a chance to respond.

"And how long will you be *visiting*?" Olivia wondered.

Hope looked at Michael, to see if he wanted to answer that question, too.

"My plans are up in the air right now," she said, when he remained silent.

"Well, if you're going to be around a while longer and want something to do, Ashley—my youngest granddaughter—was telling me that the high school drama club is gearing up for their holiday production," Evelyn chimed in. "And Tyler Hutchinson—the drama teacher—is always happy to have volunteers to help out."

"It would be a major *coup* for him to bring in a real Hollywood actor to direct his students," Angela mused.

"An unemployed Hollywood actor would be much less of a *coup*," Hope remarked.

"You won't be unemployed for long," Charles predicted. "I imagine your agent is already busy fielding calls."

"Unless you decide you don't want to go back to Los Angeles," Angela said.

"Why wouldn't she want to go back?" Olivia wondered.

"Plenty of people make career changes," her mother pointed out.

"Maybe teachers or...bank managers," Olivia said. "But not Hollywood celebrities."

"Anyway, you should stop by the high school and talk to Tyler," Evelyn told Hope, returning to her original point. "Even if you can't commit to helping out for the duration, I'm sure he'd love to meet you and introduce you to his classes."

"I'll do that," Hope promised.

"That wasn't so bad, was it?" MG asked Hope, after they'd said goodbye to everyone and were making their way back to the cabin.

"Actually, it wasn't bad at all," she said. "I really enjoyed spending time with your family."

"You looked like you were having a good time," he noted. "Especially when you were cuddling with Emeline."

"You mean when I finally managed to pry her out of your arms?" she teased.

"Holding the baby got me out of doing dishes," he said.

"I might have bought that excuse except that you were cooing and smiling the whole time you had her."

"Happy I wasn't doing dishes."

"That's your story and you're sticking to it, huh?"

"I'm not ashamed of the fact that I have fun hanging out with my nieces and nephews," he said.

"Well, it's obvious they adore you, too."

"I always figured I'd have a kid or two someday," he admitted.

"Or four," she interjected.

Because a lifetime ago, they'd talked about having a family together, and obviously she remembered.

"Or four," he said, then shrugged. "But so far, it hasn't happened."

"To your mother's great disappointment," she noted.

"What about you?" he asked, opening the door of the cabin. "Do you still want to have kids someday?"

"I do." She crouched to greet Bernie as soon as she walked through the door, and the dog happily lapped up every ounce of her attention. "Though I feel my window of opportunity is rapidly closing."

"Maybe you should have married one of your five fiancés," he said.

"I was *not* engaged five times," she told him.

"Did I miss one? Was it six? Or more?"

She rolled her eyes. "I was only engaged twice. Well, technically three times—but the third engagement only lasted about twelve hours, so I'm not sure that really counts."

"You had a twelve-hour engagement?" He poured a glass of wine for Hope and opened a bottle of beer for himself.

"It was New Year's Eve, and I had mixed feelings about the year ahead because it would include my thirty-fifth birthday. The awareness of that milestone on the horizon—and three glasses of champagne—fueled my decision to accept Seth's midnight proposal."

She settled on the sofa with her wine, and Bernie immediately jumped up beside her. "And though my birthday was one day closer the following morning, my brain was clear of the effects of the bubbly and Seth was as relieved as I was when I gave back the ring and told him I couldn't marry him."

"He proposed and you said yes—in the moment, anyway—so that definitely counts as an engagement," he decided.

She shrugged. "Well, the other two so-called engagements were merely constructs of a creative press," she told him. "One based on nothing more than the fact that I was seen looking at engagement rings with one of my costars who wanted a second opinion before plunking down big bucks on the ring he'd chosen to propose to his longtime girlfriend."

"And the second?" he prompted.

"The second was the fantasy of an ardent fan who photoshopped my face and his onto pictures taken at his brother's engagement party and sent them out with a press release announcing that a June wedding was being planned."

"You're kidding."

"I'm not."

"Okay, those two don't count," he agreed. "But still, three engagements and no wedding—why not?"

She sipped her wine. "What do you want me to say—that I couldn't bring myself to walk down the aisle because I never loved any of those men as much as I'd loved you?"

"That would certainly be a boon to my ego," he said, hoping the warmth he could feel creeping into his face wasn't visible to Hope.

"Or maybe I'd foolishly romanticized our past, turning what had been a teenage love affair into something more—something that no real adult relationship could live up to," she suggested as an alternative.

"I'd say we dispelled that theory in ten minutes in the foyer of your grandmother's house."

"*Now* you want to talk about that?" she challenged.

"No." He pushed the memory aside. "We're talking about why you never got married."

"Possibly it's because I saw too many friends and costars fall in and out of love too many times. Or possibly it was receiving an invitation to my mother's fourth wedding that made me wary of taking that step—which is what happened when Justin—fiancé number two— was pushing me to set a date for our nuptials."

"Your mother's been married four times?"

"Six," she told him. "And currently awaiting her sixth divorce while she dates a man she believes is going to be husband number seven. I think she's trying to best Elizabeth Taylor."

"Everyone should have goals," he said.

She smiled at that.

"So how was wedding number four?" he asked.

"I didn't make it," she said. "Because the big event— and despite being her fourth wedding, it was a big event—was in Saint Lucia and I was in the middle of filming in LA.

"Anyway," she said, obviously eager to shift the topic of conversation. "It occurred to me that being released from my studio obligations might be a blessing in disguise—an opportunity to live a more normal life, maybe even fall in love and get married."

"Wouldn't you miss the spotlight?" he asked.

"I never craved fame and fortune as much as I craved my mother's attention," she confided. "Though it took me a lot of years—and a lot of therapy—to realize it."

"Still, I don't imagine you could have built such an impressive career if you didn't enjoy acting."

"I did enjoy it—some days and some jobs more than others," she told him. "But maybe it's time to find something else to enjoy."

"I just find it hard to believe that you'd actually consider walking away from it all."

"I'm considering all my options," she said lightly. "And now that we've thoroughly dissected my romantic past, tell me about yours."

He had more questions about her sudden desire for a career change, but Hope was obviously eager to redirect the conversation. "There's not much to tell."

"I find that hard to believe."

He shrugged. "I've dated a lot of women over the years, but none of the relationships lasted very long. Not until Paige—and looking at engagement rings was the closest I ever got to proposing."

"I was actually wondering about that," she admitted. "About why you were shopping for a ring."

"Doesn't a woman usually expect the man to offer a ring when he asks her to marry him?"

"Usually," she acknowledged. "But what about your grandmother's ring? Why didn't you want to give that to Paige?"

"I didn't think it was really her style," he lied.

"You didn't think she'd want to wear a family heirloom from Italy?"

"No, I didn't," he said, then abruptly changed the topic by saying, "Anyway, it's lucky for you that I'm not engaged, because my fiancée might not approve of you sleeping across the hall."

"I don't think your mom would have offered Mitch's room to me if you had a fiancée."

"Don't underestimate my mother," he warned.

"I wouldn't dare." She sipped her wine. "And you shouldn't give up hope—lowercase *h*—that you'll find a woman you want to give your grandmother's ring to someday."

He managed to smile at that, though he was starting to suspect that the greatest regret of his life was giving up Hope—uppercase *h*.

Chapter Fifteen

Michael stood up abruptly. "I think I'm going to turn in."

"Already?" Hope glanced at her watch. "It's not even ten o'clock."

"Morning comes early on the ranch."

"After sleeping here for ten days, that's not exactly a revelation," she told him. "Nor is your alarm going off at five a.m. every morning."

"Should I apologize for disturbing your slumber?"

"Of course not," she said. "But I'm thinking I should apologize to you."

"For what?"

"I don't know," she admitted. "But obviously I said or did something to cause you to want to retreat to your bedroom before the seventh-inning stretch in the ball game."

"You didn't," he promised. "It's just been a long day and I'm tired."

"Are you sure that's all it is? Because it seems to me

that every time we have a meaningful conversation, every time we start to get close, you immediately back away."

His jaw tightened. "We're not going to do this, Hope."

"What are we not going to do—acknowledge that the chemistry is still there?" she challenged.

"Is it chemistry or curiosity?" he countered.

"You're going to have to explain that," she told him.

"It's been a long time. And our first time together was the first time for both of us. And while it's natural to wonder if and how it might be different now, I don't think it would be smart to indulge that curiosity."

"You don't want me," she said, surprised how much the realization hurt.

She didn't think she was so irresistible that any man would want to be with her, but Michael wasn't any man—he was the man she'd never forgotten. Their relationship was the yardstick against which she'd measured all other relationships—and the reason she'd never been able to make a commitment to anyone else.

But apparently he didn't feel the same way.

"I'm sorry, Hope."

She shook her head. "Don't apologize. It's my fault for being foolish enough to believe that what we once meant to one another might still mean something."

"Eighteen years is a long time," he said gently.

Now she nodded.

"The best thing for both of us is to move on."

"Yes." She swiped impatiently at the tear that spilled onto her cheek. "You've made that perfectly clear."

"And there's no point in starting something when we both know that you'll be returning to LA soon. You might have reasons for hiding out here now, but you're not going to stay forever. Your agent will call about a movie or another TV show, and you'll be on your way back to California."

"What makes you so sure?" she challenged.

"Because you're too talented to walk away from your career."

"It takes more than talent to be an actor—you have to want it enough to make the sacrifices. And I'm not sure that I want it anymore."

But the prospect of walking away from her acting career—not taking a hiatus, but changing her life—filled her with equal parts excitement and trepidation. Excitement at the prospect of being able to do anything that she wanted to do; trepidation at the realization that she didn't know how to do anything else.

She'd spent the past eighteen years playing different roles, pretending to be other people. In the process, she'd somehow lost herself. Forgotten who she was and what she wanted.

Not that she was complaining. How could she regret having had the opportunity to live a life most people could only dream about?

But somehow the pursuit of her career had taken over all else. Her career had become not just the focus of her life but the entirety of it.

Without her career, what was left?

If she wasn't Lainey Howard, who was she?

It was a question she continued to ponder long after Michael had turned in for the night.

"If British Columbia is 'Hollywood North' maybe Nevada can be known as 'Hollywood in the Desert,'" MG commented when he responded to the knock on his door Tuesday morning and found Colin McCarragher—

Hope's on-screen husband—standing on his porch. "The town seems to be a popular celebrity destination these days."

"I'll take that as confirmation she's here," the actor said.

"Who?" MG said, belatedly attempting to run interference for his temporary houseguest.

"Hope," Colin said. "I need to see her."

"If she is here, it might be because she didn't want anyone to track her down."

"I'm not anyone. And I drove through the night to get here. Well, I actually knocked on Edwina's door first— she sent me here."

Before he could respond to that, Hope appeared behind him.

"Colin?" His name was almost a sob as she pushed past MG to launch herself into the other man's arms.

Colin held her as she cried, making MG feel like a third wheel in his own home.

"Maybe you should come in," he said dryly, stepping away from the door.

Colin crossed the threshold, Hope still in his arms.

"It's okay, Pip." He murmured to her quietly as he stroked a hand down her back, not like a lover but like a mother soothing a distraught child.

And she was obviously distraught, MG noted. But were her tears about losing her job or something else? And what was the relationship between Hope and her former costar?

He was relieved to note that there didn't seem to be any kind of sexual tension between them. Because even though he knew he shouldn't care, he did. Because as much as he wished he could deny it, Hope was right about the chemistry between them.

Not that he had any intention of acting on it. Because MG prided himself on learning from his mistakes—and opening up his heart to the woman who had trampled on it once before would be a huge mistake.

Still, the last thing he wanted to do was to leave Hope alone in his cabin with another man. Unfortunately, there were chores to be done and his brother and cousins were expecting him to show up to help do them.

So he put on his hat and boots and slipped out of the cabin without either Hope or her visitor realizing that he'd gone.

"Good thing I've got a change of clothes in the car, because you've almost soaked through my shirt with your tears," Colin said, settling onto the sofa with Hope in his lap.

She drew back, still sniffling, to survey the damp garment. "Apparently I'm hazardous to wardrobes these days."

"Sounds like there's a story there," Colin remarked, offering her the box of tissues from the end table. "But what I really want to know is why you didn't call to tell me what was going on."

"I did call." She plucked a handful of tissues to mop her face and blow her nose. "Several times. But all my calls immediately went to voice mail."

"Which is when most people leave a message."

"I didn't know what to say," she admitted. "And I was afraid that if I fell apart on your voice mail, you'd cut your vacation short and come home to try to put the pieces together."

"Instead, I had to wait until I was back in LA to hear that you'd been fired and left town—and that the vultures outed your location."

"My mother outed my location," she muttered.

"Didn't I just say that?"

"Ouch," she said, even as a smile tugged at the corners of her mouth.

"I know Debra's your mother," Colin noted. "But no one has picked more meat from the bones of your career than she has done."

And no one had ever defended her more fiercely than Colin had always done.

"Tell me what happened, Pip."

Her heart squeezed at his use of the familiar nickname—short for Pipsqueak—the moniker he'd bestowed upon her when they first met, because the top of her head barely grazed his chin. After eight years, the name was as familiar to her as her own, and the thought of not hearing it every day—because she would no longer be working with Colin every day—made her want to cry again.

"What did you hear?"

"That you asked for a meeting with the producers, because you had some concerns that the show was going in a direction you didn't like and, when they wouldn't back down, you decided it was time for you to move on."

"Well, the first part is true," she told him. "But it wasn't so much the story line as the casting that I had a problem with."

"Donovan Kessel?" He seemed surprised, and then the pieces clicked together. *"Sonofabitch."*

Hope swiped at the fresh tears that spilled onto her cheeks.

"Oh, Pip." He hugged her closer. "Why didn't you tell me?"

"Because I knew that you were—if not friends at least friendly—and I didn't want you to feel as if you had to take sides."

"We worked on a couple of made-for-TV movies together, before he hit big with the *Shadow* series," Colin said. "And I had no complaints about him as an actor, but as a human being, I saw enough to know that I wouldn't let him date my sister. Or my best friend."

"Too bad I didn't know you way back when."

When she'd been new to Hollywood—not just young but incredibly naive and starstruck in the presence of the rising star.

"Did you tell Larry? Or Tony or Greg or Fallon?" Colin asked gently, naming each of the show's producers.

She shook her head. "Not the details. And they didn't ask."

"Because they want Donovan Kessel on board to jack up the ratings, and it's all about ratings."

She nodded.

"Apparently they haven't paid any attention to the reckoning that's been happening in Hollywood," he remarked dryly.

"Anyway, I'm out and he's in."

"It doesn't have to be that way," Colin told her.

Tell your story. The whole story, her agent had urged.

"Now you sound like Jenny."

"She's a wise woman."

But Hope shook her head again. "I've already torpedoed my career—there's no point in blowing up my reputation, too."

"I'm not here to browbeat you into changing your

mind—or to drag you back to LA, though that's what Nisha suggested I should do."

"Why are you here instead of home with Nisha, anyway?"

"Because I needed to see you, to know that you're okay—and to let you know that I've got your back. Always. Whatever you decide to do."

"You're going to make me cry again."

"Please don't," he said. "This is my favorite Prada shirt."

"I know. You have about a dozen of them in different colors." She grabbed a fresh tissue and dabbed at her eyes again. "By the way, congrats on your engagement."

"Can you believe she finally said *yes*?"

"I can," Hope confirmed. "Because I know Nisha loves you as much as you love her."

"Then why did she say *no* the first two times I asked?"

"I think she just wanted to be sure that you were going to stick."

"That's what she said," he admitted.

"And now she's probably eager for you to get back so you can start planning your wedding. Not to mention that shooting is scheduled to start this week," she suddenly realized.

He shrugged, clearly unconcerned. "The way I see it, Thorne's going to need some time to mourn the death of his wife."

"I figured they'd kill me off," Hope admitted. "Which is marginally better than being locked in an asylum."

"Apparently Lainey tumbled off a cliff."

"So not just dead, but a painful and gruesome death."

"I wouldn't be so sure," he told her. "Recovery crews were unable to find her body, so obviously our writers—

regardless of what they might have been told—aren't willing to close the door on the possibility of your return.

"But enough about what's happening in *Rockwood Ridge*," he decided. "Tell me what's happening at the Circle G—which, by the way, is a really impressive piece of property."

"One of the biggest cattle ranches in the state," she told him.

"I can believe it," he said. "And if you have to hide out, there are much worse places to do it."

"Still, I'm not particularly proud of the fact that I'm hiding."

"So forget about your reasons for being here for a minute and tell me about the cowboy," he suggested.

"Michael?"

"Is that his name? We weren't officially introduced."

"That's Michael," she confirmed.

"Wait a minute… Michael was the name of the guy you fell in love with when you were thirteen," he suddenly remembered.

She felt her cheeks color. "That was a very long time ago."

Colin grinned. "It's him, isn't it? Your cowboy bodyguard is your childhood sweetheart, your first lover, the only man you've ever loved?"

She sighed. "I really don't have any secrets from you, do I?"

"We've spent a lot of time together over the past eight years—we had to talk about something."

"But your life is so much more interesting than mine."

"Obviously not," he told her. "Now tell me—is your bed the one his boots have been under?"

She rolled her eyes at his mangled interpretation of the Shania Twain song lyrics. "No."

"And why not?"

"I wish I could say it's because my life is a mess right now and I'm not in a place to get involved with anyone, but the truth is, Michael doesn't want me. He doesn't even seem to like me very much these days."

"Whatever gave you that idea?" he asked curiously.

"He's made his feelings perfectly clear."

"Honey, if that's what he told you, the man was lying. Because I saw the way he looked at you, and it was *not* with dislike or disinterest."

"Why would he lie?"

"Why do any of us lie? To protect ourselves."

"Even if that's true—so is the rest of what I said. My life is a mess."

"So straighten it out."

"I'm working on it."

"And if you don't want to tell your story to the whole world, at least tell your cowboy."

When MG returned to his cabin several hours later, Hope's visitor had gone and she was standing at the stove, stirring soup in a pot.

"I was beginning to think you might not make it back for lunch today," she said, when he walked through the door.

"I wasn't sure I would, either," he told her.

"Did you run into some kind of problem with the cows?" She dropped a cheese sandwich—waiting to be grilled—into the hot pan on the stove.

"No." He lathered up his hands at the sink, then rinsed

and dried them. "I just didn't want to interrupt your visit with your...friend."

"Colin is a friend," she confirmed. "One of the best I've got."

"And yet it seems you didn't let him know that you were coming to Haven for a vacation."

She managed a smile. "Are we still pretending I was on vacation and not running away?"

He shrugged. "One doesn't necessarily preclude the other."

"Either way, I ordinarily would have told Colin about my plans, but he was out of the country at the time and out of cell phone range." She flipped the sandwich. "Completely incommunicado."

The suggestion being that if the other man had been reachable, she would have reached out to him. And maybe then she wouldn't have felt the need to hide out in Haven. And though MG still wasn't sure exactly what she was hiding from, he had no doubt that there was something. Hope wasn't the type of woman to shy away from a few unflattering headlines.

She ladled the soup into bowls while the sandwich browned in the pan. He didn't bother to ask why there were two bowls but only one sandwich—they'd shared enough meals over the past week for him to know that she avoided carbs like the plague. Making him realize that her impulsive act of ordering garlic bread at Diggers' that night had been, if not really the act of a wild woman, at least wildly out of character for her.

He carried the bowls to the table while she turned the sandwich out onto a plate and cut it in half. It was a simple meal—comfort food, his mother would call it—but he heartily enjoyed it. Of course, he'd found that he enjoyed any meal he shared with Hope and every minute he spent with her.

Were those minutes coming to an end now that Colin had been here to see her? Would she go back to LA soon?

The thought made the sandwich settle like a lead weight in his stomach.

Hope swirled her spoon in her soup. "Do you have any plans this afternoon?"

"Nothing specific," he said. "Why?"

"I was hoping maybe we could go for a ride."

He was surprised by the suggestion. Though she'd been encouraged to ride any time she wanted, as far as he knew, she had yet to do so. He was also pleased by the invitation to accompany her—and perhaps just a little bit worried that his leg would choose today, when he was with Hope, to stiffen up. But it felt pretty good right now, and the opportunity to spend some time with Hope was one he could not resist.

So they tidied up the kitchen together, then went out to the barn to saddle up a couple of horses. MG chose Travis, a bay gelding with black mane and tail, for himself and Dolly, a palomino mare, for Hope.

Hope might have been a little tentative at first, but Dolly wasn't. The mare knew the drill, and eagerly trotted after the gelding when he turned toward the mountains.

They followed the path of Crooked Creek—which was also the dividing line between the Circle G and the Blakes' namesake property. In the spring, the creek would flow easily, abundant with snowmelt. Now, in mid-October, the water was little more than a trickle through a dry channel.

They'd been riding for about half an hour when they

reached a stand of trees. Aware that Hope hadn't been on the back of a horse in a lot of years, MG drew Travis to a halt and dismounted, then waited for Hope to do the same.

She didn't move. "I think I'm stuck."

"You're not stuck."

"Okay, but I don't remember how to get down."

So he talked her through the steps, grinding his teeth as she swung her right leg over the horse's flank—putting the sweet curve of her butt right at his eye level.

"Are you there?" she asked, because now she was facing away from him and couldn't be sure.

"I'm here." He put his hands on her hips, to reassure her of his presence, and she finally removed her left foot from the stirrup and hopped to the ground.

She turned around then, and found herself in the narrow space between the horse at her back and MG at her front.

He immediately took a step back, cleared his throat. "Okay now?"

"Okay except that I can't feel my butt."

"You'll feel it tomorrow," he promised, untying the blanket that he'd secured to the back of his saddle.

"No doubt," she agreed.

He shook out the blanket and spread it out on the ground, beneath the trees, then gestured an invitation.

She stretched out, leaning back on her elbows and crossing her feet in front of her. He joined her, keeping as much space between them as possible, and uncapped his canteen, offering the water to her first.

"Thanks." She swallowed a mouthful, passed it back to him.

They sat in silence for several minutes before she

spoke again. "I've forgotten how beautiful it is out here. How peaceful."

"Most beautiful place in the world," he agreed.

After another minute, she shifted onto her side, so that she was facing him. "Aren't you going to ask me about Colin's visit? Or my meltdown?"

He shrugged. "I figured if there was something you wanted me to know, you'd tell me."

"I want you to know," she told him. "I owe you an explanation for why I'm hiding out on your ranch."

"I'm willing to listen to whatever you want to say, but you don't owe me anything, Hope."

Her gaze met his, and what he saw in her eyes tangled him up inside. "Maybe I owe it to myself."

Chapter Sixteen

After everything they'd shared over the years, it was hardly a surprise that Hope was willing to trust Michael with her truth. She knew it wasn't going to be easy to tell him, but she needed him to know that she wasn't the same girl she'd been when she left Haven eighteen years earlier—and why.

"Obviously you know that I was fired from *Rockwood Ridge*?"

He nodded. "The headlines were kind of hard to miss."

"Unless you were in Tanzania's Ngorongoro Conservation Area, which is where Colin and Nisha—his fiancée—were when the news broke. They flew back to the US yesterday."

"And he abandoned her as soon as they arrived to hop in his SUV and chase after a former lover?"

"You shouldn't believe everything you read," she chided. "Colin and I were never romantically involved.

And apparently it was Nisha's idea that he come to Haven. She would have come, too, but she had back-to-back meetings scheduled today that she couldn't miss.

"Anyway, back to me getting fired—I know it's just a TV show and losing my job probably doesn't seem like a big deal to you, but it was my dream job. The entire cast and crew were a joy to work with, every day. And, after eight years together, they were more than friends and colleagues—they were like a second family to me. Nisha, through her connection to Colin, was part of that family, too.

"Of course, there are always cast changes in any show," she continued. "New characters are introduced and others depart. But at the heart of *Rockwood Ridge* is the Chesterfield family. When Thorne Chesterfield fell in love with Lainey Howard, it cemented her position on the show. Their relationship had ups and downs, but Thorne and Lainey were as iconic a television couple as Derek and Meredith or Randall and Beth."

"Who?"

She had to smile. "You don't watch a lot of TV, do you?"

"Do you want me to recite the Angels' starting lineup?"

"Okay, so you watch a lot of baseball," she allowed. "I would come home from set and watch episodes of *Grey's Anatomy* and *This Is Us* that I'd saved on my DVR. But my point is, I thought I would get to play Lainey Howard for as long as *Rockwood Ridge* was on the air. And considering the show has a strong foothold in all the key demographics, that should be a very long time.

"But while *Rockwood Ridge* continues to be a solid performer, all network shows are losing viewers to streaming services. In an effort to lure back those viewers, the producers decided to court some big names for guest spots or recurring roles.

"One of those big names was Donovan Kessel. When I first heard whispers about the possibility of him being signed on, I went to the producers and asked them to reconsider. I confided that there had been some…friction…between us in the past and I wasn't really comfortable with the idea of working with him."

A muscle jumped in Michael's jaw and it seemed that he had to consciously unclench it before he could ask, "What kind of friction?"

"I'm getting to that," she promised. "But in the meeting, they reminded me that Donovan Kessel was a much bigger draw than Hope Bradford and that if I forced them to choose between us, I wasn't going to like their choice.

"I thanked them for their time and walked out. I mean, I was a professional. I'd shared the screen with plenty of other actors I didn't necessarily like, and I was sure I could tolerate working with Donovan Kessel if our paths had to cross. Until I had lunch with a couple of friends one day, including Sidney Westcott. Sidney's a writer on the show, and she mentioned that one of the story lines being considered for the upcoming season was another extramarital affair for Lainey—this time with the new character portrayed by Donovan Kessel."

Sidney had violated her sworn silence to keep the upcoming story lines under wraps, because she was excited and convinced it would be a great plot twist for Lainey. Hope had managed to smile and nod, then excused herself from the table and gone to the bathroom to throw up. Because while she could have handled exchanging a few lines with the actor, there was no way she wanted to be close enough for him to touch her and kiss her, as such a story line would obviously necessitate.

"And I couldn't do it. I wouldn't do it. Because—" she blew out a breath and hugged her knees to her chest "—when I was eighteen years old, Donovan Kessel sexually assaulted me."

She gave Michael a minute to consider the revelation. Then another minute.

"I want to say something," he finally responded. "Something supportive and reassuring—but I'm having trouble finding the right words because my brain is focused on all the possible ways that I could kill him."

"I wouldn't ever want you to go to jail on my account," she assured him.

"*He* should be in jail," Michael said. "Jesus, Hope. You were eighteen?"

She nodded.

"Barely more than a child."

She managed a smile. "We both know *that's* not true."

He didn't smile back.

"So why isn't he in jail? Was he even arrested?"

She shook her head slowly.

"Why the hell not?" he demanded in a shocked tone.

"Because… I never reported the assault," she admitted.

"I don't understand."

Sometimes, she didn't either. And her weakness—her cowardice—continued to be a source of shame to her.

"It was a long time before the #MeToo movement and… I felt responsible for leading him on. Because he was Donovan Kessel and I was thrilled when he invited me to have lunch with him.

"While we were eating, he mentioned that he was

considering a script for his new production company and that there was a part he thought could be perfect for me. When he asked if I wanted to see the script, of course I said *yes*. So we went to his office, and when we got there…he kissed me. And it was a little exciting at first, being kissed by Donovan Kessel, but when he started to slide his hands under my skirt, I told him *no*.

"But I guess he wasn't used to hearing that word from a woman, because instead of backing off, he pushed me onto the sofa and ripped open my top. I was shocked—and starting to panic. I pleaded with him to stop, and he…he told me that I wasn't a good enough actor to convince him I didn't want it, because he knew that I did.

"And then the door opened and his assistant walked in." It was an effort to keep her tone level, dispassionate, as she recounted the events of that nightmarish day. "He hadn't turned the lights on, so she probably thought the office was empty, and she gasped when she saw us on the sofa. He yelled at her to '*get the hell out*' and she backed away quickly, apologizing profusely for interrupting. But that brief moment when he was snarling at her was enough for me to wiggle out from under him and rush past her and out the door."

She chanced a glance at Michael and saw his eyes burning with a fury unlike anything she'd ever seen before. In that moment, he looked capable of murder—but Hope wasn't afraid. Because she knew his anger wasn't directed at her. Because despite their history—or maybe because of it—she knew that he would never hurt her. And maybe it lifted her heart a little to know that he still cared enough about her to want to take apart anyone who did hurt her.

"It could have been so much worse," she acknowledged. "Believe me, I'm aware of how much worse it could have been. But it was bad enough."

"Did you tell anyone what happened?" he asked her now.

"Not right away. I eventually told Jenny—my agent. But that was a few years later, when she wanted me to read for a part in another Donovan Kessel movie."

"She didn't tell anyone?"

"I asked her not to. I mean, nothing really happened." She shook her head. "Of course, that's not true. He sexually assaulted me, betrayed my trust and destroyed my confidence. But I didn't want my career to be over before it had really started."

"His career is the one that should have ended."

"But that's not how things work in Hollywood—or at least it's not how they worked seventeen years ago."

MG started to reach for her, then dropped his hands to his sides. "I want to hold you," he confided. "But after hearing what you went through, being subjected to another man's unwanted touch—"

"I'd really like it if you held me."

The words were barely out of her mouth before he was hauling her close. She leaned into him, breathing in his familiar masculine scent and relishing the strength of his arms around her, and felt more at peace than she'd felt in a very long time.

"I think, if he'd been the first man to touch me, it might have taken me a lot longer to get over what happened." The confession was whispered against his shoulder. "But thanks to you, I knew how it felt to be with someone I loved—and who loved me."

His hold tightened. "If I can't kill him, can I at least beat him to a bloody pulp?"

"No." She tipped her head back to kiss his cheek. "But I appreciate the sentiment. Sincerely."

"I'm so sorry you had to go through any of that. And on your own."

"It was almost enough to make me come home. But I knew that if I ran away, I'd be letting him win." She exhaled a weary sigh. "But that's exactly what I've done now, isn't it?"

"Maybe you didn't run away so much as made a strategic retreat to figure out your battle plan."

"I think you're giving me more credit than I deserve."

"There's nothing wrong with taking some time to think about what you want—and if it's worth fighting for. And you're welcome to stay at the Circle G as long as it takes."

"You might regret making that offer," she warned.

"No." He shook his head. "I don't think I will."

"We'll see," she mused. "But right now, we should head back and figure out dinner."

She felt better after she told Michael. Unburdened, somehow. Which was odd, Hope thought, because absolutely nothing else in her life had changed. But by telling him what happened to her, the usual heaviness in her heart felt a little bit lighter. Almost as if taking control of the narrative to set the story straight took back some of the power that had been taken from her so many years before.

Over the next few days, as she enjoyed the new routines that she'd established since coming to the Circle G, she found more of the heaviness lifting away. Maybe it was the quiet solitude of the ranch, maybe it was Michael, but whatever the reason, it was a good feeling.

Part of her new routine was cooking dinner. Though Michael insisted that he didn't expect a meal on the table when he came in at the end of the day, she knew he appreciated finding one ready. Saturday morning, he'd left early to make a trip to Reno with his dad. Apparently one of the automated gates wasn't working and they could either order the necessary replacement part from the manufacturer, to be delivered in one to two weeks, or pick one up directly from a supplier. It was an easy decision.

The round trip would take more than six hours—plus whatever time they spent in Reno—so Hope knew that he'd be gone most of the day but she expected he'd return in time for dinner. She'd recently dug up a favorite recipe for sesame chicken that she wanted to make except that several key ingredients were absent from Michael's kitchen. Which left her with one of two options—find a different recipe or venture into town to get what she needed from The Trading Post.

She opted for the latter—along with the dark wig again. And a jacket, because the fall weather was already cooler than Hope was accustomed to.

Thankfully she had her car, as Edwina and Dennis had driven it out to the Circle G the previous afternoon. And while she felt pretty confident that the local reporters and gossip bloggers had moved on to other stories, she knew that it might only take one random #celebritysighting by a fan with a cell phone and a social media account to have them descending on Haven again.

On her way to the grocery store, she passed Anthology Books and impulsively pulled into a vacant parking spot nearby. She'd been doing some reading at the ranch, slowly making her way through the popular fiction on

Michael's bookshelves. He seemed to be a fan of Quinn Ellison, and soon Hope was hooked on her books, too.

She pushed open the door and immediately turned to the New and Hot section. There it was—at eye level with stickers indicating it was a Staff Pick and Local Author.

"Hope?"

She let her hand fall back to her side and turned to face Michael's sister.

"It *is* you," Olivia said. "I wasn't sure, because you look totally different with the wig."

"Obviously not," Hope said dryly.

Olivia laughed. "No, you do," she assured her. "The only reason I did a double take is that I fell in love with the shirt you're wearing when I saw it in one of the designer shops in Vegas last year and I couldn't imagine anyone else in town who would drop that kind of money on a top."

"Betrayed by my weakness for pretty clothes," Hope said with a sigh.

"Anyway, I'm glad I ran into you," Olivia said. "I was planning to come out to the ranch later today to see you, but this saves me a trip."

"Why did you want to see me?" she asked curiously.

"Because... I wanted to talk to you about something."

Hope couldn't help feeling wary after their last encounter in town. "What?"

But Olivia's attention had shifted to another customer browsing on the other side of the store.

"Can you excuse me for just a minute?" she said to Hope.

"Sure."

Hope picked up the book she'd come into the store for and turned it over to read the back cover copy and pretend she wasn't watching as Olivia greeted—and hugged—the other woman. She recognized her as Paige Gallagher, Michael's ex, from The Night at Diggers'—as it would forever be denoted in her mind.

The two women chatted for a few minutes, then they hugged again and Paige returned to browsing while Olivia made her way back to Hope.

"You plan on doing a lot of reading?"

Olivia glanced at the stack of books in the crook of her arm—the Quinn Ellison title and three more she had no recollection of picking up. "I like to read, and I don't currently have any scripts requiring my attention."

"Does that mean you have time for lunch?"

She glanced at her watch, though she had absolutely nothing on her agenda for the rest of the day, and nodded. "Um, sure."

Olivia paid for her purchases, then Hope did the same and they walked over to Diggers' together.

"I owe you an apology," Olivia said, picking up the thread of their earlier conversation after their food had been delivered, "for telling you to stay away from MG."

Hope shook her head as she poked at the lettuce in her Caesar salad. "You don't need to apologize for looking out for your brother."

"That's what I told myself I was doing," the other woman confided. "But if I'd really been looking out for him, I would never have encouraged him to take the next step in his relationship with Paige when I knew he was still in love with you."

"I can't claim to know why the proposal never happened," Hope said. "But I can assure you that it wasn't because your brother has any residual feelings for me, because he's made it perfectly clear that he doesn't."

"And you believe him?"

"He was quite convincing."

"He hurt you," Olivia realized.

Hope shrugged. "It was my own fault for having expectations."

"Because you still love him, too."

"We were kids when we fell in love," Hope reminded Michael's sister. "Then we grew up and grew apart."

"You didn't grow apart—*you* moved away."

Hope could hardly deny it. "The point is, we both moved on. Even if the engagement didn't happen, he was planning to ask Paige to marry him."

"Yeah," Olivia noted. "But I'm pretty sure that was only because he felt he owed her for saving his life."

It was almost seven o'clock when MG finally got back from Reno Saturday night. It had been a long day and his leg would have been screaming in pain if he'd had to be in the driver's seat the entire round trip, so he was happy he'd had his dad for company. He was even happier to be home now, and he realized—when he opened the front door and found Hope reading a book in the living room—that she was the reason why.

He was starting to get used to her being there, and he knew that was a dangerous thing. The initial awkwardness of the first few days was long past, and now they found themselves talking for hours, like they used to. She seemed genuinely interested in what he had to say, and though she was open-minded when it came to listening to other ideas, she didn't hesitate to voice her own opinion when it conflicted with his.

He'd always known she was beautiful, and now that she was a Hollywood star, the rest of the world knew it, too. Watching her on the screen, seeing her take on the role of various characters, he'd discovered that she was also incredibly talented. But listening to her speak the words others had written for her, he'd somehow forgotten how smart she was. Not only smart but curious to learn and eager to grow.

He'd also forgotten how quickly and completely he'd fallen for her—though since she'd moved into the bunkhouse, he'd been careful to remind himself every day. Because falling for Hope Bradford might have been inevitable when they were both young and foolish enough to imagine forever, but they knew better now.

Most important, he knew that Hope would soon grow bored with the slow pace of life in Haven and return to Los Angeles.

But even accepting that her departure was inevitable, he knew that he'd miss her like crazy when she was gone.

And he wasn't the only one. His dog had fallen head over heels for their temporary houseguest and followed Hope from room to room around the cabin, as if he couldn't bear to let her out of his sight. So MG wasn't surprised to discover that Bernie was on the sofa, too, snuggled against her.

She glanced up when she heard the door open and offered him the familiar easy smile that never failed to take his breath away.

"You're back."

"I'm back," he confirmed. "And that's the new Quinn Ellison book in your hands."

"It is." She marked her page before setting the book aside.

"Does that mean you went into town today?"

She nodded. "I wanted to make sesame chicken for

dinner and you didn't have sesame oil. Or rice vinegar. Or fresh ginger. Or chicken."

"And then I texted to tell you that I wouldn't be home for dinner," he said, feeling an unexpected twinge of guilt.

"That's okay," she said. "I'll make the chicken tomorrow."

He'd reminded her, more than once, that he didn't expect her to cook for him. And each time, she assured him that she liked to cook—especially when she had someone to share a meal with.

"What did you have for dinner?" he asked her now.

"I didn't," she admitted. "But I had a big lunch. With Olivia, in fact."

"You had lunch with my sister?"

She nodded. "We crossed paths at the bookstore."

"The boys must be at their mom's this weekend," he remarked. "Olivia doesn't have time to catch her breath, never mind go out for lunch, when she's chasing after them."

"She mentioned that," Hope confided. "But in a way that made me think she loves every minute of it."

"She does," he agreed.

"She mentioned something else, too."

"And you said that in a way that makes me think you weren't happy to learn about this something else," he noted.

"You're right. I'm even more annoyed that you didn't tell me."

"Okay," he said cautiously. "But will you at least tell me why you're mad before you start yelling?"

"I'm not going to yell," she assured him.

And she didn't.

Instead, she just looked at him for a long minute, and then her eyes filled with tears.

He would have preferred the yelling.

"Hey." He knelt by the sofa and tipped her chin up, forcing her to look at him. "What did she say to you to bring this on?"

"She told me that you…you…*almost died*."

Bernie, picking up on her distress, lifted his head from her lap to rub it against her arm.

"Old news," he said lightly. "And I *did* tell you about the accident."

"You didn't tell me that you *almost died*."

"In my defense, it's not really something I like to dwell on. And—" he gestured to himself "—as you can see, I'm fine."

"You're not fine," she denied. "You've got a rod and six screws in your leg—and you probably shouldn't be kneeling like that."

"Compound fracture," he said with a shrug, though he did get off his knees to perch on the coffee table.

He might have chosen to sit beside her, but Bernie gave no indication of relinquishing that spot any time soon.

"I've seen you wince," she confided. "Even if you're not aware of it, I know you still experience some pain."

"And I limp sometimes, when the leg is bothering me," he admitted. "But all things considered, I really am fine."

"Olivia also told me that Paige saved your life."

"That's what the doctors said," he confirmed.

"That you might have bled out—or frozen to death—if she hadn't found you."

"Obviously my sister talks too much."

"She didn't want to tell me. When she realized I didn't know any of the details, she tried to change the subject, but I wouldn't let her."

"Because you wanted all the evidence she could give you to justify being mad at me?" He was teasing, of course, trying to make her smile.

And it almost worked.

Her lips started to curve, then they trembled, and her eyes filled again.

"I wasn't really mad," she told him now. "I was scared."

"Scared?" he echoed, surprised by this revelation.

"Scared to realize that I could have lost you forever... and I didn't even know it."

He rose to his feet then and drew her into his arms— and immediately remembered why he'd been keeping a careful distance from her over the past couple of weeks. Because when he was close to her, he wanted to be closer still. When he was touching her, he wanted to touch her all over. And now that he was holding her, he didn't ever want to let her go.

She buried her face against his chest, sniffling a little.

Then her arms snaked around his middle and she squeezed him tight. And he was suddenly and achingly aware of the fact that her body was plastered against his.

After a long minute, she tipped her head back to look at him. Her lashes were wet and spiky from her tears, her eyes as clear and blue as the sky on a perfect summer day.

Awareness crackled between them.

Now would be a good time to step back. To put some distance between them.

But his arms remained around her, his feet glued to the ground.

It was Hope who finally made a move—lifting herself onto her toes to touch her mouth to his.

Chapter Seventeen

She shouldn't have kissed him.

She was an uninvited guest in his home and while Michael had made it clear that he was prepared to tolerate her presence, he'd also told her that he didn't want her in his personal space. But she'd ignored all of that and deliberately breached the boundaries he'd established.

And while it was true that he'd kissed her back—expertly and very thoroughly—Hope had been the one to initiate contact. But she'd also been the one to draw back, even when all the hormones in her body were clamoring for her to move in the opposite direction.

She spent the better part of Sunday with her nose buried in Quinn Ellison's book, but not even the engaging characters or fast-moving plot of the story could banish the memory of that kiss. She made sesame chicken for dinner that night, and the whole time she was chopping and sautéing, the memory of that kiss teased her mind.

Monday morning, Hope woke up with her lips tingling and knew that she'd dreamed about the kiss—and more. It was lucky that she had a plan for the day—and after lunch, she headed into town to meet Tyler Hutchinson at Westmount High School.

Ty happily gave up his prep period for Hope—and he seemed thrilled by the possibility that she might be willing to help with the after-hours drama club. Which happened to be meeting after school that day if Hope wanted to hang around and say hi to the students.

Since there was nothing else on her calendar, Hope agreed. She returned to the auditorium at 2:40, when the final bell sounded, and was chatting with Mr. Hutchinson when the members of the drama club started to filter in. There were some excited whispers as a few of the students spotted and recognized that there was a "celebrity" in their midst, but Mr. Hutchinson quickly got them quieted down.

"Some of you might know Ms. Bradford from her role as Lainey Howard on *Rockwood Ridge*," Mr. Hutchinson said by way of introduction when the teens were all seated on the stage.

There was a smattering of applause over which one of the students said, "You mean *formerly* of *Rockwood Ridge*."

"What you may not know," the drama teacher continued, pointedly ignoring Missy Sutherland's remark, "is that Ms. Bradford grew up in Haven. She went to school at Westmount and was a member of the drama club—and a star of many of its productions. In fact, it was while she was playing Juliet on this very stage that she was discovered by a Hollywood director."

That revelation was followed by another round of applause.

"And we are very fortunate that Ms. Bradford has expressed an interest in helping out with the drama club while she's in town. Now, we've got less than eight weeks until opening night, so we're going to want to get down to business as soon as possible. Those who want to audition for parts in the play can pick up a copy of the script on their way out. The sign-up sheet will be posted at eight o'clock tonight—please pick a slot that works with your schedule, indicate the part you want to read for and show up when you say you're going to show up. Those who are here to sign up for set design or the lighting crew or any of the other essential backstage roles, thank you. Sincerely. We couldn't put a show on without you.

"Auditions will take place Wednesday and Thursday. Callbacks, if necessary, on Friday and the cast list will be posted by eight o'clock Sunday night. Drama club will not meet next Monday. Rehearsals will commence with a read-through of the script on Thursday. Any questions?"

Several hands shot up.

"Theo," he said, calling on a tall boy sitting at the back.

"What play are we doing this year?"

"A good question," Mr. Hutchinson noted. "And the answer is *A Christmas Carol*—a holiday classic."

"In which all the major parts are male parts," Missy grumbled.

"In Shakespeare's day, all the actors were male," Ashley pointed out.

"*A Christmas Carol* wasn't written by Shakespeare," Missy said.

Ashley rolled her eyes. "I know that. I was just making the point that a good actor can play any role, regardless of gender."

"And it's a good point," Mr. Hutchinson agreed. "But whether a character is understood to be traditionally male or female and however a student might identify, they can audition for any part."

"Good," Tori said. "Because I want to be Scrooge."

"Good luck with that," Missy told her friend. "Because if Sofia wants it, Sofia will get it."

Several students turned to look at a slender dark-haired girl with big eyes sitting beside Theo—the aforementioned Sofia, Hope presumed.

"Any other questions?" Mr. Hutchinson asked.

There were a few exchanged glances, some head-shakes, then Missy's hand shot into the air.

"Yes, Missy?"

"Can I ask Ms. Bradford a question?"

The teacher deferred to Hope.

"Of course," she agreed readily.

"Is it true that you didn't want to work with Donovan Kessel because you slept with—"

"Missy!" The sharp tone of Mr. Hutchinson's interjection clearly expressed his disapproval of the girl's question.

"—him and then he dumped you?" Missy forged ahead, ignoring her teacher's admonition.

"It's okay, Mr. Hutchinson, I'll field this one." Hope stared Missy down, then smiled at the rest of the group. "I'm happy to answer questions about my experiences working in Hollywood, but I'm not going to answer questions about my personal life—especially when they are based on nothing more than tabloid headlines or rumors."

"Perhaps it would be best if we adjourned early today," Mr. Hutchinson suggested.

There were groans and protests that would never follow a teacher's suggestion of ending a class early.

"I just want to say that I think you're an incredibly talented actor and Lainey Howard was my favorite character on *Rockwood Ridge*," Tori said in a rush, obviously eager to say her piece before the opportunity was lost.

"And when Lainey gave Thorne back his ring, because she didn't want to cause strife in his family, I cried as hard as Lainey did," Whitney confided.

The boy sitting beside her scoffed at that, to which Whitney responded with an elbow to his ribs. (Hope noted that he seemed rather pleased with the attention.)

"And then Edward Chesterfield tried to pay you off to leave town, because he knew that so long as you were in Rockwood Ridge, his son would never be able to love anyone else."

"And you told him, very clearly and very coolly, that you weren't for sale."

"Apparently season five was a popular one," Hope mused.

"Season six was the best," Nicole declared. "When Lainey finally marries Thorne."

Missy seethed as her friends heaped praise on Hope.

"My dad has an old videotape filled with TV commercials that you did, before you made it big," a girl with spiraling red curls volunteered. "He said everyone knew you were going to be a star and maybe he'll sell the tape on eBay someday and get rich."

"That's…flattering," Hope decided.

"And maybe a little creepy," Mr. Hutchinson said under his breath, so that only Hope could hear.

She didn't disagree.

"My mom says she was your best friend in high school," a slender girl with blond hair and Laurel Walsh's dark eyes said.

"Then you must be Madison Gibson," Hope guessed.

Madison's eyes went wide and her peers looked at her with new respect.

"Does anyone have any *questions* about *acting* that Ms. Bradford might be able to answer?" Mr. Hutchinson asked, attempting to steer his students back on track.

And for the next half hour, Hope responded to their queries about a day in the life of an actor before Mr. Hutchinson finally shut down the Q&A and sent everyone home.

"This is an unexpected surprise," MG said, when Hope walked through the door with two pizza boxes in hand.

Bernie obviously thought so, too, because the dog roused from his slumber and padded across the floor to greet Hope, his nose twitching in the air.

She was smiling as she reached down to rub the top of the dog's head. "I stayed late to talk to some of the students, so I figured I'd pick up dinner rather than try to figure out what to cook when I got hom—back," she quickly corrected herself.

"You do know it's not your job to put dinner on the table, don't you?" he asked.

"I know, but I don't mind cooking and it seems the least I can do to compensate for the fact that I'm invading your space."

"You're not a horrible roommate," he said.

"Such flattery is going to turn my head," she cautioned.

"And I'm never going to complain about Jo's pizza," he told her.

"I didn't think you would."

"But you've got two boxes there," he noted. "So you must be really hungry."

"I thought *you* probably would be—and I knew you wouldn't want to share my pizza."

"What's on yours?"

"Grilled chicken, green peppers and red onions."

"That doesn't sound so bad."

"It's what's under the toppings that I suspect will make your nose wrinkle."

"What's under the toppings?"

"Cauliflower crust."

He definitely wrinkled his nose, making her laugh.

"I didn't even know there was such a thing on the menu."

"Apparently it was Lucy who added it—against her mother's wishes. But it was so popular that Jo had no choice but to keep it."

"Hmm," was all he said.

"Do you want to try it?"

"No." His response was immediate and definitive, making her laugh again.

"Bernie doesn't seem to be turning his nose up at it," she noted, as the dog hadn't left her side since she walked through the door.

"Bernie's a mooch—who has already had his dinner," MG said pointedly.

With an audible sigh, the dog lowered his head and slunk away from the table.

"So how did things go with the drama club?" MG asked, when they were eating their pizza.

"Pretty well, I think," Hope said. "Mr. Hutchinson is certainly willing to let me help out while I'm in Haven."

He reached into the box for another slice of pepperoni and sausage pizza. "Have you figured out yet how long that's going to be?"

"No, but I have been thinking that I should probably move back to my grandmother's," she said. "No one's talking about my 'sudden and abrupt departure' from *Rockwood Ridge* anymore and the last of the paparazzi have surely left town."

"I wouldn't count on it," he said.

"Why would you say that?"

"You haven't talked to your grandmother today?"

"No. Why? What happened?"

"Apparently she caught someone peeking through her living room window early this morning."

"Why didn't she call me? And how do you know?"

"She ran into my mom at The Trading Post."

"She must have been terrified."

"My mother's not *that* scary."

Hope rolled her eyes. "You know I wasn't referring to her encounter with your mother but finding someone peeking in her window."

"Apparently she screamed and Dennis chased off the Peeping Tom wearing nothing more than boxer shorts."

"Who was wearing boxer shorts—Dennis or the Peeping Tom?"

"Dennis. I think."

"I need to call her," Hope said, reaching for her phone.

"I hate to think that her privacy was violated because of me."

"Are you kidding? According to my mother, Edwina was retelling the story to anyone who would listen and basking in the attention."

But she was already connecting the call.

While she was on the phone, MG wrapped up the remaining pizza. He would likely finish his at lunch the next day. Hope, if she continued to eat one slice at each sitting, would be able to dine on her leftovers for the next week.

"You're right," she said, when she'd finished her call. "Grams is more excited about the attention than concerned about the Peeping Tom."

"But you're concerned?" he guessed.

"Of course, I am," she told him. "Though a lot less than I would be if I didn't know Dennis was there with her."

"Would you feel better if you went back to her house?"

"I'd feel like a third wheel if I went back to her house," she admitted. "Do you have any idea how embarrassing it is to realize that your grandmother has a more active sex life than you do?"

"I can't say that I've given my grandmother's sex life much thought—and I really wish you hadn't put the question in my head now," he confided.

"I'm sorry," she said, her cheeks flushing prettily. "For some reason, I seem to lose my conversational filter when I'm with you."

"It might be because there was a time when we could talk to one another about anything."

"It might be," she acknowledged. "Anyway, I think

it would be better if I stayed here...unless I'm interfering with your sex life."

"You're definitely interfering with my sex life."

And every other aspect of his life.

"I'm...sorry?"

"Maybe it would be better if you went back to your grandmother's," he said.

She seemed surprised—maybe even a little hurt—by his response, but she nodded. "If that's what you want... I'll go pack my things right now."

But MG stayed where he was, blocking her path. "I didn't say it was what I wanted."

Electricity crackled in the air.

She swallowed. "What do you want?"

He'd been fighting his desire for weeks, trying to convince himself that it would be a mistake to give in to his feelings for her. And maybe it would turn out to be a mistake. But right now, with Hope close enough to touch, it was a mistake he wanted to make.

"I want you, Hope. I've always wanted you."

Then he dipped his head to cover her mouth with his own.

When he touched the tip of his tongue to the seam of her lips, she parted willingly for him, and lifted her arms to link them behind his head as her tongue tangled with his.

After what seemed like an eternity and somehow not nearly long enough, he eased his mouth from hers.

"What are we doing here?" Hope asked, when she'd managed to catch her breath. "Is this just about having fun again?"

He knew what she was asking.

But he didn't know what she wanted his answer to

be—and he didn't dare let himself think beyond this moment.

"I could certainly do with some fun in my life," he said. "If you're okay with that."

She tipped her head to the side, as if considering. "Does fun include me getting to see you naked?"

"Hopefully in the next five minutes."

Her lips curved. "Then I'm very okay with that."

He responded by lifting her into his arms.

"Michael," she protested. "Your leg—"

"My leg is fine," he promised.

He carried her to his bedroom, then set her on her feet beside the bed to kiss her again. He made quick work of her clothes—yanking her sweater over her head and then tugging her pants down her legs, leaving her clad in a couple of scraps of wispy lace designed to make a man beg. And he might have been tempted to do just that, if he didn't clearly remember what had happened the last time he dropped to his knees in front of her.

His shirt and jeans were added to the growing pile of clothes on the floor, then they tumbled onto the mattress together. But now that she was here in his bed, now that the moment he'd been fantasizing about since that first night at Diggers' was finally at hand, he had no intention of rushing. Instead, he was going to savor every second, every kiss, every touch. He was going to love her like she'd never been loved before, so she'd remember this night—and him—long after she went back to LA.

But first, he needed to touch her. He was so eager— almost desperate—that his hands trembled as they skimmed over her body. He tried to be gentle, but his palms were hard and callused—courtesy of the manual labor he did every day. He opened his mouth to apologize for their roughness, but Hope's sigh of pleasure assured MG that she didn't mind. So he forgot about apologies and focused his attention on exploring every dip and curve of her delectable body.

He trailed kisses along her jaw, down her throat, over her collarbone. He nuzzled the hollow between her breasts, his unshaven jaw abrading her skin, but she didn't protest. Her nipples were already peaked, and when he brushed his tongue over one tight point, through the barely-there fabric barrier, he heard her breath catch. He unfastened the front clasp and peeled back the cups, baring her flesh to his hungry gaze and hungrier mouth. She gasped when he captured a nipple and moaned when he began to suckle.

Her hands clutched at his shoulders, her nails scoring his skin. He didn't care.

He tugged impatiently on the scrap of lace that stretched across her hips and heard the fabric rip. She didn't care.

He dipped a finger into the soft folds between her legs to test her readiness. She wasn't just wet but dripping—a mind-blowingly arousing discovery. His finger advanced again, sliding into her this time. She moaned again. A second finger joined the first, moving in and out as his thumb massaged her most sensitive spot. Her hips instinctively lifted off the mattress, moving in concert with his ministrations. Her release came hard and fast, and she cried out his name as evidence of her pleasure poured out of her.

When the aftershocks of her climax began to subside, he shifted away from her.

Her hand clamped onto his arm. "Don't you walk out

on me this time, Michael," she said, in a tone that was somehow both breathless and fierce.

"I'm only going to get a condom," he promised, simultaneously amused and incredibly, almost painfully, aroused.

"Okay," she relented, letting her hand drop away.

He returned with a little square packet less than thirty seconds later.

She took it from his hand, carefully tore it open and rolled the latex over his erection. Then she stood up to push him onto the bed and straddled his hips with her knees. Next she leaned forward to nip at his jaw and slide down his body, letting her breasts rub against his chest.

He groaned.

She looked at him, the self-satisfied smile of a woman who knew she was in charge curving her lips before she resumed her seductive torture, kissing her way down his body, trailing her tongue over the ridged muscles of his belly, lower. She nipped playfully at his hip, nibbled on his thigh. He knew when she'd found the scar that ran along the outside of his leg, almost from hip to knee, because the touch of her searching fingers suddenly gentled, then her lips skimmed over it.

"Does it hurt?"

"Not right now."

She seemed to take his word for it, as her mouth moved to the inside of his thigh, slowly inching upward.

"Hope." It was all he could manage through gritted teeth as he desperately fought not to lose control while her tongue traced the length of him, from base to tip, and back again.

"Turnabout's fair play," she said, then took him in her mouth.

His hands fisted in the sheets and stars exploded behind his eyelids.

"If you want me inside you…you need to stop that," he told her. "Now."

She released him slowly, taking him perilously close to the edge as she pulled her mouth away.

"I want you inside me," she said, and positioned herself so that the tip of his throbbing erection was at her entrance. Then she slowly advanced…inch by inch…by inch…until he was buried to the hilt inside her. Finally she began to move, rolling her hips in a torturously slow pace that he feared would kill him—albeit with a smile on his face.

He caught her hips, halting her movements and holding her against him as he rolled, reversing their positions.

She let out a breathless laugh. "You've got some moves, cowboy."

"You ain't seen nothin' yet," he promised.

Then he thrust into her, hard and deep, driving them both toward a release that was already too close. She moaned with pleasure as they moved together, faster and harder. He was holding on to the last fraying thread of self-control with a slippery fist, but he was determined to ensure she found her pleasure again first. Reaching between their bodies, he zeroed in on her pleasure point again. He felt her muscles clench around him, then the pulsing waves of her release, and let himself plunge into the abyss alongside her.

Making love with Michael as a teenager had been all hearts and flowers. Making love with Michael as a grown woman was earth tremors and fireworks. When he got up to dispose of the condom, Hope remained sprawled on the mattress, not sure she could move or even if she wanted to.

She had absolutely no regrets about what had happened. She did, however, have questions—most notably: what came next?

Did "naked fun" allow her to spend the night in his bed?

Or would he want her to go to her own room so that he could sleep?

After all, morning came early on the ranch.

And what did she want?

Hope was hardly a stranger to sex, but she'd rarely spent the night with a man. To her mind, sleeping with someone was almost more intimate than sex, because in slumber, she had no way of maintaining her carefully cultivated image, and there were pieces of herself she was reluctant to let anyone see.

But Michael wasn't anyone. She trusted him not only with her life but with all her secrets. But though their lovemaking had been off-the-charts spectacular, he'd made it clear that they were only having fun. That what they'd shared tonight wasn't the start of some kind of reunion romance but merely a release of the tension that had been building between them as a result of living under the same roof.

Spending the night in his bed, in his arms, might blur the lines of their relationship—if only in her own heart. So it would probably be best if she slept in her own bed across the hall.

So resolved, she started to gather up her scattered clothing.

"What are you doing?" Michael asked, returning from the bathroom.

"Looking for my underwear."

He scooped the torn lace panties off the ground, dangled them from a fingertip. "I think you're going to need a new pair."

"That's two pairs now," she told him.

"I'll buy you a dozen pairs."

"They're La Perla."

"I don't know what that means," he admitted.

"It means they're expensive."

"I'll be more careful next time."

"Is there going to be a next time?"

He took the garments she'd gathered out of her hands and tossed them toward the chair in the corner of the room, then drew her into his arms. "There is very definitely going to be a next time."

She felt his erection pressed against her belly as he murmured the words against her lips.

"Right now?"

"Right now," he promised, easing her back down onto the bed.

MG awoke before his alarm sounded the next morning, with Hope's warm naked body sprawled on top of him. He blindly reached a hand out, fumbling for the switch so it wouldn't go off and disturb her slumber.

For a brief moment, he considered pretending that he'd forgotten to set the alarm, so he could enjoy another hour or more in bed with her. Unfortunately, he knew the reprieve wouldn't last that long before his brother or one of his cousins came knocking on the door.

And while he didn't think that hooking up with Hope was a big deal, he didn't necessarily want his family to know about it. He could handle the ribbing he might get from Mitch or Caleb or Liam, but if his mom found out, she would have *expectations*.

So he carefully shifted Hope's body away from his and rolled out of bed, then pulled the covers up over her. As he settled the blankets, an empty condom wrapper fluttered to the ground. He scooped it up and carried it to the bathroom, to toss it in the wastebasket with the others.

Except there was only one empty wrapper in the trash.

A trickle of unease skittered down his spine.

He returned to the bedroom to look all around the bed and even under it.

Nothing.

He swore.

Hope stirred. "Michael?"

He hadn't meant to wake her, but now that she was awake, he didn't have to panic alone.

She eased herself into a sitting position, the covers falling to her waist, baring her sweetly curved, rosy-tipped breasts and making him forget, at least for the space of a heartbeat, that he was panicking.

"Is something wrong?" she asked.

He nodded. "We made love three times last night— but we only used protection twice."

Chapter Eighteen

Hope was grateful that she'd promised to be at the high school for auditions that afternoon, because she needed a distraction to get her mind off the fact that she and Michael had apparently been so eager to be together that they'd forgotten to use a condom the third time. Because that meant she could be pregnant—and she was reluctant to consider the possibility, no matter how remote.

Not because she didn't want to have a baby, but because she very much did. She hadn't given the idea a lot of thought when she was in LA, partly because she'd worried that having a baby might limit her prospects but mostly because there hadn't been anyone special in her life that she wanted to have a baby with. But being back in Haven, seeing how parenting had opened a whole new world for other people she knew, had made her reconsider. Suddenly the prospect of being blessed with a baby filled her with joy. And the prospect of having Michael's baby filled her heart to overflowing.

Unfortunately, he didn't feel the same way. When he'd pointed out the discrepancy between the number of times they'd made love and the number of condoms they'd used, he'd clearly been freaking out. And though she was sorry that the prospect—however miniscule—of having a baby with her could induce such a negative reaction, she couldn't offer him false assurances when he'd asked if she was taking any other form of birth control. She did point out, though, that the chances of her being pregnant after only one time without a condom were slim, especially when she didn't even know if it was the right time of the month for her to be able to conceive.

She'd held her breath then, waiting for him to suggest that she go to the pharmacy to get the morning after pill—just to be safe. But he didn't say anything and she certainly didn't bring it up, because if there was even the teensiest, tiniest chance that she might have conceived a child, she didn't want to extinguish it.

But now she was feeling guilty about her silence. Because she knew it wasn't fair to keep him in the dark about all the options. And though it made her heart ache to even consider that he'd want her to take the emergency contraceptive, she knew that she had to stop at the pharmacy on her way back to the ranch.

But first, she had auditions to sit through.

For the most part, they were pretty good. A couple of students showed real promise, and a couple others would definitely be cast in the ensemble, but she nevertheless enjoyed watching them all on stage.

Mr. Hutchinson was chatting with Mrs. Doyle— an English teacher who frequently helped out with the drama club—when Hope excused herself, exiting the auditorium just as Missy Sutherland was walking past.

"Missy—can I talk to you for a minute?"

The teen looked at her warily. "What do you want?"

"I was just wondering why you haven't signed up to audition for the holiday production."

"Why do you care?"

"Because I thought you wanted to be an actor."

"Mr. Hutchinson says it's important for an actor to know the ins and outs of a production and working on stage crew is just as important as being on stage."

"I don't disagree," Hope said. "But acting skills are honed by acting."

"Well, I don't want to be stupid Mr. Scrooge or Jacob Marley or Bob Cratchit."

She nodded slowly. "I understand. Sometimes our fears hold us back from stepping outside of our comfort zones."

Missy tossed her head. "I'm not afraid."

"My mistake," Hope said easily.

"And anyway, there's no point in trying out for the lead because Mr. Hutchinson always gives Sofia the best parts."

"Always?" She had to wonder if there was any truth to the claim or if it was simply the opinion of a disgruntled actor. (Or perhaps disgruntled *actors*, considering this wasn't the first time Hope had heard a similar remark.)

"*Always*," Missy confirmed.

"Because it was Mr. Hutchinson who told me that you were pretty good as Abigail Williams in *The Crucible* your sophomore year."

"I was a lot better than pretty good," Missy said immodestly. "But I was Sofia's understudy. The only reason

I got to be Abigail is that she came down with tonsillitis the day before opening."

"Well, I just wanted to let you know that there are still a few open spots, if you change your mind about auditioning."

"You just want me to try out so that you can tell Mr. Hutchinson all the reasons you don't think I should get a part."

"I do think your attitude needs an adjustment," Hope told her. "But I can assure you that I've managed to work with plenty of actors I didn't get along with when the cameras weren't rolling."

"Like Donovan Kessel?" Missy asked with feigned innocence.

Hope knew she was being baited, and she kept her expression carefully neutral as she responded.

"Check the website if you want to audition, because once those slots are filled, the opportunity will be lost." She glanced at her watch. "Now I have somewhere I need to be."

And she exited stage left.

"Good timing," MG said, when Hope followed the scent of grilling meat to the barbecue at the side of the house, where he was flipping burgers.

"So I see." She could also see that Bernie was at his side, no doubt hoping that one of the burgers would fall off the grill. "Optimistic, isn't he?"

He followed her gaze to the dog. "Eternally."

"Is there anything I can do to help?" she asked.

"These are just about ready, so you can go on in and get the condiments out of the fridge."

She nodded and disappeared into the house.

Bernie looked from the grill to Hope's retreating form and back again.

"You're torn now, aren't you, buddy? Not entirely sure what smells better—the pretty lady or the grilled meat?"

The dog whined in his throat.

MG chuckled. "Come on," he said. "If you're really lucky, Hope will drop a piece of her burger under the table. And if *I'm* really lucky, she won't make me sleep in the doghouse."

She glanced up when he walked in with the plate of burgers.

"You didn't only grill—you made a salad."

"As my mother would say, a man might want to live on meat alone but a woman needs vegetables."

Her lips curved. "Your mother has a lot of interesting sayings."

"She does." He set the burgers on the table and reached for Hope's hand, drawing her toward him. "And I wanted to do something nice for you to make up for this morning."

"You mean for freaking out over the fact that your little swimmers were possibly doing the front crawl in my fallopian tubes?"

"I don't think those are the words I used, but yeah." He lowered his head and touched his lips to hers. "I overreacted, and I'm sorry."

"You don't need to apologize." She stepped out of his arms to take her seat at the table. "The prospect of an unplanned pregnancy—however remote—is scary."

He sat down across from her. "I didn't see you freaking out."

She shrugged as she scooped salad onto her plate. "Maybe because, in recent days, I've started to give some thought to the idea of having a baby and discovered that it's something I really want."

"Even so, I'm sure you didn't envision a scenario in which you might end up coparenting a child across a distance of six hundred miles."

"No, I didn't." She nibbled tentatively on her burger.

"There's something else on your mind," he guessed.

She nodded. "As much as I love the idea of having a baby, I realized that it would be better for everyone—especially the baby—if both potential parents were on board with the plan. So if you're still freaking out on the inside—"

"I'm not," he hastened to assure her.

"Okay, but in case you have any doubts at all… I stopped at the pharmacy and picked up the morning after pill."

He set his burger back on his plate. "Did you take it?"

She shook her head. "I wanted to talk to you first."

He was silent for a minute, considering.

"Do you want to take it?" he finally asked her.

"No." She poked at a slice of cucumber with her fork. "But I think whether I do or don't take the pill is a decision we should make together."

"Don't take it." He hadn't known what he intended to say until the words spilled out of his mouth, but he didn't regret them.

She looked at him—her expression a combination of uncertainty and relief. "Are you sure?"

"No," he admitted. "But I've been thinking about it all day, and about the fact that I have never, in the whole of my life, had unprotected sex with a woman. And I wondered if maybe it wasn't an accident that I forgot last night but…fate."

"Fate?" she echoed dubiously.

"Do you have a better explanation?"

"Half-aroused and half-asleep?"

"*Half*-aroused?" he said indignantly.

She managed to laugh at that, but he could tell that there was something else weighing on her mind.

"We could get married," he said. "If that would make things easier for sharing custody—"

"Before you start making plans and throwing around proposals to do the right thing for a baby that might or might not exist, there's something else I have to tell you."

"Okay," he said cautiously.

"I saw Paige in town. At the pharmacy."

"Did she say something to you? About us?"

Now she shook her head. "I don't even think she saw me."

"So why are you telling me this?"

"Because I saw her checking out and…she was buying a pregnancy test."

A four-letter word that—even at his current age—would have his mother reaching for the soap—flashed in MG's head in capital letters and neon lights.

Oh no, this could *not* be happening to him.

Not now.

Hope *had* to be mistaken.

Even as he tried to convince himself of that, he heard the echo of Paige's voice in the back of his head.

I want a baby.

But that was the night they'd broken up—and they'd never had unprotected sex. The only time he'd ever slipped up and forgotten to use a condom was last night—with Hope.

Unfortunately he knew that they were only ninety-eight percent effective, even when used properly every time. Which meant that two out of every one hundred women who relied on condoms as contraception could get pregnant.

And there was that four-letter word again.

And again. And again.

He swallowed. "Are you sure?"

"Do you think I would have said anything if I wasn't sure?"

No, she wouldn't have.

Because they'd only just found their way back to one another—however temporarily—and learning that he was going to have a baby with someone else (and possibly Hope, too!) changed everything.

"She could have been buying it for a friend," he pointed out.

"That's a possibility," Hope acknowledged.

"And even if the test was for her, there are two potential outcomes, right? Isn't it just as likely that the result could be negative as positive?"

"Except that I don't imagine she would have bought the test unless she had reason to believe it could be positive."

"And even if she is pregnant, the baby might not be mine," he said, desperately searching for an out to this potentially disastrous situation.

"Another possibility," she allowed. "But I think, instead of making yourself crazy wondering *what if*, you need to find out."

She was right, of course.

He needed to know.

And sooner rather than later.

He pulled out his cell, retrieved Paige's contact information.

Can we talk?

The thirty seconds he had to wait for a response seemed like an eternity.

What's up?

He exhaled an unsteady breath.

Not via text. Or on the phone. Can I come over?

I'm actually headed to Vegas for the weekend.

Vegas?
Paige had definitely nixed the idea when he'd once suggested heading to Sin City for a quick getaway, so he was admittedly surprised to learn that she was making a trip now.

When will you be back?

Late Sunday night.

Can we talk Monday?

Sure.

Which meant he had three days to wonder and worry.

Hope couldn't blame Michael for being preoccupied.
His whole world had been turned upside down in the space of twenty-four hours, and she couldn't help but feel partly responsible.

She had no regrets about anything that had transpired between them, but she could understand how he might be freaked out by the possibility that he could conceivably (ha!) end up the father of two babies born within a couple months of each other—one with his ex-girlfriend and one with the woman he was currently sleeping with.

Except she wasn't sure that was an accurate description of their relationship, considering that they'd only spent one night together. And when ten o'clock—the usual time that he turned off the television and headed to bed—came and went and he remained on the sofa watching the baseball game, she decided that he probably wanted some space.

So she got up and retreated to her own room, leaving the door open so that Bernie could follow. But he seemed to know that Michael needed him more than she did, because he settled on the floor by his master's feet.

Hope went through her usual bedtime routine—washing her face, brushing her teeth, braiding her hair so it didn't tangle in the night. She crawled beneath the covers, wishing she had a book to read to help focus her thoughts, but she'd already finished the new Quinn Ellison. After tossing and turning for nearly an hour, she decided to check out Michael's bookshelves again—and found the man himself standing by the window, looking out at the starry night.

He turned when he heard her approach, and she halted in her tracks.

"I didn't realize you were still up."

"I couldn't sleep," he admitted.

But he'd tried, she realized now. Because he was wearing pajama pants low on his hips—and nothing else. In the glow of the moonlight, she could clearly see the outline of his broad shoulders, and felt a familiar stirring low in her belly.

"Do you want to be alone?"

"No."

She took a few steps forward, out of the shadows. "Do you want a distraction?"

She felt the heat of his gaze as it raked over her, as tangible as a caress.

"I want you, Hope."

His words—stark and honest—eased some of the tightness that had taken hold of her chest when she saw Paige in the pharmacy and started to question what the other woman's potential condition could mean for them.

"I wasn't sure you still would…after …everything."

"I've got more questions than answers right now," he said, tugging on the belt of her robe to draw her toward him. "But that is the one thing I know for sure."

The knot easily came undone, and then his hands were inside her robe, stroking her through whisper-thin silk and lace. (Because when there was even the slightest chance of spending the night with a man, a smart woman donned something sexier than boxer shorts and a tank top.)

"Is this from the fancy place where you get your underwear?" he asked.

"La Perla," she said. "And yes."

"Then you should probably take it off before I do."

"Good idea."

"I was surprised to get your text message the other day," Paige said, when she opened the door in response to MG's knock Monday night.

It would be polite to respond with a similarly casual

remark—or maybe by asking how she'd been. But one question had been hammering in his brain for the past three days and he needed an answer now.

"Are you pregnant?"

She blinked. "What?"

"Hope saw you buying a pregnancy test at the pharmacy," he admitted.

Now she sighed. "I knew I should have gone to a drug store in Battle Mountain."

"Are you pregnant?" he asked again.

"Yes."

He managed to ignore the tightening of the knots in his stomach and nod. "Obviously we've got some things to figure out."

"No, we don't," she told him.

"There's no way I'm going to let my baby grow up without a father," he assured her.

"Seven weeks ago, you stood in almost that exact spot and told me you weren't ready to be a father," she reminded him.

"Seven weeks ago, I didn't know you were pregnant."

"Because I wasn't."

He frowned. "I don't understand."

"It's not your baby, MG."

"I don't understand," he said again.

"When we broke up—"

"You mean when you dumped me?"

"I didn't think I'd ever get over you," she continued, ignoring his interjection. Then she shrugged, a small smile playing at the corners of her mouth. "I was wrong."

"You're saying that you're with someone else now?"

"I'm with someone else now," she confirmed, holding up her left hand to show him the wedding band on her third finger. "Someone who loves me and wants a future with me—and our baby."

MG was stunned by her admission—and perhaps a little put out that she'd gotten over him so quickly. At the same time, he was sincerely happy for her—and desperately relieved to learn that the baby she was carrying wasn't his.

"That's why you went to Vegas," he realized.

She nodded.

"Can I ask…"

"Gavin's the father of the baby—and now my husband."

"And you're happy?"

"Very happy," she assured him.

"Then I'm happy for you."

"I'm happy for you, too," she said. "I always suspected you and Hope would find your way back to one another someday."

"I'm not…we're not…she's just staying at the Circle G until she goes back to California."

"You're a smart man, MG, but ridiculously stubborn sometimes. If you want her—and we both know that you do—then don't let her get away this time."

"It was good to see you." He kissed her cheek. "And congrats again."

She sighed. "Here's an idea, MG. Instead of waiting for her to leave, why don't you ask her to stay?"

"Because she won't," he said, resigned to the fact.

"Ask her," Paige urged again. "Give her a chance to surprise you."

The possibility that Paige might have been pregnant with his baby had sent his mind spinning because he knew that a child was a lifelong connection between their parents. The idea of having a baby with Hope (once he got over the panic) sent his heart soaring for the same reason. And now that the question of Paige's had been answered, he could focus on making plans with Hope.

Who was sitting on the porch with Bernie when he got home, obviously waiting for him, wanting to know.

"She's pregnant," he confirmed, before Hope could ask. "But it's not my baby."

"I can tell you're relieved," she remarked.

"Was it the grin on my face that gave me away?"

"That was my first clue," she confirmed.

He knelt on the step in front of her and leaned forward to kiss her.

"I've got some more good news for you," she said, when he finally ended the kiss.

"Tell me."

"I got my period."

He leaned back. "That's good news?"

"Don't you think so? A baby would have been a big complication for both of us right now."

"I guess you're right," he agreed.

But it didn't feel like good news.

It felt like his fledgling hope for a future with Hope had just slipped through his fingers.

Chapter Nineteen

It was fun to be involved in theater again—and a big change from what Hope had been doing for the past eighteen years. Putting on a play was different than filming a TV show. There was no director calling to cut a scene, no retakes if an actor forgot a line, no second chances to get it right. So the actors had to be able to hold up under pressure and go with the flow when something went wrong. Because something always went wrong.

Mr. Hutchinson was a dedicated teacher who seemed to want his students to succeed as much as he wanted the play to be a success. And aside from some disagreements with respect to casting (he wanted to give Sofia Rivera the lead and she'd argued against it, with Mrs. Doyle backing Hope's choice of Missy Sutherland—who had ultimately decided to audition for the role), Hope was mostly impressed with his knowledge of theater work and generally approved of his direction. So she didn't know why, after several weeks of rehearsals, it suddenly started to bother her that he was very hands-on with his students. Holding Missy's hips to position her on stage, tucking a strand of hair behind Sofia's ear so the audience could see her facial expressions more clearly, and accidentally (?) brushing the side of Nicole's breast with the back of his hand when he helped her position the prop crutch under her arm.

But she kept her concerns to herself. None of the actors seemed obviously bothered by his actions, though she'd noticed that Missy would sometimes sidestep when she saw him coming—deliberately moving to the opposite side of the desk, if they were blocking a scene in Scrooge's office, or positioning herself more closely to a castmate, if there was no furniture on the stage.

Working with the students also had Hope giving serious consideration to the direction of her own acting career. Jenny had been in touch regularly to discuss options—mostly short-term guest spots on established TV shows—and she'd couriered some movie scripts for Hope to peruse. And while it was reassuring to know that being fired from *Rockwood Ridge* hadn't meant the end of her career, she wasn't particularly excited about any of the options presented to her.

"You got another package from your agent today," Michael said, when she arrived back at the ranch after a lunch date with Laurel on a Wednesday afternoon late in October.

She ignored the envelope on the counter. "Another script she wants me to take a look at."

"You don't sound very excited," he noted.

"I don't feel very excited," she admitted. "And I know

I should. This one's a rom-com with a big star already cast as the female lead. I would potentially play her best friend."

"So what are your reservations?"

"I think they're more about the timing than the project," she said. "Obviously I'd have to go back to LA to read for the part and I don't want to abandon the drama club at this stage."

"You're really enjoying working at the high school, aren't you?"

"I don't actually work at the high school," she reminded him. "I'm just helping out."

"What if you could work there?"

"I think you actually need to graduate from teacher's college to be a teacher."

"Something to think about," he said.

She frowned. "Don't you think thirty-five is a little old to be starting college?"

"Not at all," he assured her. "But if you don't want to go the teacher's college route, you could run your own drama program. Nobody would question that you have all the credentials you'd need for that."

"Do you really think a town this size could support something like that?"

"If you build it, they will come."

She rolled her eyes. "I could have guessed that if you were ever going to quote a line from a movie, it would be a baseball movie."

"Just think about it," he said.

So she thought about it.

And she was still thinking about it the next day when she was sorting through a box of old costumes that had been donated to the school by the local community theater, looking for suitable pieces for the holiday play.

"Ms. Bradford—are you in here?"

She stepped out from behind the curtain. "Missy?"

The teen made her way down the aisle toward the stage. "I know I'm early for rehearsal."

Hope glanced at her watch. It was 12:20 and rehearsal was scheduled to begin at 2:45 p.m.

"A little bit," she agreed.

Missy managed a smile. "The windows of my Spanish class overlook the parking lot, so I saw you arrive, and I was hoping to speak with you in private."

"Sure." Hope abandoned the box of cast-off clothing and sat on the edge of the stage to give Missy her full attention. "What's up?"

Though they'd admittedly gotten off to a rocky start when they first crossed paths at The Daily Grind, the chip on Missy's shoulder had been whittled down significantly since she won the lead role in the holiday production. Hope had been gratified to discover that her instincts about the girl were right, as Missy proved herself eager to learn and willing to work hard, and Hope knew she was going to be a fabulous Scrooge.

"I was just wondering…when you first started auditioning for roles, did the casting directors want to see… pictures of you?"

Pictures?

"Do you mean headshots?"

The girl hesitated a fraction of a second before she nodded.

"Absolutely," Hope told her. "A good headshot provides the casting director with a sense of who you are as an actor. A good headshot will also help you get an agent, who ensures your headshot is seen by those directors."

"And how did you know…" Her follow-up question trailed off when the auditorium doors opened again, and Ty Hutchinson strolled in carrying another cardboard box.

"More donations from the community theater," he announced. "Lots of hats and gloves and stuff like that in this one."

"Let's take a look," Hope said.

He dropped the box on the stage, only then noticing that Hope wasn't alone.

"Shouldn't you be in class, Missy?"

She shook her head. "It's my lunch period right now."

"So why aren't you in the cafeteria?"

"I just wanted to talk to Ms. Bradford—about how to play Scrooge's reaction to the Spirit of Christmas Yet to Come."

Which wasn't at all what the girl had been talking to her about, and the blatant lie set Hope's internal alarms screaming.

"We can talk about it some more at rehearsal later," she said to Missy.

The teen sent her a look of relief and gratitude, then nodded and made her escape.

And her hasty retreat so closely on the heels of the teacher's arrival triggered more screaming. Or maybe it was the way she'd seen Tyler look at Missy—and the way Missy had avoided looking at him—that set off her alarms again.

Or maybe she was imagining things.

Everybody she'd talked to at the school—teachers and students alike—had great things to say about Mr.

Hutchinson. In addition to teaching four classes and running the drama club, he was also an advisor to the yearbook committee and the unofficial photographer for many school events.

But most everybody in Hollywood had great things to say about Donovan Kessel, too—except perhaps the naive young women who'd been invited back to his office under the pretext of looking at movie scripts.

Hope pushed the uncomfortable comparison aside and lifted the flaps on the box.

"There's some great stuff in here," she said, digging through the contents. Not just hats and gloves, but scarves and shawls and waistcoats.

"I thought so, too, when I took a quick peek. It's almost as if this is a box from the community theater production of *A Christmas Carol*."

"Lucky for us," she said.

"Someone really needs to sort through the mountain of costumes backstage and figure out what's worth keeping and what should be gotten rid of, but in the four years I've been at Westmount, I haven't managed to find the time to do it."

"I should be able to make some headway over the next few weeks," Hope told him.

"That would be great," Ty said gratefully.

"So this is your fourth year teaching here?"

He nodded. "I was at Gordon Black in Reno for three years before that."

"You left Reno to come to Haven?"

"My wife wanted to raise our girls in a smaller town."

"It is a good place to grow up," she said. "And Westmount is fortunate to have teachers who put so much time and energy into extracurriculars."

"Extracurriculars are an important part of the high school experience," he noted.

"I remember," Hope told him. "Though I put all of my eggs in the drama club basket."

"I'd say that paid off for you."

"I've been very fortunate in my career," she agreed.

"Anyway, I should get back to my creative writing class," he said, then he turned and walked out of the auditorium the same way he'd come in.

Hope stood where she was for another minute, wondering if she'd misread the situation. If she'd misunderstood the strange vibe between Missy and the drama teacher.

Ty was a good guy. A married man who absolutely doted on his gorgeous wife, the mother of his two beautiful daughters.

But Hope knew from her own experience that monsters came in all shapes and sizes.

"Since coming back to Haven, I have never missed LA more than I do today," Hope said, sliding into the vinyl bench across from Laurel at the Sunnyside Diner. "I had to scrape my windshield this morning—with my driver's license, because I don't have a windshield scraper."

"You ain't seen nothing yet," her friend warned.

Hope whimpered at the thought.

Laurel laughed. "It's not so bad—if you dress for the weather."

"Apparently I'm going to need a new wardrobe."

The other woman's expression brightened. "I'm always up for shopping."

The prospect of browsing through the stores with her

old friend immediately lifted Hope's mood, too. "Okay, before we leave here today, we're going to pick a date and put it in our calendars."

"Why not right now?"

"Because right now, I need coffee."

As if on cue, a server appeared with a pot in hand to fill their cups.

After they'd placed their orders (an egg white omelet with feta and spinach for Hope; a fruit plate with yogurt and granola for Laurel), they settled on a date for their shopping excursion and then chatted about the upcoming holidays while they waited for their food.

When their breakfast was delivered, Laurel made a face at her plate and Hope knew the reason—even before her friend isolated the three slices of kiwi.

She nudged her own plate closer to the middle of the table, and Laurel transferred the fruit.

"I can't tell you how much I appreciate this," Hope told her friend, as she dug into her omelet.

"It's just a couple of slices of kiwi."

She smiled. "I wasn't referring to the fruit, though I am a big fan of kiwi."

"I'm a big fan of Chris Hemsworth." Laurel speared a strawberry with her fork. "Does that count?"

"He's from Australia not New Zealand, so no," Hope said.

Her friend shrugged. "Oh, well."

"I actually met him once." Hope sprinkled pepper on her eggs. "Sort of."

Laurel's eyes went wide. "Tell me everything."

"It was four or five years ago, at a restaurant in Malibu. He was with his wife and kids. I was with some friends."

"And?"

"And I was coming out of the ladies' room at the same time he was on his way into the men's room with his twin boys. He was paying attention to whatever one of them was saying and bumped right into me."

"Ohmygod. You had actual. Body. Contact. With Thor?"

"Completely inadvertent, but yes." Hope nodded. "And let me tell you, that chest is every bit as solid as it looks onscreen."

"Ohmygod," Laurel said again, fanning herself with her hand.

"I'd stopped in my tracks, because I saw him coming even if he didn't see me, and still I stumbled back from the impact. He instinctively grabbed my arms, catching me so I didn't fall, and apologized, sincerely, in that unbelievably sexy voice."

Now Laurel whimpered.

Hope grinned. "Let me tell you—it was two-and-a-half seconds of pure magic."

"I can imagine. I *am* imagining." Her friend closed her eyes. "Just give me a minute."

The server refilled their coffee mugs.

Laurel finally opened her eyes again and scooped up a spoonful of yogurt. "Actually, I've had some celebrity encounters of my own," she said. "In fact, I've slept with an Emmy-winning actor more times than I even remember."

She laughed. "Those childhood sleepovers were always a lot of fun, though we didn't always get a lot of sleep."

"Sleepovers aren't about the sleeping but the bonding," her friend pointed out.

"Actually, that's what I was trying to thank you for," Hope said now. "Not the kiwi, but for being my friend. I never imagined that we'd be able to pick up right where we left off."

"I never imagined anything different," Laurel said.

"Really?"

"We did it all the time when we were kids. Every September, I'd come back to Haven after being gone for the whole summer, and we'd pick up without missing a beat."

"I'd forgotten about that," Hope admitted.

"Well, those summers away are the reason I was so determined to keep things civil—as much as possible—when Christopher and I split. I didn't want him to feel as if he had to move halfway across the country, resulting in our kids being shuffled around like me and my brother were."

It had been hard on her friend, Hope remembered now. And she hadn't been very sympathetic—because it was difficult to feel sorry for Laurel, whose parents fought over spending time with her, when she'd never even known her father and her mother had willingly abandoned her to be raised by her grandparents.

In retrospect, Hope could be grateful to Debra for making the choice that was best for her daughter, even if that hadn't been her primary motive. Growing up in Haven—with friends like Laurel and Michael—had meant a childhood filled with happy memories.

"But speaking of actors and acting," Laurel said. "I hear you're helping out with the drama club's holiday production this year."

"I am," she confirmed. "And I'm having a lot of fun working with the kids."

"Does that mean you'll be here at least until Christmas?"

"That's the plan."

"And after?"

"I'm trying not to think too far ahead."

"Well, for what it's worth, there are a lot of people in this town who would be overjoyed if you made Haven your home again."

"Maybe. If you and my grandmother are 'a lot of people.'"

"You're underestimating the number of friends you have here," Laurel chided. "You didn't even include MG in your very short list."

"I'm not sure that Michael considers me a friend."

"Do you think he'd invite someone who wasn't a friend to stay in his house?"

Hope pushed her half-eaten omelet aside and reached for her coffee. "There really are no secrets in this town, are there?"

"None at all," her friend agreed. "And there shouldn't be any secrets between friends, either."

"You think I'm holding out on you?"

"Are you?"

"Maybe I am," she allowed. "But I didn't know if you wanted to know that Michael Gilmore has a chest that is every bit as swoonworthy as Chris Hemsworth's."

"And now you're just bragging," Laurel grumbled.

Hope laughed, because even if she didn't have a lot of friends, she had the very best ones.

Something was going on with Hope.

Though MG would never claim to be the most astute observer, even he'd noticed that she'd been preoccupied for the past few days. But when he asked what was on her mind, she only said "drama club stuff."

He wanted to believe it was true, but he couldn't help but wonder if she was thinking about the latest script her agent had sent—and thinking about going back to California. Which was something he definitely didn't want to think about.

She didn't seem to miss her life in Hollywood, though she'd remarked—on more than one occasion—that she missed the weather. He'd responded to her complaint by promising to keep her warm, Hope had then asked how he intended to do that, and he'd answered her question with a demonstration. Afterward, she'd assured him that she could happily learn to tolerate the cold weather again if she got to spend long winter nights in his bed.

It sounded like a perfectly good plan to him.

But then, this afternoon, she'd sent him a cryptic text message:

Some things to deal with at school. Will be late tonight. Possibly very late. Don't wait up. XO

As if he could even consider going to bed before she was home, especially after a message like that.

It was just after ten o'clock when Bernie lifted his head, obviously having heard the crunch of gravel as Hope's vehicle turned into the driveway. The dog rose from his bed and made his way to the door to greet her.

MG got up, too, but he went to the kitchen to pour the glass of wine he suspected she was going to want after she removed her coat and boots and hat and gloves and fussed over the dog, as she did every time she walked through the door.

When she was finished greeting Bernie, she moved into MG's arms—and held on for a very long time.

"Rough day?" he guessed.

"You have no idea."

"Anything you want to talk about?"

"First, I want a glass of wine," she said.

He handed her the glass.

Her eyes filled with tears.

A very rough day, he realized.

She settled on the sofa and sipped her wine.

To MG's surprise, Bernie plopped down by Hope's feet, allowing him to take the seat beside her.

"Did you eat?" he asked.

She shook her head.

"But I'm not hungry," she said, pre-empting his next question.

He put his arm around her, and she tipped her head back against his shoulder.

"The condensed version of the story is that Linda Doyle is taking over supervision of the drama club, effective immediately, because Tyler Hutchinson is definitely going to lose his job and probably going to jail."

A very rough day, indeed.

"Can you expand on that at least a little bit?" he asked cautiously.

She sipped her wine again. "I actually liked him," she said. "And I'm not the only one. He was voted Teacher of the Year his first year at Westmount. Reputed to be tough but fair and happy to spend extra time tutoring the students who needed it. In addition to working with the drama club, he attended various other extracurricular events—pep rallies and sporting events and music concerts, usually with a camera in hand, taking pictures for the yearbook."

He squeezed her a little tighter, a silent offer of encouragement.

"And he was a good photographer. So when he invited his drama students to his home studio to sit for headshots, of course they said *yes*. Because he was their teacher and they were grateful he was willing to help them out. *'Tilt your head a little to the side.' 'Smile a little wider.' 'Maybe undo another button.' 'Why don't we try some photos without the bra?'*"

MG swore.

She nodded. "As far as I know, it didn't go any further than taking pictures. But for those girls—at least half a dozen, probably more—it was far enough."

And the teacher's actions, MG was sure, were also a reminder to Hope of her experience with the actor he still wished he could throttle.

"I should have asked questions." Hope swiped at the tears that spilled onto her cheeks. "The more time I spent with him, the more I couldn't shake the feeling that something was off. But I ignored my instincts. Or maybe I was afraid that my own experience was making me see something that wasn't there."

"I'm thinking you must have asked questions—or how else did this all come out?"

"One of the drama club students approached me. She didn't actually tell me what happened, not at first, but when I followed up with her later, she confided about her experience.

"But she didn't want me to tell anyone else—and she freaked when I suggested contacting the sheriff. Because she didn't want to get him in trouble—she just wanted him to stop pressuring her to pose for more pictures.

And because she's going to be graduating in June, she figured that she'd never have to see him again after that."

"How did you change her mind?"

"I wish I could take the credit," Hope said. "But the truth is, when she talked about going away to school and getting away from him, she seemed to realize that while the distance would stop what he was doing *to her*, it wouldn't stop *him*. And it turns out she's got a sister who will be starting high school in September, and she refused to stay silent and give him the opportunity to do the same thing to her.

"So I went with her to talk to her mom first, then we all went to the principal and he called the sheriff."

"Whoever the student is, she's obviously a very brave young woman."

Hope nodded. "Maybe, someday, I'll be as brave as her."

MG was careful not to disturb Hope when he slipped out of bed the next morning. She'd had an emotionally exhausting day and a restless night and he wanted her to get some sleep before she headed over to the high school later in the day. And he knew she'd be going back to the school, to preserve the illusion of normalcy for the drama club students.

Some of them would be shocked to hear the rumors that were likely already circulating about their teacher. Some of them already knew the horrible truth.

But there was nothing for MG to do about it, so he attempted to put it out of his mind and focus on his work. It was a surprisingly warm and sunny day for early November—a good day for fixing fence—and he was happy to have his cousin Liam's company to do it.

They'd spent a lot of time together, growing up in close proximity on the ranch, though Liam had decided a few years back that he wanted to be a hotelier rather than a rancher, creating a rift between him and his dad that was only mended after David Gilmore's heart attack.

Liam had come back to help out then and discovered he didn't hate ranching so much as he'd wanted to make his own choices. He still owned the Stagecoach Inn in town, but it was his wife, Macy, who was in charge of the boutique hotel now, somehow managing the upscale property and their triplets with a steady hand and ready smile.

"How are things going with your new roommate?" Liam asked.

"No complaints," MG said.

Something in his tone must have given him away, because his cousin grinned. "Caleb figured it wouldn't take you long to hook up again."

"Do the two of you always gossip like a couple of old ladies?"

"Not always," Liam said, unchastened. "But when the hottest rumors involve one of our favorite cousins, absolutely."

MG responded to that by hammering a post.

His cousin waited until the hammering had stopped to pick up the thread of their conversation. "I heard she's been helping out with the drama club at the high school."

"You heard right."

"Apparently she's a big hit with the kids."

"An actual celebrity in their midst."

"Do you think she'll stick this time?"

It was the question MG had been asking himself for weeks. In the beginning, he wouldn't have hesitated to answer with a resounding no, because he knew that Hope had a life and a career in LA. A glamorous life and successful career that he felt certain she intended to return to as soon as the media circus surrounding her departure from *Rockwood Ridge* died down.

And when he'd first taken her to his bed, they'd both been in agreement that this—whatever this was between them—was only temporary. But somehow, over the last few weeks, what had once seemed clear had become a lot murkier.

As the days turned into weeks and she gave no hint of any plans to go back to California, he found himself wondering. When she showed little interest in potential projects that her agent tossed in her direction, he'd started to consider that maybe she wasn't eager to return to her former life. And every night, when they came together in his bed, he found himself hoping that she'd choose to stay—even as he cautioned himself against giving all of his heart to her again.

He finally responded to his cousin's question with a shrug. "I think, right now, she's taking some time to figure out what she wants."

Liam wiped the sweat from his brow. "You tell her what *you* want?"

"She needs to make her own choices."

"Obviously that's a *no*," his cousin said, shaking his head.

"You know, this work would get done a lot faster if you talked a little less," MG told him.

"What I know is that being noble only gets you so far," Liam countered. "You need to seize the day."

"You need to seize that box of nails."

"Go after what you want."

He took the box of nails his cousin proffered. "What I want is to get this damn fence fixed."

As he pounded nails, he wanted to pound on Liam. And Caleb and Mitch—though they weren't currently within pounding distance. Because they were all too eager to dish out advice—all of them smug and happy with their pretty wives and their perfect families.

Well, he was happy, too. Happier with Hope than he'd imagined he could be.

And at the same time, there was a part of him that continued to hold back, that was reluctant to admit the truth of his feelings, because he feared this happiness couldn't last. A part of him that didn't dare tell her that he wanted a future for them together—the same future they'd planned eighteen years earlier because he was afraid that what he had to offer wasn't enough for her. That a northern Nevada rancher couldn't possibly entice a Hollywood celebrity to stay.

It turned out to be a self-fulfilling prophecy, though another two weeks passed before MG walked into the cabin at the end of a long and grueling day—his body sweaty and his leg throbbing—and found Hope packing.

Panic seized his heart in a desperate grip even as a voice in the back of his head reminded him that he'd known all along this was coming. That eventually she would leave. And that they'd had weeks more than he'd dared hope for when she first moved into his cabin.

Her suitcase was open on top of the bed and she was neatly folding and tucking various items of clothing inside. Beside the suitcase was the envelope with the latest script that her agent had sent a few days earlier.

"Going somewhere?" he asked.

She jolted at the sound of his voice, then laughed and pressed a hand to her heart. "I didn't hear you come in."

"Just now."

"Yes," she said, finally responding to his initial question. "A quick trip back to LA. I've got some things to do—things I've put off for too long already."

"What about the drama club?"

"Mrs. Doyle has kept everyone on track with barely a hitch," Hope assured him. "I have no doubt that she can manage on her own for a few days."

"It's a long way to go for only a few days," he remarked, wondering if she really expected him to believe that her trip would be of short duration.

"That's why I decided to fly," she said. "It won't be all that much faster, factoring in the drive to the Reno airport, but Grams and Dennis are going to take me."

"When did you tell your grandmother that you were leaving?"

"When I had lunch with her today."

"Who else knows?"

"Your mom and dad." She closed the lid and zipped up her suitcase. "I stopped by their place on my way back to return your mom's lasagna pan and say goodbye."

"And when were you going to say goodbye to me?"

"Tomorrow morning—before I left." But something in his tone must have warned her that there were a lot of emotions churning beneath the surface, because she turned to give him her full attention now. "What's going on, Michael? Why are you acting so strange about this?"

"Only one of us here is an actor," he reminded her.

"Are you upset that I'm going back to LA?"

"Nope," he lied. "Not upset and not the least bit surprised. We both know that you've just been putting in time here until your agent found a project worth your while."

"I have not been putting in time," she denied.

"What would you call it?" he challenged.

"Figuring out what I want the rest of my life to look like."

"And now you know—and you're going back to LA."

"For a few days," she said again.

"You don't have to pretend for my sake," he told her. "You've built a successful career and you should fight for it."

She shook her head. "How did I ever fall in love with such an idiot?"

His heart jolted.

Was she saying…she loved him?

"Make no mistake," she told him now. "I do intend to fight for what I want—but it's not a decent part in a rom-com or even the resurrection of Lainey Howard—it's you."

"We agreed that this—whatever this is between us—was only temporary."

"No," she said again. "*You* said it was only temporary and *I* chose not to argue with you about it because I was hopeful that, in time, you would fall in love with me again as I was already falling in love with you."

"Your life has taken some unexpected turns the last few months," he reminded her. "And maybe your work on *Rockwood Ridge* made you believe in happy endings, but this is the real world, Hope. And in the real world, the movie star doesn't fall in love with the country boy."

"And what makes you an expert on the real world?" she demanded to know. "You can tell me that you don't feel the same way, but *don't you dare* tell me that my feelings aren't real.

"I've loved you for most of my life, Michael. Even when I was seventeen, I didn't go to LA because I didn't love you enough to stay—it was because I loved you too much. Because what I felt for you was so big, and so real, it scared me even more than the prospect of starting a new life in a new city."

He wished he could believe her. He wanted to trust that what she was saying was true. But by her own admission, she'd come to Haven to hide out. And he couldn't help but think that her sudden declaration of feelings for him was only a justification to continue hiding, because if she really did intend to come back, he had to guess that would be the reason.

"And now you're a star, Hope. And you deserve to take your place with the biggest and brightest in LA, where you'll shine far brighter than you ever could here."

She stared him down. "I've never denied that I was running away when I left LA, Michael. But I'm not running anymore. I'm finally ready to face my fears—and my feelings." She lifted her chin defiantly. "Maybe someday you'll be ready to do the same."

Chapter Twenty

Olivia responded to his SOS promptly. Less than fifteen minutes after MG sent his text message, his sister's SUV was pulling into his drive. As soon as the vehicle came to a stop, the doors opened and her three boys spilled out.

Bernie barked happily—the first time MG had seen a spark of joy in his dog since Hope had walked out with her suitcase three days earlier.

His sister got out more slowly—with a tray in her hands.

Apparently she'd been at their parents' house when he'd messaged, asking her to bring Easton, Hudson and Colton out to play with Bernie, who'd been moping around the house.

"Mom warned me that the dog probably isn't the only one moping and that I should visit at my own risk. But she also sent these—" Olivia gestured with the tray of cinnamon rolls "—to sweeten your disposition."

"My disposition is just fine," he lied.

She walked past him and into the cabin, before popping a coffee pod into the machine.

"Make yourself at home," he said dryly.

"I always do." She wandered over to the window while she waited for her coffee to brew. "Who do you think tires out first—the boys or the dog?"

"Does it matter?"

"Not really." She returned to the kitchen and wrapped her hands around the mug of coffee. "It's cold out there today. I'm thinking we might actually get the snow that's been forecast."

"So now we're talking about the weather, are we?"

"Isn't it a favorite topic of ranchers? That and the price of beef?"

"You're right about that," he confirmed.

"Plus, I wasn't sure if you were ready to talk about Hope."

"Nothing to talk about."

"You are moping."

"No, I'm not."

"I've been here five whole minutes and you haven't scarfed down half that tray of cinnamon rolls," she pointed out. "Definitely moping."

He deliberately lifted one of the soft, gooey pastries and took a big bite.

"Yeah, that proves me wrong," she said dryly.

He took his time chewing and swallowing—because it gave him an excuse not to respond to her pithy remark.

Olivia's phone buzzed.

She set down her mug to pull it out of her pocket, a furrow etching between her brows as she read the message on the screen.

"Turn on the TV."

"What?"

Huffing out an impatient breath, she moved past him to pick up the remote control and do it herself.

"Channel Five, Mom said."

He opened his mouth to ask what was on Channel Five, but the picture on the screen answered his question.

Hope.

She was sitting in some kind of conference room in what looked like an office building, the floor-to-ceiling windows behind her providing a view of the city outside. No less than a dozen microphones—many of them with network logos—were propped on the table in front of her to catch her every word.

A press conference, he realized.

She looked…beautiful. As always. The most beautiful woman he'd ever known. The dress she was wearing was from her Hollywood wardrobe, as he called it. Something that showed her to be the star that she was. And when she smiled at the cameras—he felt like he'd been kicked in the gut by an ornery horse.

Somehow he managed to catch his breath and focus on what she was saying.

"…seventeen years old when I first came to Los Angeles, and absolutely fearless. Or so I thought. In reality, I was incredibly naive. Up until then I'd lived a relatively sheltered life in a small town in northern Nevada, so I didn't know that there were reasons I should be afraid, people I shouldn't trust. My naivete didn't last long."

She paused, glancing at the notes in front of her. Then, for the first time, she publicly recounted the story of Donovan Kessel's invitation to lunch—and the assault that followed.

When she paused again, it was to reach for the water

on the table in front of her. The bottle trembled slightly in her hand as she twisted off the cap, then she lifted it to her lips and sipped.

"I didn't want to be assaulted, but that's what happened. He didn't rape me, though I have no doubt that's what he intended. Lucky for me, his assistant walked into the office while I was struggling with him, and I managed to escape.

"I was lucky to get away, and still, that assault changed me. I was no longer naive. I definitely wasn't fearless. In fact, I was terrified to tell anyone what happened, and for a very long time, I didn't.

"Recently, I had the privilege of meeting a young woman who reminded me—just a little bit—of who I used to be. Though she isn't nearly as naive as I was at the same age, and she recently proved herself to be a lot braver than I've ever been.

"She is my inspiration for being here today. Not to tell you my story, but to tell you the truth. And to apologize to any other young women who might have been victimized because I wasn't brave enough to speak up sooner.

"I'm also here because I wanted to set the record straight for fans of *Rockwood Ridge*, but after today, I don't intend to say anything more on the subject of my history with Donovan Kessel. Being assaulted was a horrible experience, but it's in the past. I'm ready to move forward and I'm not going to let it hold me back."

She nodded then, not to the reporters in the front row, but to the people standing at the back of the room. Jenny and Colin and Nisha and several other members of the cast and crew of Rockwood Ridge.

Her heart was pounding, as if she'd just completed a marathon. And perhaps, in some ways, she had. She'd been running from the story—from the truth—for years. And now, finally, the running was over.

As she'd told Michael before she left the Circle G, she was ready to face her fears and her feelings. Ready to look forward to the future—and she really hoped, with everything in her heart, that he would be part of that future.

But she didn't have time to think about that now, because the assembled reporters had a lot of questions in the wake of her revelations. Questions they shouted at her now, though Dolores Chen, her longtime attorney, held up a hand, indicating that she was retaking control.

"Hope came forward today to tell a truth that she's kept hidden for a long time, and she knows that Mr. Kessel will come forward now, too, most likely to deny the allegations against him. He might claim that the assault never happened or he might decide to spin it as a misunderstanding of a consensual encounter.

"But this isn't a case of she said/he said," Dolores assured the group. "It's a case of the truth finally coming to light, and in support of that truth, there's someone else here who would like to make a statement."

The lawyer looked over her shoulder toward a cluster of people standing in the corner. One woman extricated herself from the rest to take a seat at the table, on the other side of Hope's lawyer.

She took a moment to settle in, then leaned slightly closer to the microphones and began to speak. "My name is Allison Pinter. Seventeen years ago, I worked as a personal assistant to Donovan Kessel…"

After the press conference, Jenny drove Hope back to the Courtland Hotel in West Hollywood, parking her

Lexus in the employee parking lot so they could sneak in through the service entrance and avoid the press who were camped out by the main doors.

As soon as she stepped into her suite, Hope kicked off her shoes and dropped onto the closest sofa. Jenny headed straight to the minibar. She retrieved two bottles of water and handed one to Hope.

"How are you feeling?" she asked her friend and client.

"Exhausted." Hope tipped the bottle to her lips and drank deeply. "Liberated. Vindicated."

Jenny settled beside her, kicking off her shoes now and propping her feet on the glass-topped coffee table. "Did you know that Dolores had tracked down Donovan Kessel's assistant?"

She shook her head. "I didn't even know she was looking for her. It never occurred to me that, after so many years, she might remember—or be willing to admit that she did."

"The golden boy is going to have a much harder time talking his way out of this now," Jenny mused.

"It doesn't matter," Hope said. "And I mean that sincerely. It really doesn't matter to me what Donovan Kessel says or does anymore."

"I'm happy to hear that. I had some concerns, when you told me what you wanted to do, but obviously you knew that this was the right thing for you now."

"I had some concerns, too," Hope admitted. "But I really do feel better now that it's done. I know there's going to be fallout, but I feel confident that I can handle it."

Jenny glanced at the phone that was always in her hand—a permanent accessory no matter what she was wearing. "Your mom released a statement expressing regret that she couldn't be there today but assuring the world that her daughter has always had her complete support."

"I had a good conversation with her earlier," Hope confided. "I didn't want the press conference to be the first she heard about it."

"You really never said anything to her when it happened?"

She shook her head.

"I wish I'd known you then," Jenny said. "And I like to think that if I had, I would have encouraged you to report the assault."

"I don't know that you would have succeeded," Hope said. "Because I didn't want to be known as the wannabe actress attempting to claim fifteen minutes of fame by accusing a celebrity of trying to rape me."

"Now the world knows, but he won't be held accountable because the statute of limitations has passed."

"He'll be held accountable," she said confidently. "Just not by the law."

"The studio released a statement, too," Jenny told her. "They're shocked and appalled to hear about what happened to you. They were under the impression that, quote—'Ms. Bradford's conflict with Mr. Kessel was rooted in a long-ago disagreement'—and they're sorry if any of their actions added to your pain and suffering."

"But mostly they're sorry that the optics of the situation don't make them look good," Hope added.

"No doubt about that," her agent agreed, muting her phone and setting it down on the table. "Should we order dinner?"

"Dinner sounds great. I was so twisted up about the

press conference that I've barely eaten the past three days."

"I could go for a burger." Jenny rose from the sofa and made her way to the desk, to check the room service menu on the tablet provided to guests.

"A burger sounds good," Hope said. "But you need to go home and have dinner with your husband and kids."

"My husband and kids are going out for pizza and a movie tonight, because there was no way, after a day like this one, I was going to leave you alone."

"I'm fine," Hope assured her.

"I'm staying anyway," Jenny said firmly.

So Hope gave up trying to send her friend away, and after they had dinner, Jenny went back to her car to retrieve her overnight bag—proof that she'd planned to stay all along—while Hope gave her grandmother a call.

"Anyone else you need to check in with before we kick back to watch a movie?" Jenny asked.

Hope thought fleetingly of Michael. She'd wondered if he might call her—or at least send a text message—after the press conference. Of course, it was possible he knew nothing about it. And even if he had seen it, he'd made it clear that their lives were worlds apart.

"Nope, I'm good."

Someone was knocking on the door.

Hope pulled the covers over her head, wishing that the someone would go away—or that Jenny would respond to the summons. Because she couldn't imagine that her agent, who'd slept on the sofa in the living room, was actually sleeping through the ruckus.

With a muttered oath, she dragged her weary body out of bed and padded into the other room. Of course,

Jenny wasn't sleeping. She was on the balcony, phone against her ear, obviously working already.

"You better have coffee," Hope grumbled. "If you're going to knock on my door at this ungodly hour, you better have—"

The rest of the words stalled in her throat when she opened the door and saw Michael.

"A latte from Urth Caffé?" he suggested, completing her unfinished sentence.

"How did you… Colin," she realized.

Michael nodded. "He told me where you were staying. And warned that I better not show up at your door before eight a.m. without your favorite coffee."

She accepted the cup he offered, noted that there were two more in the carryout tray.

"He guessed your agent might be here with you and told me that I could score points if I picked up coffee for her, too."

"She's out there—" Hope gestured toward the balcony "—undoubtedly fielding calls from people on the East Coast who don't appreciate that there's a three-hour time difference between there and here."

He remained standing in the hall, holding the tray with the two cups.

"I suppose you want to come in?"

"I wouldn't mind."

She stepped away from the door to allow him entry.

He dragged his left leg a little as he crossed the threshold.

"Long drive?" she guessed.

"You know it is."

She peeled the lid off her cup. "Where's your cane?"

"I'm fine, Hope. I've been walking around for half an hour to loosen up."

"Looks like you could use a half hour more."

"Maybe. But I couldn't wait any longer to see you."

She sipped her coffee as he made a quick survey of her hotel suite.

"So this is how the other half lives."

"The Gilmores aren't exactly paupers," she noted.

"No," he agreed. "But I think I'm only realizing now just how much of a difference there is between cattle rancher wealthy and Hollywood star wealthy."

"Did you come all this way to remind me again that we live in different worlds?"

He shook his head.

"And anyway, my agent booked the room."

"Obviously you're making a lot of money for her, too."

"Hope's the reason my kids are in private school," Jenny said, stepping into the suite and into their conversation.

"Michael, this is Jenny Stanwyck. Jenny, meet Michael Gilmore."

A wide smile spread across her agent's face. "The infamous Michael Gilmore."

He looked at Hope questioningly. "Infamous?"

"Jenny isn't just my agent—she's been one of my closest friends for the past fifteen years."

"Hope is very special to me," Jenny said. "And I'll say lots of nice things about you, too, if you tell me that one of those coffees is for me."

"It is," Michael confirmed, lifting the cup out of the tray and offering it to her.

"This one's a keeper," Jenny said.

Hope sipped her coffee. "He's not interested in being kept."

"Well, I can't imagine he came all this way to ask for your autograph. Maybe you could hitch a ride back to Haven with him," Jenny suggested. Then to Michael she said, "Hope has decided she'd rather volunteer with the Westmount High School Drama Club than make gobs of money on *Rockwood Ridge*."

"They offered you a new contract?" he asked Hope, reading between the lines.

"*Gobs of money*," Jenny said again.

"They did," Hope confirmed.

"And you turned it down?"

Jenny cleared her throat. "You obviously have things to talk about, so I'm going to go home to remind my husband that he has a wife and my kids that I'm their mother."

Hope set her cup down to hug her agent. "Tell them I say thanks for letting you hang out with me last night. And thank *you* for everything."

"It was always my pleasure." Jenny slung the strap of her overnight bag on her shoulder and toasted Michael with her coffee. "It was nice to meet you—and thank you for this."

"I saw your press conference yesterday," Michael said when Jenny had gone. "It took a lot of courage to stand up there and tell the world what he did."

"It was necessary," she said.

"That's only one of the many things I've always admired about you," he said. "That you step up to do what needs to be done and say the things that need to be said. Such as calling someone out for being an idiot."

"Are you referring to any idiot in particular?"

"I think you know I am."

"Maybe I want to hear you say it."

"I was an idiot. And I love you, Hope."

Her eyes filled with tears, and her heart—as battered and bruised as it was—immediately started to heal. "I didn't think I'd ever hear you say those words again."

"I'm sorry I didn't say them sooner. I thought by not acknowledging my feelings, I could prevent myself from being hurt again. Because as much as I enjoyed the time that we spent together at the ranch, I didn't believe it would last. No matter how good everything seemed, I was convinced you were going to leave."

"And then I did leave."

"And now I know why."

"I wanted to tell you, but you weren't exactly in a listening kind of mood."

"I saw the suitcase and… I panicked," he admitted.

"It wasn't your most shining moment." She moved into his arms and lifted her hands to link them behind his neck. "But so far, this one has potential."

"Any ideas about how I might ensure it realizes its potential?"

She drew his head down to whisper in his ear.

He responded by lifting her off her feet and carrying her to the bedroom.

Epilogue

Hope and Michael returned to Haven the day before Thanksgiving. Despite the lateness of the hour when they arrived, Hope insisted on stopping at Morgan's Glen so they could pick up Bernie, who had been staying with Olivia and Adam and the boys while they were out of town. Although the dog had been lavished with attention by Easton, Hudson and Colton for four days—and enjoyed lots of extra treats—he was overjoyed to be reunited with his two favorite people. (MG acknowledging that he'd been relegated to number two in Bernie's affections since Hope had come into their lives—but he wasn't going to complain, because he was just as happy to have her home with them.)

The next day, the whole family gathered at Angela and Charles's house, and when Michael's mother enfolded Hope in her embrace and said, "I'm so glad you're home," she finally felt as if she was home.

Not just in Haven, but at the Circle G, with Michael and his family.

In addition to Michael's siblings and their spouses and kids, Shirley Morgan—Adam's mom—was in attendance, as were Edwina and Dennis. Conversation throughout the meal touched on a number of subjects, but it wasn't until dessert was served that Olivia asked Hope what everyone was wondering.

"Are you ever going to go back to *Rockwood Ridge*?"

"They killed off my character," Hope reminded her.

"Yeah, but it's TV," Michael's sister pointed out. "They're always bringing characters back from the dead on TV."

"There's even a whole show about people back from the dead," Easton chimed in.

"*Rockwood Ridge* isn't *The Walking Dead*," Adam told his son.

"Does it have *any* zombies?" Hudson wanted to know.

"None."

The boys were visibly disappointed by this revelation.

"It would be better with zombies," Elliott declared.

"And anyway," Angela said, steering the conversation back on track, "there was no proof that Lainey died."

"You're right," Hope acknowledged. "And as it turns out, my agent is in the process of negotiating a short-term return for Lainey, to give proper closure to her story line."

"What a wonderful gift to your fans," Grams said approvingly.

"And a happy end to my career in the spotlight," Hope said.

"You don't think you'll ever be tempted to go back?" Lindsay asked curiously.

Hope looked at Michael as she shook her head. "I've got everything I ever wanted right here."

The next three-and-a-half weeks passed in a whirlwind of drama club rehearsals and preparations for the holidays. When Hope wasn't at the high school, she was either shopping with Laurel or decorating with Grams or baking with Angela. And somehow, between all those other tasks, she and Michael—and Bernie—found time to hike through the snow to cut down their own Christmas tree. Finding the time to decorate it took a little bit longer.

But finally it was December 21—the night of the last performance of *A Christmas Carol*.

There was an energy and excitement in the theater that was unlike anything else Hope had ever experienced, and she loved every minute of it. And Westmount High School Drama Club's holiday production had already proven to be an enormous success, with the auditorium packed every night and the actors rewarded with standing ovations at the conclusion of each performance.

Hope didn't expect tonight to be any different, so she was surprised to find Missy hovering backstage when the other students were already in the wings, waiting for the curtain to go up.

"Is something wrong?" Hope asked.

"No." The teen shook her head. "I just wanted to tell you that I'm sorry.

"I saw the press conference," Missy continued, not pausing long enough to give Hope a chance to respond. "I didn't know... I never would have taunted you about... him...if I'd known what he did to you."

"You don't need to apologize, Missy."

"But I am sorry. You were there for me, and—I know you probably think I'm just a kid, but I wanted you to know that I'm here for you, too."

Hope felt an unexpected lump rise in her throat. "Thank you." She gave the girl a quick hug. "Now go out there and break a leg."

Michael had a bottle of champagne chilling in the fridge that he wanted to uncork when they got back to the house, in celebration of Hope's successful directorial debut. (After Ty Hutchinson was ousted—and arrested—Linda Doyle had happily turned over the directorial reins to Haven's Hollywood star.)

"I appreciate the thought," she said. "But let's hold off on the champagne for a minute."

Then she took his hand and led him into the living room, gesturing for him to sit while she retrieved a present from beneath the Christmas tree.

"Why are there presents under the tree?" he asked with mock disapproval. "Christmas isn't for another four days."

"It's only one present," she said. "Because this is one that can't wait until Christmas."

"You mean *you* can't wait until Christmas," he teased.

"Just open it," she urged.

"It's too small for a tie," he said, as he tore off the festive paper. "And hopefully you know me well enough by now to know that I don't wear ties very often, anyway."

"You wore one tonight," she noted.

"You didn't give me a choice."

"And you looked very handsome," she told him. "But no—it's not a tie."

He lifted the lid of the narrow box to reveal…

"Not a tie," he echoed.

It was a pregnancy test—with a distinctive plus sign in the window.

He looked at Hope. "Is this…for real? Are you… pregnant?"

She nodded, the smile tugging at the corners of her mouth reflected in the sparkle in her eyes.

"We're going to have a baby."

Though it wasn't a question, she nodded again.

Obviously this was why she'd nixed the champagne.

It wasn't a big surprise—because they'd decided to stop using birth control when they returned from California—but it was a happy one, and his heart filled with joy as his own lips curved.

"This is the best Christmas present ever," he told her.

Her smile widened. "Do you really think so?"

"I really do," he assured her. "I mean, I kind of hoped we'd have to try a lot more before it happened, but I'm not at all disappointed. And, as it happens, I have something for you, too."

"It's still four days until Christmas," she reminded him.

"But since you gave me an early present, it only seems fair that I should be able to give one to you."

He reached into his pocket and presented her with…

"It's my grandmother's engagement ring," he said.

As if she might have forgotten.

As if she hadn't dreamed—more times than she could count—of this man placing this very ring on her finger.

He glanced from the ring to Hope's face, his expression serious.

"She wore it from the day my grandfather proposed until the day she died as a symbol of the love they shared.

When it came to me, I knew I wanted to put it on your finger someday, as a symbol of my promise to love you, faithfully and forever, like my grandfather loved my grandmother.

"I'm hoping today's that day, because I've never loved anyone else as much as I love you and I want to spend every day of the rest of our lives together as husband and wife."

Hope wondered if he felt her hand tremble as he lifted it from her lap.

But it wasn't just her hand that trembled—every part of her was quivering with excited anticipation. Because *this* was the moment she had been dreaming of her whole life.

Maybe it wasn't her first proposal—or even the second or third—but it was the only one that mattered. Because Michael was the only man she'd ever truly loved.

"Hope Bradford, will you marry me?"

"I thought I couldn't possibly be any happier than I was when I saw the plus sign on the pregnancy test," she said, her eyes blurred with happy tears. "I was wrong."

"Is that a *yes*?" he prompted.

"That's a definite *yes*."

He slid the ring onto her finger—a symbol of the promises they'd made to one another and of the love they'd share forever.

* * * * *

Look for Finley Gilmore's story,
the next installment of Brenda Harlen's Haven series
Coming soon to Harlequin Special Edition!

And catch up with recent titles in
Brenda Harlen's Match Made in Haven series:

Meet Me Under the Mistletoe
The Rancher's Promise
The Chef's Surprise Baby
Captivated by the Cowgirl
Countdown to Christmas
Her Not-So-Little Secret

Available now, wherever Harlequin
books and ebooks are sold.

#3013 THE MAVERICK'S HOLIDAY DELIVERY

Montana Mavericks: Lassoing Love • by Christy Jeffries

Dante Sanchez is an expert on no-strings romances. But his feelings for single mom-to-be Eloise Taylor are anything but casual. She knows there's a scandal surrounding her pregnancy. But catching the attention of the town's most notorious bachelor may be her biggest scandal yet!

#3014 TRIPLETS UNDER THE TREE

Dawson Family Ranch • by Melissa Senate

Divorced rancher Hutch Dawson has one heck of a Christmas wish: find a nanny for his baby triplets. And Savannah Walsh is his only applicant! Who knew that his high school nemesis would be the *perfect* solution to his very busy—and lonely—holiday season...

#3015 THE RANCHER'S CHRISTMAS STAR

Men of the West • by Stella Bagwell

Would Quint Hollister hire a woman to be Stone Creek Ranch's new sheepherder? Only if the woman is capable Clementine Starr. She wants no part of romance—at least until Quint's first knee-weakening kiss! But getting two stubborn singletons to admit love might take a Christmas miracle!

#3016 THEIR CONVENIENT CHRISTMAS ENGAGEMENT

Top Dog Dude Ranch • by Catherine Mann

Ian Greer is used to finding his mother, who has Alzheimer's, anywhere but at home! More often than not, he finds her at Gwen Bishop's vintage toy store. He admires the kind, plucky single mom, so a fake engagement to placate his mother—and her family—seems like the perfect plan. Until a romantic sleigh ride changes their holiday ruse into something much more real...

#3017 THE VET'S SHELTER SURPRISE

by Michelle M. Douglas

Sparks fly when beautiful PR expert Georgia O'Neill brings an armful of stray kittens to veterinarian Mel Carter's small-town animal shelter. Mel has loved and lost before, and Georgia is only in town short-term, so it makes sense to ignore their mutual attraction. But as they open up about their pasts, will they also open up to the possibility of new love?

#3018 HOLIDAY AT MISTLETOE COTTAGE

The McFaddens of Tinsley Cove • by Nancy Robards Thompson

Free-spirited photojournalist Avery Anderson just inherited her aunt's beach house. And, it seems, her aunt's sexy, outgoing neighbor. Hometown hero Forest McFadden may be Avery's polar opposite. But fortunately, he's also the adventure she's been searching for.

HSECNM0923

Get 3 FREE REWARDS!

We'll send you 2 FREE Books <u>plus</u> a FREE Mystery Gift.

FREE Value Over **$20**

Both the **Harlequin® Special Edition** and **Harlequin® Heartwarming™** series feature compelling novels filled with stories of love and strength where the bonds of friendship, family and community unite.

YES! Please send me 2 FREE novels from the Harlequin Special Edition or Harlequin Heartwarming series and my FREE Gift (gift is worth about $10 retail). After receiving them, if I don't wish to receive any more books, I can return the shipping statement marked "cancel." If I don't cancel, I will receive 6 brand-new Harlequin Special Edition books every month and be billed just $5.49 each in the U.S. or $6.24 each in Canada, a savings of at least 12% off the cover price, or 4 brand-new Harlequin Heartwarming Larger-Print books every month and be billed just $6.24 each in the U.S. or $6.74 each in Canada, a savings of at least 19% off the cover price. It's quite a bargain! Shipping and handling is just 50¢ per book in the U.S. and $1.25 per book in Canada.* I understand that accepting the 2 free books and gift places me under no obligation to buy anything. I can always return a shipment and cancel at any time by calling the number below. The free books and gift are mine to keep no matter what I decide.

Choose one: ☐ **Harlequin Special Edition**
(235/335 BPA GRMK)

☐ **Harlequin Heartwarming Larger-Print**
(161/361 BPA GRMK)

☐ **Or Try Both!**
(235/335 & 161/361 BPA GRPZ)

Name (please print)

Address   Apt. #

City   State/Province   Zip/Postal Code

Email: Please check this box ☐ if you would like to receive newsletters and promotional emails from Harlequin Enterprises ULC and its affiliates. You can unsubscribe anytime.

Mail to the Harlequin Reader Service:
IN U.S.A.: P.O. Box 1341, Buffalo, NY 14240-8531
IN CANADA: P.O. Box 603, Fort Erie, Ontario L2A 5X3

Want to try 2 free books from another series? Call 1-800-873-8635 or visit www.ReaderService.com.

---

*Terms and prices subject to change without notice. Prices do not include sales taxes, which will be charged (if applicable) based on your state or country of residence. Canadian residents will be charged applicable taxes. Offer not valid in Quebec. This offer is limited to one order per household. Books received may not be as shown. Not valid for current subscribers to the Harlequin Special Edition or Harlequin Heartwarming series. All orders subject to approval. Credit or debit balances in a customer's account(s) may be offset by any other outstanding balance owed by or to the customer. Please allow 4 to 6 weeks for delivery. Offer available while quantities last.

Your Privacy—Your information is being collected by Harlequin Enterprises ULC, operating as Harlequin Reader Service. For a complete summary of the information we collect, how we use this information and to whom it is disclosed, please visit our privacy notice located at corporate.harlequin.com/privacy-notice. From time to time we may also exchange your personal information with reputable third parties. If you wish to opt out of this sharing of your personal information, please visit readerservice.com/consumerchoice or call 1-800-873-8635. **Notice to California Residents**—Under California law, you have specific rights to control and access your data. For more information on these rights and how to exercise them, visit corporate.harlequin.com/california-privacy.

HSEHW23

HARLEQUIN
PLUS

Try the best multimedia subscription service for romance readers like you!

Read, Watch and Play.

Experience the easiest way to get the romance content you crave.

Start your **FREE TRIAL** at
<u>www.harlequinplus.com/freetrial</u>.